"I suppose you do everything at the last minute?"

Bette asked.

Paul's eyes dropped to her lips. "And I suppose *you* have your Christmas shopping done by Labor Day?"

"Of course."

He shuddered, and she laughed.

"Some years," she confided, "I get really crazy and wait until Halloween. And you, I suppose, are out there on Christmas Eve, madly buying." She smiled slyly at him. "Of course, you realize that by the time you go shopping on the twenty-fourth, you're just looking at my leftovers. I've already snatched up all the perfect presents out there."

His wounded expression drew a triumphant chuckle from her that he joined with easy, warm laughter.

It was crazy, she thought. The whole thing. Walking on a beach in her work clothes in the middle of October, with a man she'd known exactly thirty hours, and whose drawbacks easily reached double digits. And enjoying it. A lot....

Dear Reader,

Welcome to Silhouette **Special Edition** . . . welcome to romance. Each month, Silhouette **Special Edition** publishes six novels with you in mind—stories of love and life, tales that you can identify with—romance with that little "something special" added in.

And may this December bring you all the warmth and joy of the holiday season. The holidays in Chicago form the perfect backdrop for Patricia McLinn's *Prelude to a Wedding,* the first book in her new duo, WEDDING DUET. Don't miss the festivities!

Rounding out December are more stories by some of your favorite authors: Victoria Pade, Gina Ferris, Mary Kirk and Sherryl Woods—who has written Joshua's story— *Joshua and the Cowgirl,* a spinoff from *My Dearest Cal* (SE #669).

As an extraspecial surprise, don't miss *Luring a Lady* by Nora Roberts. This warm, tender tale introduces us to Mikhail—a character you met in *Taming Natasha* (SE #583). Yes, Natasha's brother is here to win your heart—as well as the heart of the lovely Sydney Hayward!

In each Silhouette **Special Edition** novel, we're dedicated to bringing you the romances that you dream about—the types of stories that delight as well as bring a tear to the eye. And that's what Silhouette **Special Edition** is all about—special books by special authors for special readers!

I hope you enjoy this book and all of the stories to come.

Sincerely,

Tara Gavin
Senior Editor

PATRICIA McLINN
Prelude to a Wedding

Silhouette Special Edition

Published by Silhouette Books New York

America's Publisher of Contemporary Romance

To Ginni,
who believed even when there were no endings,
and who gave the best advice of all:
Just Get It Done

SILHOUETTE BOOKS
300 East 42nd St., New York, N.Y. 10017

PRELUDE TO A WEDDING

ISBN: 0-373-09712-3

First Silhouette Books printing December 1991

Books by Patricia McLinn

Silhouette Special Edition

Hoops #587
A New World #641
Prelude to a Wedding #712

PATRICIA McLINN

says she has been spinning stories in her head since childhood, when her mother insisted she stop reading at the dinner table. As the time came for her to earn a living, Patricia shifted her stories from fiction to fact—she became a sports writer and editor for newspapers in Illinois, North Carolina and the District of Columbia. Now living outside Washington, D.C., she enjoys traveling, history and sports, but is happiest indulging her passion for storytelling.

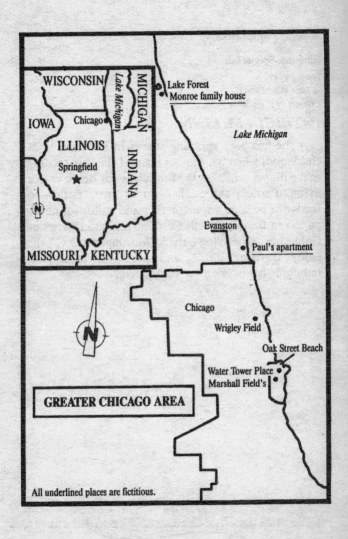

WISCONSIN

Lake Michigan

MICHIGAN

Lake Forest
Monroe family house

Lake Michigan

IOWA

Chicago

ILLINOIS

INDIANA

Springfield

Evanston

Paul's apartment

MISSOURI KENTUCKY

Chicago

Wrigley Field

Oak Street Beach

Water Tower Place
Marshall Field's

GREATER CHICAGO AREA

All underlined places are fictitious.

Chapter One

"**P**aul, I'm having the baby."

Paul Monroe stared in disbelief at the woman standing at the far side of his old-fashioned desk. A ripple of panic swept through him, but he swallowed and tried a chuckle. It sounded feeble. "You gotta be kidding, right?"

"No. I'm not kidding."

He saw the strain in Jan's young face, backing up her words, but still he hoped for a reprieve.

"I mean, you told me all along that this would happen sometime—"

"I told you it would happen today."

He'd heard that exasperated tone enough to ignore it. "And I've seen it coming for a while, so I knew you'd have the baby someday—"

"Not someday. Today. And not sometime. Now."

Paul stared at Jan and wished he'd had an urge to make calls outside the office this morning, or an impulse to play hooky. The day had sure been tempting enough, with Indian summer casting sparkling October light across Chicago. Surely he could have found something he had to do outside the office. Maybe an appraisal in the country, down winding lanes between half-bare trees revealing bites of blue sky. Not that he minded coming to his office most days. Building and office alike held an ambience Sam Spade would have recognized immediately. Paul liked that.

But some days he just didn't feel like being confined by four walls, and he was lucky enough and good enough in his field so that those days he could find something else to do. He wished he had today, because then he wouldn't be here facing his very pregnant and soon-to-be-beyond-pregnant-and-into-motherhood secretary, wondering what in the hell he was supposed to do next.

Hospital. That's what he was supposed to do. Get her to the hospital. Damn, this should have been Ed's job. Fathers-to-be had a moral responsibility to make this panicked drive to the hospital—not bosses.

"Are you—"

"I'm sure. I've been timing the contractions for a while and they're getting close now. Plus my water broke."

He might not know much about women having babies, but anybody who'd ever watched TV knew that phrase meant business. "Have you called—"

"I've called the hospital," Jan informed him, still efficient even when her skin went pale and her breath came hard with a contraction. Contraction—that seemed a mighty polite word for what appeared to be just plain agony. "They're expecting us." With a smile that shone even through the pain, she patted her protruding stomach. "And I've called Ed's office. They're trying to track him down and he'll meet us there."

He should have known she'd have everything taken care of. She scheduled everything so darn efficiently, so why couldn't she have scheduled this moment for about three hours earlier or six hours later so she'd be at home? Then he wouldn't have to be the one saying, "Okay, I'll dri—"

"I appreciate your driving to the hospital." He also should have known her ability to anticipate his sentences wouldn't abate even in the throes of childbirth. Jan Robson might be only twenty-five, but sometimes she awed him. What awed him most was how she ran his office to her own exacting standards without impinging on his freedom. She was amazing. She never let up.

Nearly before the thought finished forming in his mind, she spoke. "But before we leave for the hospital, you have a phone call to make."

"Aw, Jan."

"You've been putting it off and putting it off, and there's no more putting it off now. It's exactly the way you're dealing with the proposal from the Smithsonian, too. Eventually you won't be able to ignore that, either."

He ignored her second statement. "This wasn't supposed to happen until Halloween."

"No. I've told you all along that the due date was October 7. And I'm right on time—"

Of course she was, Paul thought. Jan was always right on time.

"—but you chose to pretend it would happen at Halloween because you'll be out of town then. You wouldn't make the call before, so you have to make it now."

"But Jan—"

"You promised, Paul."

"I know, but this isn't the time—"

"This is the time."

"After I get you to the hospital—"

"No. Now, while I can make sure you do it."

"I'll talk Centurian into giving me somebody on loan like they did when you had flu two years ago and for your honeymoon and—"

"Disasters, every time. Besides, no secretary from Centurian will work for you now that they know better and—"

"But they all like me," he protested with a faint satisfaction at, for once, getting to interrupt her.

It would be easiest if he could use one of the Centurian Insurance secretaries. Even as an independent contractor, he did enough work for them that they'd rented him this cubbyhole office. A Centurian secretary would have at least a basic understanding of what he did, besides knowing where to find the copying machine.

"Of course they like you. Everybody likes you, but they all know what you're like to work for and they won't do it. You'd run wild with a regular temporary, and I won't have you— Ah!"

The way she broke off and clutched her hand to her stomach propelled him out of his chair and to her side in record time. Then there was nothing to do but give her the support of an arm around her shoulders until he felt the tension ease out of her.

"Jan, we need to get you to the hospital."

She looked up at him through eyes glazed with pain, joy and determination. "You promised."

Hell! Hell and damnation! He pivoted and reached the phone in one stride. "You don't play fair, woman."

"That's the only way to win with you."

"What's the number?" he grumbled, a grin fighting against the churning in his stomach. She did know him well.

She gave it to him. "And the person you want to talk to is Bette Wharton." She pronounced the first name as one syllable.

He repeated the name when the voice on the other end of the line identified herself as Top-Line Temporaries and asked how she could help him.

He heard the click of the phone as he was transferred, then a new voice answered, "Bette Wharton."

This voice sounded crisp and cool on the surface with the hint of something smooth and hot inside, and it made him think inexplicably of the spicy cheese concoction his mother used to stuff celery. Despite his tension over Jan, he almost grinned. How might this unknown woman on the other end of the telephone line react to being compared to stuffed celery?

"This is Paul Monroe. I'm calling because—"

"Ah, yes, Mr. Monroe. I've been expecting your call."

"You have?" He looked up, prepared to skewer his secretary with a look. She *would* have him call somebody with the same trick as hers of not needing him to finish sentences. And why in the world did he have to make this call if Jan had already lined things up?

"Yes. I have a list of candidates."

But Paul wasn't listening. His dirty look had changed to one of worry.

"Tell her," Jan ordered. She exhaled with a breath he supposed she'd learned at that birthing class she and Ed had attended.

"I need a secretary," he blurted out.

"I know. As I said, I have several candidates. But I think you should make the final choice. If you'd like to stop by our office, or I could come by your office—"

"I'll come there…sometime. Maybe today or—I don't know— We have to get to the hospital. Now! We're having a baby!"

Bette Wharton held the receiver long after the fumbling click had severed the connection, as if the instrument in her hand could reveal to her the scene on the other end. Only when the dial tone pierced her fog did she hang up.

So Jan Robson was having her baby. And Paul Monroe needed a temporary secretary. Which meant she'd finally meet him.

She'd been intrigued since the brisk young secretary had first come to her office five months ago and explained that she would be going on maternity leave eventually and needed a very special temporary secretary for her very special boss. Bette had regarded the news as propitious. For two years, she had been steadfastly guiding Top-Line toward just that niche in the marketplace—matching special needs with special service. Providing a replacement for Jan Robson could be the perfect gauge of how well she and Top-Line were doing.

Bette had wondered at first if there was more between secretary and boss than dictation, but Jan Robson saw Paul Monroe's faults all too clearly to be romantically involved with him. It had been Bette's observation that women in love lost the ability to reason when it came to the men involved.

No, Jan simply had a very high regard for her boss of six years. Bette wondered why, when the man Jan described sounded so little like a businesslike adult, but she couldn't doubt the secretary's feelings.

In deference to those feelings and with an eye to her company's future, she had conducted the search for Paul Monroe's temporary secretary personally. The results pleased her. All the employees at Top-Line were just that, but the ones she had selected for Mr. Monroe's approval were the top of the top.

Now all she had to do was wait for the enigmatic Paul Monroe to make his appearance so he could make his selection.

Darla Clarence closed Bette's office door behind her. "There's a Paul Monroe out front asking for you. I can tell him you've left for the day."

Bette recognized the offer as part of Darla's long-running campaign to get her to work less. And that meant it must be nearing six, since that was when Darla usually started encouraging her to go home; most nights Bette didn't follow the advice until two or three hours later.

"That's all right, Darla. I'll see him now. He could turn out to be a very important client for us."

"Just a one-man office," Darla said with a hint of a sniff.

"True, but he has pull with Centurian. He's our first contact with them, and you know what a prestigious account that would be. That could open a lot of doors."

In her overall plan, Bette had targeted such large corporate clients for her fifth year in business. Having the opportunity this soon felt like winning the lottery. Even so, she wouldn't trust to luck to make the most of it. She'd already drafted a proposal of what she could offer Centurian. But first Top-Line had to impress Paul Monroe enough that he'd recommend her company.

Darla gave an almost silent click of disapproval, but started to open the door.

"He doesn't look like any important client I've ever seen. At least not for our kind of business." She hesitated with her hand on the doorknob and glanced back at Bette. "Funny business is what he looks like he's best suited for."

The soft chuckle Darla left behind puzzled Bette as much as her words. Neither prepared her for Paul Monroe, who started talking the minute he came through the door.

"Hi. Whew, what a day. And this is only the middle of the week! I don't know if I'll make it to Friday at this rate. Hard to believe when people spout off about you-really-should-have-a-family they're talking about putting you through this 2.5 times. Once is enough to cure anybody."

Before Bette could rise from behind her desk to greet him properly, he'd crossed the room and flopped into the padded armchair. Eyes closed, legs extended, arms dangling over the arms of the chair, he looked as if he didn't have a bone in his compact body. At least not a self-conscious bone. He acted as if they'd known each other for years.

She swallowed her surprise. On second thought, he *did* look as if he'd had a rough day. In fact, he looked as if he'd spent it reenacting *Romancing the Stone*.

His dark gray suit was top quality, but the jacket—now critically rumpled—was dangling from two crooked fingers. His slacks bore multiple creases and seemed oddly wrinkled at the knees. The knot of his silk tie rested at midchest level, and his limp shirt showed a coffee stain on one rolled-back sleeve. The third button from the top had been matched with the second buttonhole, giving him a lopsided air.

His shining chestnut hair would do a racehorse proud, but any self-respecting Thoroughbred would demand a better brushing than this mane seemed to have gotten, she thought with a private grin.

"Sure, go ahead and laugh at someone who's been through eight of the nine levels of hell today," he said.

At the sound of his voice, she stifled a start and killed the grin. Great. Nothing like laughing at a new client to impress him. He'd opened his eyes, but only halfway, as if he could manage no more. When she met his look, however, she saw his eyes were dancing. She'd always thought that was only a figure of speech, but his truly did. The green flecks that showed against a gray background performed something lively and agile. If he'd been through eight levels of hell, well, she could believe he'd brought a bit of the devil back with him.

"You're the most cheerful martyr I've ever heard," she surprised herself by saying.

His grin widened in satisfaction—with himself, or her, or both, Bette didn't know. "That's the only way to go—singing at the stake."

"A variation on singing for your supper, I suppose."

"For my sup—? Ah, I get it. Stake turns to steak, as in charbroiled. I see why Jan picked you. I'll have to mind my P's and Q's with you—and I'm not talking vegetables."

Bette shifted at the reminder of why he'd come. Wordplay was fun, but this was business. "Yes, well... Uh, how is Jan? And the baby? Your call ended rather abruptly this afternoon."

"Both doing fine. A boy. Edward, Jr. Eight pounds eight ounces, all parts fully operational. Especially the lungs. Although his father's a little worse for wear at the moment." He held up a palm as if to forestall her, his first movement other than raising his eyelids. "And yes, before you ask, he does look worse than me right now."

"You mean he was there? I thought..."

His eyes narrowed and she felt as if she'd had a spotlight trained on her. "Of course he was there. And what did you think?"

"From your appearance, and from what you said, I thought..." Hesitating, she met his gaze and came to the conclusion that evasion was not a viable option if she wanted to stay on good terms with this man. "I thought you must have been in the delivery room somehow."

His eyes popped wide open. "The delivery room? Good Lord, woman, are you crazy?" His body seemed to sag in reaction to the energy he'd expended in astonishment. "It was bad enough in the waiting room. I never would have made it in the delivery room!"

She tried not to laugh. She really did. It was no use. In the end, she had to wipe moisture from her eyes and take three deep breaths to get her voice under control.

"I see." Another deep breath might get rid of the final quiver of amusement in her words, so she gave it a try, avoiding Paul Monroe's gaze. She had a feeling his dancing eyes would surely pave the road to relapse. "I imagine the hospital personnel wouldn't let you in there."

One eyebrow rose in a quizzical expression that invited her to share his amusement. "Actually, they all presumed I was Jan's husband at first, and for once in her life Jan was too preoccupied to straighten out the mess. I filled out some forms they shoved in my hands, then they kept telling me to follow this corridor and turn that way and check in with this desk and see that nurse. Ed arrived just in time. I tried to explain, but they were making threatening noises about my scrubbing and joining my wife in the labor room when he showed up. When they realized he was the father, they got all huffy, as if I'd been trying to worm my way into some secret place, and they kicked me out to spend the rest of the miserable afternoon in the waiting room."

"That must have been very difficult for you." Bette had had time to damp down the laughter, but apparently he didn't fall for the straight face she'd assumed.

"It was," he said in a tone that had just enough humor to escape self-pity. "I can see you think I had the easy role in this whole thing, but let me tell you, waiting rooms can really take it out of you."

She fought a grin. Business. Get back to business. "I'm sure they can. I'm glad everything went well in the end. It all turned out fine. Now—"

His groan cut her off. "Went well? Are you crazy, lady? Midway through my day I had a woman walk into my office and tell me she was in labor, and it went downhill—*fast*—from there. *Went well?*"

"I see your point. One expects one's secretary to better arrange such matters."

She regretted the teasing words as soon as they were out. Nine out of ten men didn't appreciate having their egos pricked by a sharp tongue, even in jest. Not the best way to win prospective clients. She could feel her hopes for entrée to Centurian fading as fast as the October daylight. Then she saw the glint of appreciation in his eye, and sighed in relief. Paul Monroe, apparently, was the tenth man. Still, she'd be on safer ground if she got the conversation back to the matter at hand.

"That's right," he said mildly. "A secretary should do this sort of stuff on her own time."

"I can guarantee you that none of the six candidates I have selected for you to choose from will pose a similar problem for you—at least not for the next few months."

He sat up, and she became aware of the way his chest filled the misbuttoned shirt and his forearms swelled below the rolled-back sleeves. She swallowed, and remembered the things Jan Robson had told her about this man. Not her type. Not at all.

"I sort of hoped *you'd* be my secretary."

The words to slash his presumption that any woman in an office was automatically a secretary welled up in her throat. She caught the gleam in his eyes just in time. The sort of gleam a kid's eyes had as he waited for the teacher to open the desk with a frog hidden in it.

He'd baited the hook and cast it out there like an expert. And she'd almost fallen for it.

"I don't have the credentials to join the *Mission: Impossible* team," she said smoothly. She tapped the folder on her desk. "But these people do. Why don't you look at the profiles tonight and let me know in the morning whom you would like. Someone will fill in there tomorrow, then your selection should be available, say—" she checked the thick appointment book spread open on her desk "—Monday morning. Is that satisfactory?"

"Very efficient." He said the right words, but his tone didn't have the note of appreciation she might have hoped for. She could feel the "but" coming before his mouth even formed the word. "But I don't think I'm in any shape tonight to give these profiles the consideration they deserve. I'd hate to gloss over them, but I'm afraid that's what would happen."

Despite his politely tailored words, Paul Monroe was being a smart aleck. She should be irritated at him for not taking her work seriously, but he obviously didn't take himself any more seriously. That glint in his eyes seemed to invite her to find a joke to share with him.

She gave her head a tiny shake. Jokes? She couldn't afford to think about jokes. Business. "What do you propose, then?"

He grinned.

Uh-oh. She'd made the mistake of giving Paul Monroe the perfect opening, and she'd been caught.

He sat up, slinging his jacket over one forearm and tucking the folder under his elbow. "As long as you asked, I think it would be a wonderful service of Top-Line Temporaries if you came and told me all about these candidates over dinner. An oral report instead of making me wade through the written report."

"Dinner?"

"Dinner." He stood, and tipped his head as he examined what she feared was the incredibly stupid expression on her face. "You do eat, don't you?"

"Of course I eat."

"Yeah, I guess you don't look really anorexic, but you do look a little thin. My mother would love to get her hands on you and fatten you up some."

"Your mother?" What was he doing talking about his mother? He was a client. *A client.* He'd proposed a business dinner. A little unorthodoxly, perhaps, but a business dinner nonetheless.

"Yeah, Mom's a throwback to the old days. You'd think a Lake Forest matron who does charity luncheons and supports the symphony would have followed the trend into alfalfa sprouts and organic tomatoes, wouldn't you?"

Bette was vaguely aware that his hand under her elbow, warm and firm and so very much *there*, was supposed to encourage her to rise from her chair. She rose. He handed her her briefcase and she accepted it. He steered her toward the door and she followed. Too preoccupied by his comments, she paid little attention to where she was going.

So he was from Lake Forest, from the North Shore, where suburbs were pristine and upbringings well-to-do.

"But no alfalfa sprouts for Mom. She got fed up on that sort of thing as a kid herself." Surely alfalfa sprouts hadn't been big when his mother was a girl, so he must mean something else, but she had no idea what. Though she could swear she'd seen something like a grimace flicker across his face before being replaced by a grin. "She sticks to the basics of my childhood. And I'm happy to say my childhood was filled with double chocolate brownies and triple-decker sandwiches. All my buddies used to come to my house after school, just for the food. I don't think even now she's ever served granola in her life. Thank God. G'night."

He waved to Darla, who stared as they made their way through the outer office. "You're leaving, Bette?"

"I, uh—"

"She's leaving," Paul Monroe interrupted firmly. "We're going to dinner."

"Great!"

Bette cringed a little at Darla's enthusiasm, which made it sound as if Bette hadn't gone to dinner with a man in a year. And she had. Doug Burton, last winter. Once.

She tried to slow her pace against the tug on her elbow. "Uh, maybe I should wait... lock up."

"Don't you worry. I'll lock up." So much for Darla's help. "You two go on and have a nice dinner. Have fun."

The last two words might have qualified as an order.

"We will," Paul promised.

Paul liked the smooth scratch of Bette Wharton's wool tweed suit jacket against his palm, which he'd cupped under her elbow to guide her footsteps. To him the contact seemed all the stronger for the silence that rested easy around them.

Top-Line Temporaries occupied a neat, efficient suite in a neat, efficient building in the area bounded by Michigan Avenue and Lake Shore Drive, the river and Oak Street Beach. He was heading to a different neighborhood, not many blocks away, but where the mood could swing from class to crass, glass to grit in the time it took to walk from one door to the next.

That very variety drew him to the Rush Street area. You could wait to make up your mind until the very last minute and still be within walking distance of just about anything. And if something more appealing came along before you got there, so much the better.

But he knew exactly where he was going to take Bette Wharton tonight. He'd known it nearly from the start.

When he first walked in and saw the cloud of dark hair, the eyes as deep a blue as Lake Michigan and the individualistic mouth with its tilted-back top lip, he'd liked her looks well enough, but not the expression of stern concentration she'd worn. He was all too familiar with that look.

Then he'd seen her grin when she thought his eyes were closed.

It changed her. That intrigued him. Nobody with a mouth like that should be so serious.

She obviously didn't agree. One bit of flippancy escaped her and she looked appalled. He'd watched her stiffen into seriousness, and had become determined to lure out that spark of mischief again.

That was when he knew he'd take her to Mama Artemis's Restaurant. Bette Wharton's exterior, with her conservative suit in a gray wool heathered by faint blue, sensible heels and unfrivolous gold lapel pin, might match her office's neighborhood, but that glint in her eye screamed of Mama Artemis's.

"Do you know where we're going or are you making turns at random?" she asked as they rounded yet another corner.

They could have walked four blocks straight west then five north, but he preferred to mix it up with a turn here and a turn there. "I know where we're going."

He frowned. He *did* know where they were going, had set out with that destination in mind. That wasn't like him.

"I could have sworn we passed this store once before," Bette remarked.

His frown disappeared. He liked the edge of amused skepticism in her voice.

"I said I knew where we were going. I didn't say we were taking the most direct route."

She muffled a splutter of laughter, but he heard it and liked that, too.

"Trying to throw me off the track so I can't find the place again? If this is a secret hideaway, wouldn't it be easier just to blindfold me?"

"Aw, you know how nosy people are these days. I was afraid somebody'd stop us or call a cop. Besides, I gave up my handkerchief to the noble cause of mopping Ed Robson's brow hours ago, and I didn't want to risk my good tie. You wouldn't believe how many ties I've ruined by blindfolding women wearing mascara." He stopped and turned toward her as if scrutinizing her in the glow of a store's lights. "Unless you're not wearing mascara? It's not too late to use the tie...." He let his voice trail off hopefully.

"Your tie would be ruined. I'm wearing mascara." Beneath the words lurked a chuckle. He liked that, too. "But all this talk of ties reminds me ..."

Her hands rose to just above where the well-loosened knot of his tie rested. Glancing down, he saw he'd misbuttoned his shirt at some point in this frenetic day. But that didn't interest him nearly as much as the revelation that occurred when Bette Wharton's index finger brushed his chest as she finished pushing the third button through its proper hole.

She'd hardly touched him. Considerably less skin had come into contact than in a business handshake, but no one would ever have confused the sensations. The bolt of heat tightened his muscles and kicked the breath out of him.

In the uneven light of the store displays, he saw a tide of color rising along her neck and sweeping into her cheeks. The instant before she could pull her hands away, he caught them in both of his and held them, not quite pressed against his chest. If he brought her hands back to where her finger had brushed, he wasn't entirely sure what he'd do. He couldn't risk that. But if he let her pull away now, there'd always be a barrier of awkwardness between them. And he couldn't bear that.

So he simply held her hands. Long enough so that both of them could regulate their breathing and convince themselves nothing had happened. When she took a long breath and looked at him with a smile tinged with wryness, he knew she'd succeeded before he had. To mask that, he spoke the first words that came to his lips.

"Thanks. I told you those waiting rooms are rough. I think that happened when this guy grabbed me by the collar. He was one of those chicken fathers."

He saw the question flit into her eyes, shoving aside some of the confusion and discomfort, and he felt a spurt of relief almost as strong as the disappointment.

"You know," he continued his explanation, "the fathers too chicken to go into the delivery room. Although this guy had no trouble grabbing me by the shirtfront and demanding what in the hell was taking so long. As if I knew!"

Her chuckle assured him her recovery was complete.

"The worst afternoon of my life. Thank God Jan was nearly as efficient in having a baby as she is in everything else. The nurse kept telling me Jan was having an incredibly short labor—as if she thought that should make me feel better."

"Poor Paul." She smiled, apparently unaware it was the first time she'd used his name. She slipped her hands away from him. "What you need is food to fortify you after such a long day."

"Yeah." He pretended to believe the sympathy.

"So maybe we should get to the restaurant."

"Okay." But he didn't move, enjoying the flicker of uncertainty in her eyes, intrigued by the way her thoughts were alternately revealed and hidden. With eyes like that, teasing was irresistible.

"So. . ." she said again.

"What do you mean, 'so'?"

"Don't you want to eat?" she asked.

"Yeah, I want to eat."

"Then don't you think we should get going?"

"No."

"No? Why not?"

"Because if we go, we won't be able to eat."

He saw annoyance warring with amusement in her deep blue eyes and loved it. "Paul—"

"All right, all right," he gave in with a laugh. "Turn around." He saw her take in the small sign that read Mama Artemis, then laughed again when she turned back to him with a grimace.

"You're a fiend."

"I know." He took her elbow again to guide her through the door and along the narrow hallway that led between two shops before widening to the restaurant proper, tucked into the back of the building. He found that having his hand around her elbow already felt pleasantly familiar.

"Paul!" A small, round woman with gray streaking the dark hair piled on top of her head wrapped plump arms around him with enthusiasm. "It's been too long! Much too long. You must tell us how you have been all these long months we have seen nothing of you. And your mama and papa, and your dear little sister. But now you come, come and sit, you and your young lady."

Bette would barely have had time to absorb the lightning switch from the frown and scolding to the smile and invitation before she was towed along between crowded tables. But she didn't seem thrown. He admired that. When she sent a quick, questioning glance over her shoulder, he smiled, shrugged and headed after them.

In a far corner, amid deep, rich colors aglow in candlelight, Bette slid into a small booth, its seat a quarter of a circle so small that when he sat next to her their knees tangled.

"Here. Now you settle, get comfortable, and I get wine. Then we talk about the dinner and I will tell you what you must have to eat." The woman patted Bette's hand and Paul's shoulder and hurried away.

"Is that Mama Artemis?"

"No. That's her daughter, Ardith. Mama Artemis is much more forceful."

Bette shook her head as she chuckled. "Where are they from? I don't recognize the accent."

"I really don't know. Not that I haven't asked. I have. But when they start talking about it they get into a lot of complicated history, and just when I think I'm starting to follow it, they get excited and lapse into their native language. Best I can tell you is somewhere in southeastern

Europe. I guess one of those places that's been passed back and forth a good bit."

Ardith bustled back with a bottle of wine swaddled in a napkin to catch the weeping condensation.

"How is Mama Artemis, Ardith?"

"Ah, Mama. She is the same. Always Mama." She poured the pale gold liquid into the chunky clear glass in front of Paul. "She is a terror, Mama." Even if Ardith hadn't smiled, Paul could see Bette recognized the affection and admiration and knew "terror" was a term of respect.

At her gesture, Paul tasted the wine and gave wholehearted approval. "Glad to hear she's doing well," he said. "Be sure to tell her Jan had her baby today. A boy."

"Ah, a baby! Yes, yes, I will tell her. Such a happy thing, young Jan to have a baby. And you should be having babies, too. You should find a woman, marry her, settle down and have babies."

"Aw, Ardith." The refrain was so familiar he responded automatically, but underneath a memory stirred uneasily of that same refrain spoken in another voice.

"Yes, yes, many babies. Baby girls for you to spoil and baby boys to play with the toys like you do with my nephews. They ask for you. Goran has found three soldiers he wants to show you. And a new engine. You come some Sunday. And you bring your young lady."

As she launched into a description of the meal she would serve them, Paul knew it had been more edict than invitation, and if he didn't bring Bette, he'd spend all his time explaining why.

He sighed as Ardith left them, apparently satisfied that their choices—more accurately, her choices for them—were in order.

"I don't know why I come here," he grumbled, only half-kidding. A lot could be said for places where nobody asked you to Sunday dinner or cared whom you were with or speculated on when you'd get around to having babies.

"Isn't the food good?"

"The food's terrific."

"Maybe that's the reason," Bette said as if she meant it, but he spotted a glint in her eyes. "Or maybe it's because you're obviously adored here."

"You saying I have an ego problem, huh?"

She shrugged, a movement that also raised and lowered her knee a fraction of an inch where it touched his, just enough to send a shiver of sensation running up his leg. "Or maybe it's because they invite you to come over on Sundays to enjoy the children's toys."

He grinned, trying to ignore where that shiver of sensation had concentrated. "Occupational hazard."

"Occupational? It sounds more like child's play."

He tilted his head. "Didn't Jan tell you what I do?"

"Of course she did. I couldn't select possible temporaries for you without knowing what they'd be doing."

"What do I do?" He saw her resistance to stating what she clearly felt was the obvious. "Humor me, please?"

She let out a short breath. As she started to answer, part of him experienced inordinate pleasure at the idea that she was willing to humor him.

"You are an independent appraiser, with a good bit of business coming from referrals from Centurian Insurance Group as well as several other major firms, although you do a variety of noninsurance-related appraisals. And Jan mentioned you've worked with some large museums."

He nodded, and hoped he succeeded in masking the automatic frown. At least Jan hadn't mentioned the Smithsonian offer. Prestige was one thing, but you had to consider the cost, too. "That's true as far as it goes, but do you know what I appraise?"

He saw her quick intelligence consider the question and grasp its ramifications immediately. He could practically hear her thinking that insurance companies rarely hired independent appraisers for the bulk of their business—the cars, boats, houses and routine household goods that they could assess through statistics galore.

"A specialty. Something out of the ordinary."

"That's right." He waited.

"What is it? What's your specialty?"

He liked Bette Wharton a lot at that moment. She didn't want to have to ask. He figured she felt not knowing the answer represented a slipup in her preparation. But she didn't show any of that in her tone. No grudging echo tainted a single syllable.

He wanted to kiss her. Right then and there. To lean forward across the small table and let his lips explore that up-swung lip of hers, to slip his tongue along it and then inside it.

The blood quickening through his body was a warning. Better get his mind—and his hormones—off that track and on business, or he'd be doing just what his imagination had conjured up. And he had a feeling Bette Wharton was the kind of woman to take it all too seriously.

Yes, better to stick to business. Even if she wasn't likely to take his business too seriously.

He shrugged. The movement helped a little, although he knew no shrug would ease the tension that had begun to tighten certain of his muscles. "It's pretty simple. I mostly appraise cards, trains and books."

"Cards, trains and books?" she repeated blankly.

"Baseball cards, toy trains and comic books."

Bette stared at him. "You're kidding."

"Most of the time, yes. But not about this. I also operate as a sort of clearinghouse for specialists in other areas from all over the country, and I specialize in appraising other stuff myself, too. Things like original Monopoly games, nineteenth-century mechanical toys, vintage Erector sets. But I'd say those three—baseball cards, toy trains and comic books—are the most common in my trade."

"Then your occupation really is child's play."

He'd heard it before. He'd heard notes of censure a lot stronger than the faint echo in Bette's words. But they had never bothered him before.

He did his best to shake it off. He grinned and tossed out the words of truth.

"That's me, a kid at heart."

Chapter Two

Bette tried to ignore the strange frisson of relief and disappointment that touched through her.

A kid at heart. She believed he'd spoken no more than the absolute truth, and that relieved her. Because that meant the odd undercurrent of attraction would soon wither. Dependability, solidity, maturity—those were the attributes she valued. Someone who would work through the difficulties in life as she did, someone who anticipated them and prepared for them. Certainly not someone who admitted to being—*bragged* about being—a kid at heart.

So why are you disappointed? asked a voice inside her.

To quiet it, she asked, "How did you get to know Mama Artemis and Ardith?"

"I did a job for them back when I was starting out. In fact, before I'd set up the business."

"What kind of job?"

Paul gestured widely to the room around them. "Appraising." For the first time Bette noticed one wall was decorated with assorted wooden game boards, the colors mellowed and softened by age. On a shelf along the opposite wall resided arrangements of old-fashioned toys, a teddy bear appearing to pull a wagon bearing two dolls, a wooden sled next to ancient-looking skates, a hoop and stick.

"The toys? You appraised these toys?"

"These and a whole lot more. This collection's the tip of the iceberg."

"Did they bring all these things with them when they came to America?" She wondered again about the origins of Mama Artemis and her family. Not Poland; she'd heard no trace of her grandfather's speech in Ardith's voice.

"No way. Mama Artemis had just been widowed and didn't have much anyway, but she left everything behind except the clothes on her back and her two children. She came to Chicago because she had a cousin she could live with at first, though I guess it got pretty crowded."

Bette's lips curved. She could hear her grandfather's rich, deep tones and exotic accent, recounting with pride each step his family had taken toward the American Dream. As if it were a bedtime story, he would tell her again and again, each movement forward in education or position or savings.

"So Mama Artemis started looking around for a job..." Paul went on.

Like Mama Artemis, her grandparents had lived with relatives at first. How proudly he had recounted to her how soon they had rented a whole apartment for themselves. Then came moves to a better neighborhood, a bigger apartment. He would say over and over how proud he was of his daughter—Bette's mother—who had graduated from high school and married a man who owned his own home. She remembered how her grandfather beamed the day she graduated from college, and how two years later, sick as he was, he had made her sit on his hospital bed and tell him every detail of the ceremony that entitled her to the initials M.B.A.

"Are you with me?"

Paul Monroe's touch on her wrist was fleeting, but left behind a tingle of warmth.

"What? Oh. Yes, I'm with you." She wasn't surprised to discover that one level of her mind really had absorbed what he said. Many times in business she'd blessed her dual-track mind. "You were saying Mama Artemis went to work as a housekeeper for this eccentric old man."

"Yeah, and it turned out he had this terrific collection of toys and games and dolls he'd put together bit by bit for decades. When he died, he left it all to Mama Artemis."

"And that's where you came in? How did you get her as a client?"

"I didn't. At least not if you mean going out and pursuing the account. I hadn't even set up in business at that point. I'd been working for this insurance company—a rising young executive, they said. I hated it."

He said it so cheerfully she could almost doubt he meant it. "Then why'd you do it? Did you plan that as a springboard to establishing your own appraising business?"

"I used it as a springboard to paying my rent," he said dryly. "I drifted into insurance after college."

"You majored in business?"

"No. History. Probably the only history major who never considered going on to law school." The sharp note was so at odds with his usual tone that she wondered if she imagined it. Especially when he continued easily, "But that might be because I didn't intend to be a history major. I just liked history. A quarter before graduation, I looked at my courses and figured I lacked one class each to major in psych and history, and I liked the history offering better that spring, so there I was—a history major.''

Bette shook her head, thinking of her own carefully considered selections, each a plotted step along the road to owning her own business, each a piece in the foundation on which to build her future.

He took her gesture another way. ''Go ahead and shake your head. You probably already know what I discovered—there aren't any want ads in the Sunday paper for history grads.'' He shrugged. ''That's where insurance came in.''

''And then Mama Artemis?'' she prompted.

He grinned. ''I lucked into that. I'd fallen into being sort of a troubleshooter for the insurance company, getting appraisals for unusual stuff nobody else wanted to bother with. Not the real antiques, but nostalgia items and some really oddball collections. It was an excuse to get out of the nine-to-five rut at the office, so I took courses, read a lot, asked questions. A friend of a friend told Mama Artemis about me, and she asked me to help. I was too stupid to know what I'd gotten myself into until I stood waist-deep in one of the finest collections in the country. It was worth a fortune.'' He gestured to the surroundings. ''More than enough to set up a successful restaurant on the Near North Side.''

''So you helped Mama Artemis sell off some of the collection to finance the restaurant?''

''You mean as a dealer? No.'' His hands and face had stiffened and his words were crisp. Bette contemplated this new aspect of Paul Monroe with something more than surprise.

But just as suddenly he was his easy, amused self once more. "You just ran smack-dab into my hobbyhorse. I don't think appraisers should be dealers, and vice versa. If nothing else, somebody telling you your Great-Aunt Gertie's vase is worth $22.50 when that same person's in the market to buy it poses one hell of a conflict of interest. Most folks who do both are honest, but why go dangling temptation out there like a carrot?"

"And Mama Artemis's inheritance was worth considerably more than $22.50?"

He grinned at her dryness. "Considerably more. Even with a string of zeros. I tell you, I spent the first few months scrambling around trying to figure out exactly how over my head I was. By the end of it, Mama had her restaurant, I had enough contacts to get out of insurance, a couple dozen collectors and several museums had acquired rare finds and the people of Chicago had the opportunity to enjoy some great cooking."

Bette looked at Paul Monroe and considered how different his approach to business—to life itself—was from hers. He talked of drifting, luck, happenstance and scrambling. She lived by planning, forethought, diligence and persevering.

What bothered her was, despite all that, she couldn't resist smiling back at him.

Ardith's arrival made Bette jump a little at the realization that she and Paul had been smiling foolishly at each other. It must have been contagious, because Ardith wore the same kind of smile as she set platters of steaming, aromatic food on the table, fussed with their arrangement, then exhorted Paul and Bette to enjoy their meal.

They did. Both the food and the conversation.

Bette surprised herself. She seldom dived into food like this—and never during a business meal. She found herself using a business trick of drawing out her companion by asking questions. But she knew the difference between obligatory questions and a true desire to know. She'd never laughed as much as she did at Paul's accounts of his hair-raising childhood exploits. And she'd never felt so disinclined to move away from the brush of arms and legs that occurred in the tiny booth.

Replete, and with an odd sensation of content, she sat back. "You've lived a charmed life, Paul Monroe."

He considered that as he examined his half-full water glass. Maybe he *had* lived a charmed life. He had good friends, a good business. He'd benefited from a good mind and good education. And family... Well, he couldn't deny the strains and differences, but the bottom line was that he loved them and they loved him—with one exception. And he'd fought his way clear of that one exception's influence years ago, so he had freedom, too. What else could anybody need?

Without conscious thought, his gaze went to Bette's face.

Her smile pleased him at a level he couldn't explain. More than the way her lips curved—although that was nice, too—he liked the way her cheeks and eyebrows lifted, providing a new showcase for her deep blue eyes. Even more, he liked knowing *he* had lured the smile into the light. It was a shame to keep that spark locked up behind the dusty seriousness she seemed to think necessary. The challenge appealed to him.

He wanted to see her laugh again. Here, in the soft shadows of their corner.

"You sound just like Michael," he said.

"Michael? Your brother?"

"No. Friend. Michael Dickinson, Grady Roberts and I were college roommates." He told her about finding fungus growing in the closet at the end of sophomore year and, though she wrinkled her nose in distaste, she laughed. Laughter looked even better on her than a smile.

"By the time Tris came we had quite a reputation."

"Tris? Your sister?"

"Nope. Wrong again." He recognized the flick of annoyance. Bette Wharton didn't like being wrong, and especially not twice.

"But you do have a sister."

"How can you be so sure—oh, of course, Ardith. Yeah, I have a sister, but Judi's in college now. She's eleven years younger than me. Tris Donlin's my cousin. Her freshman year the three of us—Grady, Michael and I—were seniors, and we all hung around together."

"It sounds as if you had a wonderful childhood."

"Had? You look like you think I'm still going through it." He laughed, but he noted the startled look in her eyes, as if he'd caught her at something not totally polite.

"I'm sorry, I—"

"It's all right, I was kidding." He had to cut her off. He didn't want a repeat of the tone she'd used to describe his work as child's play; he didn't want a repeat of the feeling. Better, much better, to turn the conversation.

"Of course everything wasn't roses, you know. At one time I thought the only answer was to get away. I wanted nothing to do with my family." He kept words and tone light, consciously pushing aside the jumble of those old feelings threatening to rise again. Why had he brought this up?

"About sixteen or seventeen? I think every kid goes through that stage, don't you?"

"I must have been an early developer, then, because I was twelve and a half."

"Twelve?" She cocked her head and her hair swung, exposing the side of her neck in a most distracting way. She pursed her lips—an even greater distraction—and said in ponderous tones, "A manifestation of sibling rivalry, perhaps, since you were displaced by your younger sister?"

He shook his head, but more at his own thoughts than at her words. "Nah, I'd gone through that the year before. But I guess it was about being displaced in a way."

He shifted, and felt the rub of her elbow against his jacket, the sensation translating directly to a prickling along his skin.

"What happened, Paul?"

Her voice, quiet and soft, lured him.

"We'd just moved. Only across town but a world away to a kid. My grandfather had retired. Not because he wanted to kick back and relax or anything, but because the doctors gave an order he couldn't refuse." He tried to fight stronger feelings with ironic humor. He wasn't sure it worked. "Given the choice of dying or going to Palm Springs, he took Palm Springs. But that didn't mean he gave up the reins. Not Walter Wilson Mulholland."

Not a man who'd spent his whole life dictating. Not a man whose only communication with his grandson had come in the form of orders. *Sit erect. Take your elbows off the table. Straighten your shoulders. Wear a shirt and tie for dinner at my table.*

Not the man who had talked in front of Paul as if he didn't exist. *The boy needs a haircut. The boy needs discipline. James, if you and Nancy won't send him away to school, at least stop babying the boy.*

Paul propped his elbows on the table and picked up his wineglass, concentrating on the feel of its smooth, warm surface between his palms.

"He named Dad head of the firm in his place and ordered us to move into the big house on the lake where Mom had been brought up. She didn't want to go, either."

He remembered sitting on the stairs of the little suburban house he'd been born in, out of sight, listening to his parents.

Jim, we have a home here.

We'll make a home there, honey.

I don't want to go back to that house, Jim. Don't you see what's happening?

Shh, there's nothing to cry about, honey. This is a great move up for us.

"But Walter Mulholland said it was more appropriate for our new standing in the community. And nobody disobeyed him." Certainly not James Monroe. "Big, dark furniture and drapes that looked petrified. The only noise was the hall clock. God, I hated it."

His own vehemence discomfited him. Without looking at Bette, he produced a deprecating grin. "I guess I missed our old place. The neighborhood, my friends."

He remembered the tidy little house not far from the railroad tracks. His mother had baked cookies and helped him grow a tomato patch each summer. His father had taken the train into the city every day, and home every night.

"We used to play baseball together, Dad and I. He'd been a pro. He had a tough time growing up. His folks were really poor, and baseball was his only real fun. He got through college on baseball scholarships and he started law school during off-seasons from the minors. He loves the game."

In the drawn-out twilights of summer, his father had coached the Little League team or they'd just thrown the ball back and forth, an endless pendulum connecting father and son. He could still feel the lung-bursting pride at his pals' awe that James Monroe had been a pro baseball player, a gifted fielder who reached the highest level of minor leagues and come this close to being in the majors.

Until he married Nancy Mulholland and went to work in Walter Mulholland's law firm.

"He still has his glove," he told Bette, turning his wineglass around and around, "but when he took over the firm, he didn't have time for that sort of thing anymore. And Mom was busy with Judi and the move and the new house. I was a little at loose ends. When Walter Mulholland returned for his version of a state visit late that summer, it all came to a head."

Paul consciously eased the muscles in his shoulder.

"Walter Wilson Mulholland never bought the theory about letting people 'find themselves,'" he continued. He listened to himself critically. Light irony, that was the appropriate tone. "He knew what everyone should do with his life and how to achieve it—and he didn't mince words saying so."

"That can be a sign of caring," said Bette. "That someone wants only the best for the people he loves."

"Maybe." He conceded the point because he didn't want to have to consider how little he believed it. "But with him it was more force of habit. He was born and bred to be a despot." He saw the quick frown that pleated Bette's brows. Sympathy? Or disapproval? Not liking either possibility, he forged on. "When he started diagraming my life, I didn't care for the grand design, so I ran away, complete with bedroll, clean underwear and seven dollars and thirty-four cents."

Two decades later he could still remember dinner that night—a formal meal with several strangers joining them at the big, polished table. He could still hear the stern, upright old man proclaiming that he'd decided that Paul would become a litigator. He could hear the deep, determined voice of his mother's father detailing exactly where Paul would fit into the firm's roster fifteen years in the future. And each step of his life over the next two decades. The right prep school. The right university. The right law school. The right marriage. The right family. The right address. All selected by Walter Wilson Mulholland.

He'd never liked his grandfather. That night he'd started hating him.

He'd slipped out of the house while the guests enjoyed after-dinner drinks. He'd headed for the old neighborhood. He couldn't even remember which friend he'd intended to go to, but he'd ended up in front of his old house, standing in the cold, chilled rain that can bring a preview of fall to an Illinois summer and realizing his home now belonged to another family.

"Dad found me around midnight."

His father's arms had hugged him so tightly it hurt a little, but it had been a good hurt. Even as he spoke he could feel again his father's jacket shoulder under his cheek, smell the scent of his after-shave. His father's hands had been shaking slightly as they tightened a blanket around Paul's damp shoulders.

"I thought he would skin me alive. Instead, he talked." Then and now he'd have preferred being skinned alive. He could still hear the words.

Paul, what in the world got into you to run away?

I'm not going to do what that old man tells me, even if he is my grandfather.

Your grandfather is providing you opportunities most boys never have, never even dream of. An education, a profession, a position in life.

I don't want them. I don't want anything he'd give me.

You can't say that, yet. You're only a boy. You can't know what you'll want when you grow—

He made us move. Mom didn't want to move. I heard her.

He thought it best. Your mother's always had these things, so she doesn't know what it means to be without—

And he made you take that big job.

No. No, he didn't make me. I wanted that, Paul.

"He said that when I grew up, I'd understand. That being an adult meant making choices, and that meant leaving some things behind."

Someday, when you're grown-up, when you're married and have children of your own, you'll understand, Paul.

He didn't have to grow up to understand. He'd understood then. His father had made a choice to follow Walter Mulholland's rules, and what he'd left behind were twilight games of catch with his son.

He couldn't blame his father; he'd been poor a long time and now he had a chance for money and position, not only for himself but for his family. But he could blame Walter Mulholland.

He blinked away the memories and looked at Bette. Her eyes were wide and solemn, with another emotion deep in them that he couldn't read. The flicker of the candles' flames added a mysterious light. He felt his heartbeat accelerate as if in delayed reaction to some tremendous danger.

He picked up his wineglass and tilted the cool, clear liquid into his mouth. It didn't completely ease the dryness. "That's when I realized I didn't want to be a grown-up. I preferred to stay a kid."

When she blinked, he felt as if he'd been cut off from a source of warmth and light. Her left hand rested on the table between them, the fingers long and pale against the forest-green cloth. He wanted to cover it with his own, to give the connection that he thought had grown between them a physical expression.

She lowered her eyelashes a second time, and he sensed withdrawal. Maybe his own.

He quirked a grin at her, manufacturing the mischief. "Especially those next few weeks. Mom was terrific. I even got her to let me play hooky from school the first week and go to a Cubs' game."

"What a fiend. Scare them to death, then weasel special treatment out of them." Bette made a tsking sound with her tongue. "It sounds as if you have a wonderful family."

He met her deep blue eyes again, and saw recognition there. He considered his family ties—Mom, Dad, Judi, Tris, other cousins, aunts and uncles. Not perfect, and sometimes the ties chafed, but... "I do."

"Although your younger sister..." Bette gave an exaggerated shudder. "That poor soul."

He knew what she was doing, skirting away from the serious turn their conversation had taken, and he gladly cooperated. What had gotten into him to spill all this? Not his style, not his style at all.

He snorted in disbelief. "Judi, a poor soul? Not on your life." Then suspicion narrowed his eyes. "Why would you say that?"

"To have you as an older brother," she said promptly. "I have an older brother myself, and I know what instruments of teasing torture they can be, but you—" She shivered again. "It must have been a nightmare for the poor girl."

"Hey!"

She laughed, and he let the sound, low and rippling, wash over him. The pleasure of that sound could become addictive. That, and the look in her eyes, as if she were surprised he'd drawn the amusement out of her, and perhaps secretly rather pleased, too.

"So, tell me about *your* family," he invited, sliding his right hand over her left. He did it on impulse, a casual gesture that somehow didn't feel casual. Her skin was soft and warm against his. "I bet you're the oldest of twelve, responsible for all the little 'uns since you were barely able to toddle yourself. No, wait. That's right, you said you have an older brother. So you must be the oldest girl. And you grew up in the country, and spent summers at the local swimming hole."

She shook her head with another laugh. "Not even close. I grew up in the decidedly un-country atmosphere of the near western suburbs—mostly Oak Park. I'm the younger of two, and mildly coddled. My parents worked hard enough to take early retirement a couple years ago and move permanently to Arizona where they'd had a house for years. And they still worry about their little girl being 'all alone.'"

Paul looked at her, and felt a twinge of protectiveness deep within him. He could sympathize with her parents. For all her self-reliance, he didn't like the idea of Bette Wharton being without a strong shoulder to rely on—a friend, a partner.

Then it occurred to him that she might already have that, and the possibility brought a twist to his stomach that came too fast and too strong to pretend it was anything but jealousy. God. That wasn't a reasonable reaction. What did he care whether she had someone or not? He certainly wasn't auditioning for the role of strong shoulder in any-one's life.

He sat back, sliding his fingers away from hers under the pretext of placing his napkin on the table.

Bette, too, straightened and moved away. Although the warmth of his touch still lingered on her skin, it didn't take a body language expert to read good-night.

She made a show of checking her watch. "This has been lovely, Paul. Thank you. I hope you have an opportunity to check those files, and give me a call in the morning." She gathered her purse, flashed him a smile and prepared to slide out of the booth.

"Where do you think you're going?"

If he hadn't said it with such blank astonishment, she would have been irked by the Neanderthal implication. "Home. It's late."

"Fine. I'm driving you."

"That isn't necessary. I can catch a cab to the train sta-tion and the line goes right near my house." That was true; the commuter railroad line ran no more than five blocks from her home in a western suburb, though the nearest station was a couple miles from the house she rented. She'd have to try to rouse a cab, not always an easy task at night in the suburbs.

"I bet roads go right near your house, too. I'm driving you."

Protests did no good. Not even when she logically pointed out that since he'd said he lived north of the city, along the lake in Evanston, and she lived west, it would be a long drive home for him. By the time he'd wrangled with Ardith over whether or not he would pay for their meal, then they'd said their good-nights, found a cab and reached the lot where he'd parked his car, she'd about given up.

He held open the car door for her, then went around to the driver's side. Clicking home the seat belt and starting the car with smooth efficiency, he remained silent. She knew little about cars, but this one struck her as sleekly unpretentious. It seemed old enough to be well broken in and new enough to boast all the amenities.

"Paul—"

He slanted her a quick, quelling look. "I'm driving you home."

A flicker of irritation made her grimace at him. "I intended to ask if you wanted to know where I live."

The car rolled up to a red light at a deserted intersection, and he turned to her. She could see the amusement back in his eyes. "Sorry. Maybe I jumped to a conclusion. It was just that the previous twenty-three sentences you'd started had all ended with junk about taking a train. Obviously a totally unwarranted assumption on my part this time."

"Totally unwarranted," she agreed. As the light turned green and he eased the car forward, she saw his smile in profile and tried to ignore an answering twitch of her lips.

"So now that I've apologized, are you going to tell me where you live, or do you want me to start picking spots at random?"

"That could be an interesting experiment."

He nodded. "Although I do know it's west, so that trims out a third of the Chicago suburbs. And with the hint that it's near a commuter railroad, that eliminates about a third of that third. So, I figure it shouldn't take more than a month or so to find the right one."

She gave in to the laughter bubbling up in her. "All right! I live in Elmhurst. Take the Eisenhower Expressway. A month's too long on the road for me!"

"It would be a long time between showers, but it would give me a chance to get to know you."

Meeting his look for a moment, she thought his eyes held a light not entirely deviltry or reflected streetlights. She looked away, and they drove in silence until they reached the expressway and headed west.

"Tell me more about your family," he said. "How about your older brother? Where is he?"

"Married, two children, living in Minneapolis."

"So you're an aunt!"

"Two times an aunt. Ron and Clara have a two-year-old son, Ron, Jr., and they just had a little girl, Abby, last month."

He sighed. "I wish my sister was old enough to have kids. Or maybe I should say old enough to have kids without making Mom and Dad crazy. I've always wanted to be an uncle."

"An uncle? Why?"

"It seems like the perfect setup. Uncles—and aunts—have all the fun without the responsibilities. You don't have to live up to anyone's expectations of the perfect parent. No diaper changing, no worrying about childhood diseases, no sweating out death-defying escapades, no grounding them because they stayed out too late, no wondering if the roads'll ever be safe again with a sixteen-year-old maniac on the streets, no birds-and-bees talks, no college tuition."

"Sounds to me as if you're speaking from firsthand experience."

He quirked an eyebrow at her—questioning, but already primed to share her amusement.

"As if you're remembering your own youth," she explained.

The expectant look became a full-blown laugh. "I hadn't realized it, but you're right. The idea of having a kid like me would scare anybody off! Lord, when I think of the things Grady and I got into, it's amazing we made it to twenty—and without being the death of our parents."

"Just you and Grady? Was Michael the responsible one?"

"Probably. I didn't meet Michael until college. But, yeah, I'd guess he was the responsible type even as a kid. Steady. Not like Grady and me."

As she gave him directions off the expressway, a twinge drew Bette's eyebrows into a frown, but she didn't have time to consider it, because he had another question.

"How about your friends?"

She hesitated, uneasy. "I, uh, I haven't been very good about keeping up with my friends. There's one girl from high school, Melody, who always checks in when she comes through the area. And my assistant, Darla, has been a wonderful friend to me."

She broke off to give him further instructions on where to turn. She could have let the topic drop there, but she felt the need to explain further. She refused to use the word *justify* even in her own mind.

"You know how it is when you get into college and get immersed in your classes and studying." She thought back to some of his stories tonight; maybe he didn't know. "And setting up a business doesn't leave time for anything else. It takes twenty-five hours a day just to get it off the ground. To make it really fly, you have to be totally dedicated to that, and that alone."

He glanced at her as he made the turn into her street, and she knew he didn't agree.

"What's the use of having your own business if you let it run you? The whole idea is to not have a boss looking over your shoulder, telling you what to do and when to do it. Work's fine, but there are other things in life. Ambition can take over."

She bristled a little at the implied criticism at the same time that she wondered if anyone could really be that offhand and still make a go of a business. Experience had taught her the demands of a successful business. And she had done sufficient homework on Paul Monroe to know his business was successful . . . even if her research had left out exactly what he did.

"This is it," she said coolly, "the one in the middle of the block with the light on."

He pulled into the driveway. "A house? You own it?"

"No. I'm renting this one, but I'm starting to look for a place to buy." The next step in her plan. With the business apparently on its feet, it was time to stop wasting money on rent and start building equity.

"It's nice, but you could use a jack-o'-lantern."

"Jack o'lantern?"

"You know, a pumpkin, carved to look like a face, with a candle inside."

"I *know* what a jack-o'-lantern is."

"Good. Because that front doorstep of yours could definitely use one. You know Halloween's getting close."

"Yes, I know, but a pumpkin has not been at the top of my list of priorities. I've been busy at—"

"At work," he finished for her.

She glanced over, but saw no sign of the humor she might have expected. His gaze was fixed with great concentration on her bare front step.

She prepared to say her thank-yous, but he turned the engine off. For a blood-thundering instant she thought he was going to turn to her, reach across the bucket seats, take her in his arms and . . .

Before her imagination could get too carried away, he'd gotten out and come around to open her door. She thanked him, but ignored his hand.

She'd known him less than eight hours, but sometimes that was all it took to see the flaws. He'd made no effort to hide them. From his own words she'd learned he hated schedules, he put fun over responsibility. He hadn't learned that achievement followed a plan.

It added up to one message: he was a man to stay away from.

Too bad her hormones didn't agree.

"A hatchback, huh?"

She followed the direction of his gaze to the garage door windows. Hatchback. Car.

"That's right. A total suburbanite, that's me. It comes in handy for hauling things from the hardware store."

"But you don't drive in to the city?"

"Not if I can help it. It's more efficient to take the train. That way I can work during the commute and don't have to worry about parking. You always drive?"

"I like the freedom."

Stepping within the pool of light at the front door, she took a slow, steadying breath as she unlocked the door then turned to him, holding out her hand.

"Thank you, Paul. I enjoyed the evening. Dinner was wonderful, and Mama Artemis's is a real find. I—"

He ignored the hand and the speech. Grasping her upper arms, he turned her to face him, startling her into silence. He bent his head, so slowly she thought she might explode from the waiting before he ever reached her lips.

And then, when the waiting had finally ended, all he did was brush his mouth against hers—top lip, bottom, top lip again. Softly, quickly.

"Good night, Bette."

He turned her around and headed her inside. Automatically, she closed storm door and wooden door behind her. But she couldn't move any farther. She heard his car door shut, heard the engine start, heard his car back up and pull away, and still she stood, leaning against the door's wooden panels, staring into the hallway's familiar shadows.

One thought filled the yawning emptiness his touch had made of her mind.

Uh-oh.

Chapter Three

He turned the corner and caught one last glimpse of the neat neighborhood. A neighborhood where all the corners were squared, all the houses in a straight line, all the lawns trimmed and the trees big. Someone with a ruler had probably plotted out the whole thing, including the flower beds filled with yellow mums.

It suited Bette Wharton right down to the ground.

A vague vision of his apartment rose in his mind as he accelerated onto the tollway and headed north. Although he'd lived there several years he couldn't form a clear picture of it. The walls were light, maybe white, and the windows good-sized so a good bit of tree-dappled sunlight made it into the rooms. He had an old couch his mother'd given him when she redecorated the room over the garage. But he could envision it better in that hideaway of his teen years than in his own living room. Books, a TV and stereo equipment rested on shelves of boards and bricks, smacking a bit of college days. But he'd been reluctant to put up shelves. That seemed too permanent, too attached.

He rolled into the exact-change lane for the tollbooth, flipping coins in left-handed with practiced ease. Merging into the traffic, which couldn't be considered light even at this hour, he found his mind repeated his earlier thought: *That seemed too permanent, too attached.*

Maybe that was what bothered him about the museum deal.

Jobs he'd done for several museums around the country as one-shot deals had worked out fine. In fact he'd enjoyed them. The people sure weren't in the business for money, and he liked that about them. Plus, he appreciated that museums were acknowledging the lighter side of everyday life, the toys, the games, the hobbies. And he enjoyed visits to Washington, especially since they gave him a chance to visit Tris.

But now, with the Smithsonian talking about a regular arrangement... He just didn't know.

Someone like Bette Wharton would probably jump at this kind of opportunity like a shot. He suspected that, to her, it would be a building block in some great life plan.

He checked the rearview mirror as he steered toward the exit, caught sight of his half smile and turned it into a grimace. All right, so he was attracted to Bette, despite the suspicion she actually had one of those god-awful five-year plans the yuppie magazines always wrote about. Why? What was so great about Bette Wharton?

She wasn't classically beautiful or a sex goddess knockout. And he found himself absurdly glad she wasn't either one. Anybody could spot a woman like that, but he'd made a discovery not every man would be astute enough to make.

He'd listened to the crisp coolness of her voice and heard that hint of spiciness beneath. He'd touched the no-nonsense wool of her suit and felt the softness of her skin. He'd acknowledged the common sense coming from her mouth and recognized the uncommon sensuality of that maddening upper lip. He'd looked into the forthright navy blue of her eyes and seen that she had secrets there.

Secrets. Maybe that was it. Maybe that defined the whole thing. This feeling that she'd hidden her teasing and laughter beneath a life ruled by an appointment calendar, and the challenge of luring it out of hiding.

So, maybe what he felt came more from the challenge of making her see that other side of herself, the free spirit. He could handle that.

A challenge... Yeah, he could enjoy that.

"Paul Monroe's on line two, Bette."

Bette sidestepped Darla's curious look, just as she'd sidestepped earlier questions with a simple statement that she and the client had had an enjoyable business dinner. "Thank you, Darla."

She waited until her assistant closed the door behind her, took a deep breath and lifted the receiver. "Good morning, this is Bette Wharton. May I help you?" It was chicken to pretend she didn't know who was on the other end of the line, but she wanted an extra second to remind herself of how she'd decided to deal with him.

"Hi, Bette. It's Paul."

So much for formality, she thought with an unwilling and wry smile. "Good morning, Paul. I hope everything's going smoothly so far with Sally."

"Sally? Oh, the temporary temporary secretary. Yeah, everything's fine. In fact, you know what she did?"

"What?"

"She made me fresh coffee." He sounded so impressed she couldn't help but chuckle.

"No! Really?"

"Go ahead and laugh, but Jan never does that for me. She says anybody who comes and goes as much as I do deserves to drink whatever's available."

"She has a point."

"Well, just don't go telling Sally, okay? I usually only get fresh coffee about twice a year, so this is a treat."

"I promise not to tell Sally, but she won't be there much longer."

"How'd you know?"

"How'd I know what?"

"That Sally won't be here much longer."

"Because she'll be replaced by your permanent temporary as soon as you make a selection."

"Oh. I thought maybe my reputation had already gotten to her. Isn't that an oxymoron?"

"Isn't what an oxymoron, and what reputation?"

"'Permanent temporary.' I think that's an oxymoron—you know, a built-in contradiction."

"I guess it is." She hated herself for it, but she couldn't resist repeating, "And what reputation?"

"For going through a lot of secretaries fast."

She wondered if the reason for this was only his business habits. In her line of business she couldn't help but know that a certain breed of men viewed temporary secretaries as a two-birds-with-one-stone dating service. She'd have been surprised if Paul Monroe was one; she'd also have been too disappointed for her own comfort.

In her coolest, most neutral tones, she said, "I understand that's the reason Jan Robson contacted us in the first place, isn't it?"

"I guess it is." If she thought she caught an echo of sheepishness, she could also imagine a grin lurking.

"And that, I'm sure, is why you're calling this morning." She thought he mumbled "not exactly," but ignored it. "I'll messenger the files over to you immediately, since they ended up back with my papers, uh, last night. You can look them over, then let my office know before the close of business today whom you have selected and we'll make every effort to have that person in place tomorrow morning."

"I don't like the sound of that."

What was there not to like? She was being more than reasonable; getting someone lined up overnight qualified as above and beyond the call of good customer service. She decided to quell him with a single syllable. "Oh?"

"Particularly that part about the messenger and then notifying your office." He sounded singularly unquelled. "I thought we could meet for lunch and discuss the whole thing then, say about one—"

"I'm sorry, lunch won't be possible." Not if she hoped to catch up with yesterday's leftover chores.

"But you've got to eat. All I'm saying is spend that time with me. And, of course, going over these files."

"I don't eat lunch." Now why had she said that? There were certainly times she'd skipped the meal to finish some work, but she'd also had her share of business lunches. She was reacting almost as if she were afraid of Paul Monroe. Ridiculous.

"You don't eat lunch? Well, no wonder you're thin. I tell you, Bette, my mom would definitely worry about you."

"It's very kind of your mother to be concerned." What a damn fool thing to say! His mother didn't know of her existence. She was becoming a blithering idiot. "But I must go now. I'll send the files immediately by messenger, Mr. Monroe, and wait for your decision. Goodbye.''

She hung up before she could hear any answer, then stared at the instrument as if something might leap out of it to snatch away the final shreds of her composure.

Jerkily, she picked up a pencil and rammed it into the small sharpener from her drawer.

Why did she react that way? All right, Paul Monroe made her a little nervous. Yes, she felt an attraction to him, although clearly nothing serious, since she had a firm fix on the man's faults. Even though that eye-dancing smile could make the clearest of faults a bit fuzzy around the edges. But she hadn't turned him down because of that . . . exactly. She'd turned him down because she had a lot of work and he'd disrupted her schedule yesterday. It was only logical to make up the time today. Refusing his invitation constituted an ordinary, reasonable business decision.

Then why did she feel so flustered? And why had she just methodically sharpened her pencil to exactly half its previous length?

She shook her head, trying to jostle her thoughts into acceptable order.

She felt so flustered because Paul Monroe was not an ordinary, reasonable business associate. No wonder she had an odd reaction—*he* was odd.

Satisfied with that analysis, Bette turned to her delayed tasks from the day before, and tried to concentrate. All day she tried.

An annoying anticipation edged into her afternoon, lifting the edges of her concentration and peeling it away like a label that was coming unstuck. By six-fifteen she had sharpened every pencil at least twice, and accomplished little else.

At the opening squeak of her office door, she jumped, a hand to her heart. Her pulse burst into a sprint, then slowed. Only Darla. She frowned fiercely. *Only Darla?* Exactly whom had she been expecting?

"Bette? Are you all right?"

"Yes, I'm fine. What is it, Darla?"

"There's someone here—"

The door swung wide and there he was, grinning and sending her pulse off again in double time.

"Hi, Bette."

Darla looked over her shoulder, then back at Bette. "Do you want me to...?" She let the words trail off, and Bette could tell that she didn't want to do anything, that she approved of Paul's presence in her boss's office. Bette felt ganged-up on—Paul Monroe, Darla Clarence and her own heartbeat.

"It's all right, Darla. Thank you."

She waited until Paul moved into the room and Darla closed the door. That gave her a chance to prepare a cordially businesslike scold. "Paul—"

"Don't apologize, Bette."

Her prepared words vanished. "Apologize!"

"Yeah, I understand about lunch. I know some people get uptight about keeping to a schedule. They just can't help it."

"Uptight." She forced the word through clenched teeth. He went blithely on.

"So I realized I shouldn't have pushed about lunch. But now that you've had all afternoon to catch up—" he hesitated just long enough for her to remember how abysmally she'd failed to use the afternoon to catch up, and that it was all his fault "—let's go to dinner."

"I have plans."

Most men would have instantly withdrawn at the deliberate chill in those three words. She should have remembered that when it came to what nine out of ten men would do, she faced Mr. Ten.

"Plans?" He repeated the word as if he'd never heard it, and certainly had no familiarity with the concept. "Don't you want to have dinner with me?"

She opened her mouth and shut it immediately, uncertain it would deliver the sentiment she needed to express. Damn the man.

"It's not that...." A fine start, but then she didn't know what to say next. "I have a lot of work to do." Why did the truth sound so lame?

"Didn't you have a good time last night?"

"Yes, I had a good time, but—"

"I did, too. Good. I want to hear about your business, and you should probably know more about mine before we make a final choice on this permanent temporary, don't you think?" Not giving her a chance to answer, he continued. "I thought tonight we'd try this pizza place I know where they serve deep-dish by the pound. It's across the street from where the St. Valentine's Day Massacre took place back in the twenties, and legend has it one victim crawled to the front step and breathed his last right there."

Nearly four hours later Bette found herself trying to figure out exactly where she'd lost control with Paul Monroe. Somewhere, she figured, between the time he played on her sense of responsibility by mentioning the need to discuss business and the time he cast out the lure of deep-dish pizza. She dismissed as overly pessimistic the voice that insisted on whispering that control had walked out the minute Paul had walked in the day before.

The dinner had been wonderful. And so, she had to admit, had the company.

He'd regaled her with tales of the oddities he'd seen in his business and of the escapades he'd pulled in his life. He'd also drawn stories from her of her childhood and her travails in setting up her business, but she didn't enjoy that half as much as when he talked—and made her laugh.

As the cab carried them south from the restaurant toward the center of the city, she studied him. A man whose business was children's toys. A man who refused to live by schedules or plans. A man who seemed wary of committing to something as simple as choosing a temporary secretary. Logic said, a man wary of committing to anything. Or anyone?

She frowned, disturbed for reasons she couldn't explain.

"Wait a minute. Stop here," Paul ordered the cabbie as they neared the northern limit of Michigan Avenue's Magnificent Mile.

Bundling Bette out of the taxi, he paid the fare and started her off across the wind-whipped boulevard.

"What are you doing? Where are we going?"

"The beach."

"What?"

"Oak Street Beach. I haven't been there all summer." He took her hand and wrapped it securely in the warmth of his, then led her across the lanes of traffic. They'd reached the sidewalk bordering the beach before she thought to protest further. "Don't you think it's a little late in the season to be going to the beach?"

"Don't want to rush into anything," he said with a grin, still pulling her along.

"Hey. Wait a minute. I'm getting sand in my shoes." Hauling back on his hand, she managed to stop him.

"Take 'em off."

She glared. "I also have hosiery on, and besides, it's October."

"It's also probably seventy degrees, and the sand's been soaking up sun all day."

He had a point; she ignored it. "I'm not taking my shoes off and walking in the sand in my hose. And before you say it," she rushed on, "I'm not taking off my hose on a public beach, either."

He looked at her a long moment, and she had the impression that a measuring and accounting was taking place. She stood very still for the outcome.

"You want to go back?" It was an offer more than a question.

Now she felt as if she were the one doing the measuring and accounting, only she didn't know of what or by what standards. Had he experienced this uncertainty a moment ago? She considered the toes of her shoes, already awash in a wave of sand. The black leather pumps needed polishing anyhow, and their wedge heels were nearly flat. She glanced at the tall, lighted buildings standing sentinel behind them, then out to the glistening roll of the lake and finally back to Paul. He watched her without judgment, not goading, not pressuring. Just waiting.

"Could we walk a little slower?"

His eyes lit first, then he smiled. "Yeah, I think we could manage that."

She smiled back, feeling oddly happy, as they started more sedately for the edge of the water.

"Thanks, Bette." The quick words sounded almost ill at ease, as if he expected her to jump on them. "I wouldn't have wanted to miss walking on Oak Street Beach. I've done it every summer since I was fourteen."

"Summer, huh?" She made as if to pull her suit jacket closer around her, though the lake breeze felt good against her heated skin. "I suppose you do everything at the last minute?"

"Everything." He drew her close, then let loose her hand to loop an arm around her shoulders in a chill-chasing gesture.

Disconcerted by the immediate response she felt, she dredged up extra disapproval to lace with her teasing. "I suspect you're one of the people they show on the TV news, lining up to beat the midnight postmark for your tax return."

"I've met some very interesting people in that line."

She couldn't repress a grin at his blatant self-satisfaction, but it faltered as he turned his head and contemplated her. His face was too close, his eyes too observant, his mouth too... tempting. "Bet you'd never be in that line, would you?" His eyes dropped to her lips, and she felt as if her heart and lungs were operating at double time. He blinked. "And I suppose you have your Christmas shopping done by Labor Day?"

"Of course." She'd never been prouder of producing two steady words.

He gave a histrionic shudder, and she laughed. Everything had returned to normal. Almost.

"Some years," she confided, "I get really crazy and wait until Halloween. But I'm always done, totally done, by my parents' anniversary the first week of December. That way I can enjoy the holiday. And you, I suppose, are probably out there on Christmas Eve madly buying."

"Of course. The insane rush is half the fun of Christmas, as long as you go about it with the right attitude. You can't be buying to meet some quota, you have to be looking for the exactly right gift."

They'd reached the water and turned to follow the narrow path of sand, hard-packed by restless waves and gentle tides.

"Why can't you look for the exactly right gift before December 24th?"

He leaned toward her intently. "But that's just it. What if you get what you *think's* the right gift on December 14th and then find the perfect present on the 24th? Do you return the gift you bought on the 14th or do you pass up the perfect present?"

She shrugged, and his arm rose and fell with the gesture. It made them seem connected somehow, that her movement affected his. "It depends."

"On what?"

"On if you have the receipt. On how hard it is to get back to the store where you got the 14th's present or if that present might be something someone else would like or maybe even something you need yourself."

He groaned. "All those 'ifs.' I save myself all that. I take no chances. By the 24th, it *is* the perfect present, like it or not."

They'd stopped in unspoken accord. They stared out across the water. Bette was aware of how the concentrated glow of lights from downtown illuminated the right side of Paul's face, and lights strung along the city's Gold Coast were nearly as strong on her left side. Between existed a shadowed world that seemed to leave the city and its everyday life far behind. This world between had only the light of the moon to reveal it, a strange light that could make the ordinary extraordinary and mask the dangerous.

She smiled slyly at him. "Of course you realize, don't you, that by the time you go shopping on the 24th, you're just looking at my leftovers. I've already snatched up all the perfect presents out there.''

His wounded expression drew a triumphant chuckle from her that he joined with easy, warm laughter.

It was crazy. The whole thing. Walking on a beach in her work clothes in the middle of October—even if the weather seemed a flashback to August—with a man she'd known exactly thirty hours, and whose drawbacks easily reached double digits. And enjoying it. A lot.

Crazy.

The laughter and the warmth lingered. Paul turned to her, and slight pressure from his arm shifted her shoulders so she faced him. The grin still lifted his lips and fizzed in his eyes. She watched that, so fascinated by the amusement that always seemed near the surface with him that she was hardly aware when he lowered his head and brought his mouth to hers.

Her last thought, a flash, really, was how like Paul Monroe it was to kiss her with a grin still molding his lips. She felt the teasing joy in the gliding pressure of his skin against hers.

How different this was from the night before. Then he'd drawn out the moment before their mouths met like an extended question; now he swept into the first kiss, and a second, without hesitation. Then he'd whispered a caress; now he stated it boldly. She felt a sensation of warmth that came from one arm still around her shoulder, and the other across her lower back, drawing her to him and out of the lake's cooling night breeze. A sensation of heat that came from the insistent sweep of his tongue against her lips, edging her nearer to some elemental furnace.

"Bette." She heard the faint request in his voice, even as he muffled it against the skin of her cheek, jaw and throat, and when his mouth came back to hers, she parted her lips. Her hand rested high on his shoulder, so the tips of two fingers grazed the skin at the side of his neck. The fingers of her other hand wound in his hair where it topped his jacket collar. She clenched them tighter, waiting.

He took her top lip between his teeth, not quite nipping, but seeming more to test. She sighed, and his tongue lingered on her lips, finally slipping through slowly, exploring thoroughly. She felt the glide of his tongue against the sharply smooth ridge of her teeth and gave a small, smothered gasp of impatience. Then he was done with teasing, meeting her tongue and drawing it back into his mouth.

She had the notion that her nerve endings had retreated from her limbs and brain, leaving them weightless and empty. But there seemed nerve endings to spare in other parts of her body, the parts in contact with his, where the impression of his flesh seemed to pass through layers of his clothes and hers, and into her skin.

He shifted, bringing her into closer alignment with his body, so her breasts absorbed the firmness of his chest. Pressing his arm against her hips, he settled her into the narrow cradle created by his wider stance, and she recognized the sensation of another male firmness.

For an instant, an instant without consequences, without responsibilities, she felt only a responsive softening and warming.

But she had spent too much of her life following step after careful step toward a specific end not to know that with such incendiary steps as these, one thing would most definitely lead to another.

She pulled away from his mouth with a gasp that was partly driven by a need for oxygen and partly by disappointment at the separation. A step backward got her nowhere because his arms held her fast, and pushing her hands against his chest got no results. For a breath, her mind acknowledged her situation, alone on the beach with a man strong enough to hold her against her will. But she didn't truly fear him. Perhaps she would have if she hadn't realized that the deep, uneven breaths he pulled in as he rested his cheek against her temple were his method of regaining equilibrium.

He's shaken, too, she thought. His reaction steadied her, making her own responses seem less extreme. She was also, at some level, grateful he hadn't let her go. She wasn't sure she could have stood alone in those first seconds.

When, with a last long breath, he loosened his arms, she stepped clear of the heat. With quick, unconscious movements, she straightened her jacket, twisted her blouse into line, smoothed her skirt and ran her fingers through her hair. Only when her hands moved to her lips, a reflexive reaction to the burning sensation there, did she feel Paul watching her. His gaze slanted at her from the side. She stopped her gesture half-made.

"I, uh—" She stopped to clear her throat, and started again. "I think we'd better get back now."

For a man so full of teasing words and easy talk, he could be amazingly quiet. She couldn't even be sure if she heard or imagined the half sigh before he spoke the single word. "Okay."

They started across the sand toward the lights of Michigan Avenue. He seemed content to let silence stretch between them. She wished he wouldn't. It gave her too much time to wonder what he was thinking, why he was so uncharacteristically— What? Almost solemn?

Was that how he felt after kissing her? Solemn? If she'd learned anything about Paul Monroe over the past two evenings it was that solemnity lived outside his philosophy of life. She felt like a thundercloud at a picnic, and fought the ridiculous urge to shed a few raindrops right now.

"Well, one thing for certain."

His voice made her jump, but she welcomed it and, as they emerged into the brighter lights and firmer ground of the city's streets, she gladly supplied the line he'd demanded. "What's that?"

"I definitely won't be doing my Christmas shopping early this year."

"Why not?" She didn't really care, but as long as the wryness had returned to his voice, she'd encourage him.

"Who can think about Christmas when they just went through a heat wave?"

This time when they pulled into her driveway, she was ready.

She wasn't sure how she'd respond if he repeated last night's soft caress, not after tonight's disconcerting taste of another kind. Even though their conversation during the drive had been innocuous and friendly in the extreme, with no hint of a reference to the embrace on the beach, she'd take no chances.

So she laid a cool hand on his forearm to forestall his turning off the ignition, yanked it back as if she'd been burned, forced a cheerful good-night and practically sprinted to the front door. She stood inside again, listening for long, heart-thudding moments until he backed up and drove away.

Not until she slid between the crisp clean sheets did she shake those moments on Oak Street Beach long enough for other considerations.

Leaving work early—and any time before seven was early for her—and getting home too late to do any work Wednesday had put her behind. Today made it worse.

She'd have to keep a strict schedule tomorrow and Saturday to catch up. Especially since she'd earmarked Sunday for attending real estate open houses to get a fix on the market. And added to her duties Monday would be getting Paul to decide on a temporary secretary.

She frowned. When Jan first came into Top-Line Temporaries, she'd described her boss's aversion to schedules and long-term planning. "Short-term planning, too, most of the time," Jan had added. Cheerfully and amid all the teasing of the past two evenings, he'd confirmed it.

I wonder if he views women the same way he views Christmas shopping? she thought. Her frown deepened. Probably. What else could she expect? Someone who couldn't commit himself to buying a present because something better might come along surely wouldn't commit himself to a woman.

She rolled to her side and punched the already plumped pillow. Not that it made any difference. Paul was a client. Period. A client with whom she would have a few business conversations, but would likely never see again. If she was smart.

She was smart, but her heart was a moron. That was the only explanation for the way it started pumping at high speed and depleting her oxygen stores when she opened her front door to Paul Monroe at 3:25 Sunday afternoon.

This morning she'd pored over real estate ads in the *Tribune*. This afternoon she'd attended open houses. She'd studied the market for months, honing her prerequisites in a house, her must-haves and should-haves. This, her first foray into inspecting houses, constituted the next step. After several Sundays sampling the market, she would target specific areas. Then would come the nitty-gritty of offers, contracts and mortgages.

Once she completed that, it would be time for the next step. She slipped off her shoes, tucked her feet under her on the couch. She wanted a husband, a family. Just turned thirty in July, she had time. It wasn't as if her biological clock were about to expire. But she didn't want to let that pass her by. She saw the life her brother was creating with his wife and children and, although she wouldn't want a carbon copy, there were elements she longed for.

Setting up the business had been first; it was progressing well. Then a house. Once she'd accomplished that, she'd be ready for the next step. She'd be ready to look for the right kind of man.

Gray eyes flecked with green smiled into her imagination. She glowered at them, and the startlingly clear memory of the man they went with.

Paul Monroe was *not* her idea of the right kind of man.

But he is some kind of man, commented a previously unheard-from voice inside her. The voice had backing from a hundred-thousand nerve endings that retained vivid memories from two nights ago.

Damn. She thunked her feet down on the floor. Damn.

All right, maybe she did find him physically attractive. Really, it couldn't be called more than that after one kiss. One kiss, in the moonlight, on a deserted beach. A fluke. It had to be. Because, heaven knows, nothing in his haphazard approach to life or business agreed with her ideas.

She picked up one of the real estate listings from the pile on the coffee table while the TV wrapped up the Bears game she'd mostly missed. For now, what she had to do was consider the information on the houses she'd seen. With her shoes kicked off and a soft drink at hand, she would concentrate on comparing cost per square foot and making notes of her impressions. She settled back.

The doorbell sounded.

Barefoot, she carried the listing sheet and her pen to the front door. She nearly dropped them both.

"Paul!"

She'd missed him. The realization hit hard.

Afternoon sun bronzed his breeze-ruffled hair and seemed to add a special glint to gray eyes flecked with green fire. He wore a blue shirt with the sleeves rolled to his elbows, a lightweight insulated vest in green and jeans that had been worn to a state that looked as soft as she knew they'd feel. She felt her cheeks burn at the realization that she'd been thinking about touching his jeans—with him in them.

"Hi. How 'bout those Bears, huh?" Without waiting for her to invite him in, he walked right past her. "I like the running game this year, don't you?"

"What are you doing here?" She'd trailed him into the living room. His intent gaze took in her house as if he thought he'd be tested on it. The absurd urge to tell him she'd bought this furniture to go into an eventual family room and she had her eye on an elegant couch bubbled to her lips, but she turned it sternly back.

"I came to get you. You look great."

At his warm tone, she glanced down to see if she'd been transformed, like Cinderella going to the ball. No, she still had on a surplice-wrap top in a soft raspberry color, tucked into the gathered denim skirt. Her simple leather belt matched her discarded loafers and she wore plain gold hoops in her ears as her only jewelry. In deference to the warm weather she hadn't even worn hose. Clean and comfortable was about the most that could be said for the outfit.

"Get me?" She ought to be taking better control of this conversation.

"Yeah. You'd better put a jacket on. It's going to get cool tonight. I think Indian summer's about to come to a screeching halt."

"What are you talking about?"

He glanced up from turning off her TV, and she saw the devilment in his eyes. The only thought her brain could form was the refrain she had come to associate with Paul Monroe: Uh-oh.

"The weather."

"What?"

"That's what I'm talking about—the weather." He scooped up her navy cardigan sweater from the arm of the couch and her purse from the floor and held them out to her. Numbly, she accepted them. But she also shook her head, and that helped clear some of the cobwebs.

"Paul, we didn't make any arrangements to see each other today, and I have things I need to get done—"

"What you need is a jack-o'lantern, and I intend to see to it. C'mon, you'd better put your shoes on, too."

"No."

He looked at her bare feet, over to her loafers, then at her face. "I don't know, Bette, I think your feet'll get awfully cold, but if you don't want to wear shoes . . ."

"Not no to the shoes. No to leaving with you." There, that sounded firm enough. So why did she feel so rotten? Had those glints of light in his eyes dimmed?

"I thought you'd like a pumpkin."

His tone was matter-of-fact, but she felt as if she'd just kicked his puppy.

"I would like a pumpkin, but—"

"Good, I know a great pumpkin farm not too far from here."

An hour later she stood, bemused, amid pumpkins of every size, shape and construction, and thought that if

Linus of "Peanuts" fame was right that there did exist a Great Pumpkin with magical powers, then Paul Monroe had a direct line to the big orange guy.

That was the only explanation she could come up with for how she had come to be here. One minute she was sitting in her living room checking out real estate listings and the next minute she was a passenger in her own car— "You said the hatchback's better for hauling, and we're going to have a lot of pumpkins to haul," had been Paul's explanation when he snagged her keys—and the minute after that she stood here in pumpkin land, laughing.

She'd laughed so much in the past half hour that her sides ached. She would never again look at a pumpkin without remembering the outrageous personalities Paul had assigned to the gourds they'd collected. Then he and the man running the pumpkin stand had indulged in a round of good-natured wrangling over price that had set her off again.

"Boy, remind me never to have you around when I'm haggling," Paul ordered after they'd settled their orange army on the car's deck, separated and cushioned from one another by sweet straw from the stand operator.

She smiled out the window, not bothering to respond. She felt too content, as golden and glowing as the afternoon, as mellow as the approaching dusk. Fading sunlight gilded the hardier leaves still clinging to branches while their fallen brethren wove an orange and gold coverlet. The trees rose high and straight, arching their limbs in the bare outline of what had been a summer canopy.

They'd left an area of cornfields and woods interspersed with stables, and the houses now were closing ranks. The street was trafficked, but peaceful. A straight, orderly artery going... where?

"This isn't the way to Elmhurst. Where are we going?"

"I thought we'd off-load some of these guys before we went to your place."

"I wondered why you bought so many. But then I thought it was probably a whim." She meant to tease him, but she also believed him totally capable of such an impulse.

"It was."

"And now you've decided to set up your own stand somewhere else? Where?"

"That's an idea." He seemed to consider, then discard it. "Nah. I like my idea better."

"Which is?"

She saw the sign for the town they were entering at the same time she heard his words. "We'll take some to my folks. They can use some jack-o'-lanterns, too."

"Lake Forest." She read the sign aloud, heard the dread in her voice and, knowing the tone would have carried over, was grateful she hadn't said the other two words in her mind at the moment: *your parents*.

Chapter Four

She'd said the name of his hometown as if it were a toxic waste dump site. He was used to the other reaction, the one that said that anyone from Lake Forest was a rich kid, and probably a bratty rich kid. Bette had made it sound as if he were taking her into one of the less stable portions of the Gaza Strip.

"This is the downtown area," he informed her as they rolled between lines of neat red-brick buildings whose sharply angled roofs ended in green awnings or, for more adventurous establishments, green-and-white-striped awnings. He made a couple turns and brought her through the heart of the area, then completed their circuit.

"It's very nice."

He looked around at the shops, both familiar and trendy. "Yeah, it is." If he sounded a bit defensive, too bad.

From the corner of his eye, he caught her looking at him. "Really, it is, Paul. It's rather amazing. Everything's so neat. Even the gas stations and train station."

He said nothing as they passed the train station and drove along the tracks for a while. When he turned, it was into a neighborhood of older, modest homes that seemed to grow bumper crops of bicycles and skateboards. He slowed nearly to a stop in the middle of a block.

"There, the light blue one, that's where we lived until I was twelve."

"Oh."

Bette Wharton could infuse a lot of meaning into one syllable. He just wished he could interpret it. Glancing to his right as he pulled away from the curb, he caught her eyes on him and thought perhaps he saw someone truly looking at him—at *him*, beyond images, expectations. His shoulder muscles seemed to have abruptly grown tight, so he shifted position, steering with his right hand at the top of the wheel and his left elbow propped out the window. If that left less of his face open to his passenger's scrutiny, well, that was a coincidence. He turned into a narrowly twisting street, and headed toward his parents' house.

What was the big deal? So he'd had this impulse to show her where he grew up, to have her meet his parents. That was how he did things. He kept his options open and didn't like being tied down to plans.

A curse muttered across his mind.

Who was he kidding? He'd fully intended to introduce Bette to his old house, his hometown, his parents ever since he'd first had the idea on Friday. How could it be an impulse, when he'd been spending every waking hour, and more, contemplating one, solitary woman?

He'd been planning this afternoon's stops for two days. And he didn't like that fact.

Even when he'd done it for a woman whose navy-blue eyes lit at the sight of him, then shuttered themselves faster than a blink. Even for a woman who talked about plans and arrangements so stiltedly, then laughed with abandon over a pumpkin.

Worse, he couldn't find it in himself to regret any part of it, not the thinking about her, not the pumpkin ploy, not the hometown tour. None of it, because it all meant she was sitting here next to him.

"There are my folks," he said as he pulled into the circular portion of the driveway. Spotting the car, his parents waved and started toward them. Since they'd been contemplating a flower bed on the far side of the considerable front lawn, he had a moment to cover Bette's hand where it rested on the front seat between them. "They're nice people, Bette. Honest."

She met his look and gave a forced smile.

"Much easier to get along with than me. I promise."

To his relief and pleasure, the teasing light flickered into her eyes. "Thank heavens!" she said with soft vehemence.

He was still chuckling when he opened her door and they walked out to meet his parents.

"Paul! Why didn't you tell us you were coming?"

His mother's affectionate scolding as she hugged him harmonized with his father's dry interjection, "Because he never does."

"I would have made something special for dinner," his mother concluded, then barely paused as she smiled warmly at Bette and extended a hand. "Hello, I'm Nancy Monroe."

Paul knew he'd have to hurry or his mother's sociability would outstrip his manners, and for some reason he wanted to be the one to make this introduction. "Mom,

Dad, this is Bette Wharton." He placed a hand at the small of Bette's back, with some idea of encouraging her and reminding her of his support, though he knew his parents could be counted on to welcome her. But the feel of her soft sweater and the firm, smooth curve of her back gave him something, too, something indefinably pleasing. "Bette, these are my parents, James and Nancy Monroe."

"How do you do, Mrs. Monroe. Mr. Monroe."

She shook hands with them, and he glimpsed the poise she must bring to business dealings, at least ones that didn't involve him. He suspected he threw her off her usual stride.

He liked that.

"Bette's in the market to buy a house, and I thought she should see some of the other neighborhoods around, so we swung by here." He caught her dagger look of surprise and dismay. She probably wanted to tell him she certainly wasn't looking in *this* kind of neighborhood, because it was way out of her price bracket, but was constrained by his parents' presence. He'd remembered her comment Thursday about looking for a house and he'd spotted the real estate listings on her coffee table, but he hadn't known he'd make use of the observations until he'd spoken the spur-of-the-moment words.

"A house is an excellent investment," said James Monroe with an approving nod. "I wish Paul would make that move so he'd build some equity in a property."

Paul shrugged at the familiar refrain. He should have seen it coming. "I don't mind paying rent."

"You must not, since you've been doing it so long, and now you have rent on your office as well as the apartment."

"Property just ties you down." He worked to keep the words light. It was an old skirmish line between his father and him.

"Perhaps it's time you were tied down. We had owned our first home for six years by the time I was your age."

"You owned it?"

Only the blink of his father's eyes showed that the arrow had gone home. They both knew Walter Mulholland had held the title on the Monroes' first house, as he had on this house until the day he died.

"Well, I'm just glad you both came," smoothed Nancy Monroe. "I have a lovely roast in for dinner, and now we'll be saved from a week's worth of leftovers."

"Oh, no, really. Thank you, but we can't drop in like this for dinner." Bette stopped abruptly, turning wide blue eyes on Paul, and for a moment he forgot everything else. "I mean, I . . . I really should . . ."

He saw her floundering between not wanting to impose and not wanting to deprive his parents of having their son home for Sunday dinner. "We didn't mean to stay for dinner, Mom. We just thought we'd drop off some pumpkins and I'd show Bette around a little, then we'd be on our way."

"Oh, but you must stay for dinner. There's plenty of time for you to show Bette, maybe take her to Beach Park, then we can have a nice meal and get to know each other. This is such a wonderful surprise, Bette. We don't get Paul home often enough as it is, and we always enjoy meeting his friends."

Paul tried one more time against the force of his mother's beaming smile. "But we don't want to interrupt your afternoon, and—"

"Nonsense. We were just discussing the arrangement of our spring bulb garden. It's so hard to remember where things were the spring before by the time you get around to planting in the fall.''

He knew staying for dinner was all but a certainty. Maybe he'd known it when he pulled into the driveway. He refused to consider whether he'd known it yesterday when he first thought about stopping by.

He cocked an eyebrow at Bette and gave an infinitesimal shrug, indicating that if she didn't want to stay, he'd do his best, but . . . A smile edged into her eyes and he felt an easing of the muscles in her back where he was only half-surprised to realize his hand still rested. She'd come to the same conclusion and she didn't mind, at least not terribly.

Paul's father took a more direct approach in trying to make the unexpected guest feel less awkward. "Bette, how long have you known our son?"

Paul rubbed his free hand across his mouth to mask a smile. Ever the lawyer, his father had asked the question to set up some point he wanted to make. The flaming color he brought to Bette's cheeks was inadvertent, and the surprise her answer was about to administer to his parents came as a pure, unanticipated bonus from his point of view.

"Four days." Ah, another bonus. She'd been counting. Otherwise, she would have hesitated to total them or said "since Wednesday."

Paul saw his mother blink, then take a closer look at Bette. When her gaze came to him, he looked away, suddenly not so enthralled with surprising his parents.

James Monroe, however, nodded, as if he'd half expected the response to his question to be "four days," then took Bette by the elbow and started her toward the house. "I don't imagine in that time he's introduced you to any other relatives, has he? No? I didn't think so. So we can understand your being a bit taken aback by all this. We just hope you'll commiserate with us, since we've known him for thirty-two years last March, and he's never brought a young lady home to meet us before."

"Is that true? You've never taken a woman home to meet your parents?"

Paul gave Bette an extra beat to add the word *before,* but she didn't, and he felt a frown growing. The way she said it made it sound as if bringing her to the Lake Forest house today didn't count.

"There really wasn't much need to," he finally said.

He looked down the stretch of pebbly sand, then out beyond the huge, jumbled boulders that created shallow pools for summer-time beach-goers at the municipal park. This late in the year, with the sun rapidly fading, the beach and the boat ramp farther down the lake were deserted. Two distant fishermen on the pier beyond the ramp were their only companions. He narrowed his eyes as he considered the darkening eastern sky. The breeze had picked up, and if he didn't miss his guess, Indian summer's spell would soon be broken.

After a soft drink at his parents' house, he'd brought Bette here by a roundabout route through town. He'd been telling her about youthful summers he'd spent divided between this beach and his home. "I think half my high school graduating class spent three days a week at our house, so everyone I dated was there all the time anyhow. Then in college we were too busy proving we were grown-up by going into Chicago to bother coming home."

"And since college?"

His head jerked around in surprise, then he had to bite off a grin. He hadn't mistaken that note in her voice—she was more than mildly curious. But her eyes, darkening with storm warnings just like the lake behind her, told him the consequences if he dared to make anything of it.

He knew a few people who'd be surprised to hear it, but he *could* be cautious.

"Since college, there hasn't been anyone I thought my parents would enjoy meeting."

Pleased with himself—he'd told the truth and paid her a compliment without tying himself to anything—he took her arm and headed toward the pier. They could walk the length of the beach before taking another path to where they'd left her car up on the bluff overlooking the water.

He easily slipped into more tales of growing up, including one of a sailboat race when he'd had his younger sister as his crew, and had nearly thrown her overboard.

"Do you sail, Bette?"

"Not the kind you're talking about. Just Sunfish on small lakes."

"You'd like it. I'll take you next—" He broke off. He'd been out to say "next spring." He'd always believed in keeping promises, which was why he didn't make them. But he'd been about to commit himself to something six months in the future. What had gotten into him?

Bette didn't seem to notice anything amiss. She walked beside him, watching waves slip into shore, and exuded calm.

"Anyway, it was a great neighborhood to grow up in."

"I'm sure it was." She sounded as if her mind might be on another track. "It certainly doesn't look anything like the house you described."

Contemplating the upward curve of her top lip and remembering how it had felt against his own, he almost missed what she said. "Oh, the house. Mom made a lot of changes. Actually, the same fall after I ran away. I started thinking some of the workmen were going to live with us permanently."

Work had kept his father so occupied those months that James Monroe probably wouldn't have noticed if they'd blown up the house. His mother hadn't gone quite that far, but close. By the time her father had visited at Christmastime, light and color had replaced somber bulk.

"It must have been quite a job."

"Yeah. Turning a mausoleum into a home kicks up a lot of dust."

Walter Mulholland had raged, but there was nothing he could do. Even at twelve, Paul had recognized the lesson. Walter Mulholland was beatable. All it took was determination and unbending resistance.

"It really is a wonderful place now. This whole area..." Bette made an all-encompassing gesture, then apparently remembered a complaint. "But what possessed you to say I was looking at a house in this neighborhood? I can't afford this area. And even if I could—what are you smiling about?"

"Nothing. Let's get going. I'm hungry and we have pumpkins to unload. I wonder if the neighbors need jack-o'-lanterns this year?"

"Would you like more, Bette?"

"No, thank you, Mrs. Monroe. This was wonderful, but I couldn't eat another bite."

"Are you sure? I don't think you young people who live alone get enough to eat. I'd hate to think you'd be hungry later."

Paul's chuckle spluttered into his glass of water and, Bette thought she heard something resembling "told you so."

Giving him a quelling look, she politely declined once more, then helped Mrs. Monroe clear the table. In the kitchen she put a few things away while her hostess prepared coffee and chatted of cooking, gardens, the symphony and family.

" . . . I'll have to show you a portrait of my father after dinner. Paul looks so much like him at the same age."

Bette wondered if Paul had ever heard that comparison. Considering his views on that relative, he wouldn't like it.

In Nancy Monroe's mostly gray hair, Bette could see the vestiges of Paul's chestnut color. Although he shared a lot of mannerisms with his father, Bette saw that many of his features had come from his mother. Physical features, but also the ability to make people comfortable in an instant.

Bette could admit to herself now that she'd been a bit awed. Not only by meeting Paul's parents so unexpectedly—so *soon*, she was tempted to add, as if it were an occurrence she'd seen coming—but by the house, with its sweeping, dignified exterior, its views of Lake Michigan through multiple sets of French doors, its casually elegant furnishings.

But Nancy Monroe melted away the awe. She was a very nice woman. In fact, Bette thought as she prepared to take the cream and sugar in to the dining room, they were a very nice family. Not so unlike her own.

As she stepped into the dining room, she became aware that the Monroes were not unlike her own in other ways. She felt the tension immediately. Between her and her parents, the topic was her living alone. Between Paul and his father, it apparently concerned his business.

"Contact with a prestigious museum like that can't help but enhance your reputation and that can only aid your business. It's the sort of opportunity you should cultivate." James Monroe took a breath, and Bette could tell he was repeating a question, more to drive home a point than to get an answer. "So, are you going out there to discuss this opportunity with them?"

"I'm going out there." Paul's voice surprised her. Cooler than she'd ever heard before.

"But are you—"

Paul caught sight of Bette. Rising to take the sugar and creamer as if they were too heavy for her, he cut off his father. "Ah, good. Now all we need is something to mix them with."

Without the usual amusement lighting his face, the words fell flat. He seemed to realize that. As he returned to his chair, he went on immediately. "Did you know my dad was a heck of a shortstop thirty-five years ago? Reached the top of the minor league system. Would have made it to the majors, too, only—"

Paul looked up as his mother came through the door with the coffee on a tray, and broke off.

"Are you two talking about baseball again?" she asked with fond exasperation.

"No," answered her husband. "I was trying to pin him down to make a decision, with as little success as ever. Or at least to find out if he's making a trip to D.C." He faced his son again, and his voice seemed to gentle. "And I was a borderline shortstop at best. My making the majors was extremely doubtful."

Nancy Monroe looked from one man to the other. If she forced her smile, she did it very well. "Well, if you do go to Washington, Paul, be sure to give Tris our love, won't you?" She turned to Bette in explanation. "Tris is Paul's cousin. James's sister's girl. She and Paul were always close. When they were children . . ."

Nancy Monroe went on, skillfully drawing Paul and his father into the newly directed conversation, and soon any lingering tension dissipated.

Nearly an hour later, as they said their thank-yous and good-nights at the door, Bette thought James Monroe was about to question his son once more, but his wife touched him lightly on the sleeve, and he let it fade.

As Paul pulled the car out of the drive, it was obvious he, too, had seen the interplay. "Parents trying to push their kids into making the same mistakes they did," he muttered.

"I always thought parents tried to prevent their kids from making the same mistakes they did," she commented mildly.

He frowned at her, but then seemed to relax. Before he turned back to the road, a quirk of humor lifted his mouth. "That's one of those lines all parents are taught to feed their kids, along with clean-up-your-plate, don't-play-with-that-or-you'll-poke-your-eye-out and someday-you'll-have-children-of-your-own-and-you'll-understand."

"Ah, the famous 'School for parents' where they learn one thousand and one ways to say no."

He laughed, and the sound warmed Bette. She'd brought him laughter. She'd changed his mood from bad to good. She couldn't remember ever having done that for someone before.

Instinctively, she reached for him. But she let the gesture fall short, her hand dropping to the seat between them.

"That's the one," he answered. Without taking his eyes off the road, he settled his right hand over hers where it lay on the seat.

The rest of the drive was accomplished in easy silence. Easy was about all Bette felt capable of at the moment.

Occasionally, the wheel demanded both of Paul's hands, but his right always returned to hers. Resting her head against the top of the seat, she watched the lights go by without bothering to focus. She felt surrounded by the scent of pumpkins, straw, dried leaves and Paul Monroe. She was replete with delicious food and the satisfaction of laughter.

Languor seeped into her, until she wondered if she'd have control over as simple a movement as raising her arm. Did astronauts feel like this when they experienced weightlessness, when a twitch translated into some large, slow, ungovernable gesture and a step became a floating trip to unknown destinations?

When they reached her house, Paul drove the car directly into the garage, turned off the engine, pressed the button to close the automatic door and shifted to face her. She tipped her head just enough to see him.

"Bette?"

His voice came, husky and near. He trailed the knuckles of his right hand down her neck, then pushed her hair back, behind her shoulder. Her cocoon of languor took on heat and sensation. She knew she should be thinking ahead, considering what might come next. But she couldn't. She should be alert, prepared. But she wasn't. For once the present moment filled the screen of her mind so fully that there was no room to preview the future.

"Bette."

Slowly she shifted until she could see his features, strong and marked by lines of humor in the slash of artificial light slanting in through the garage window. She didn't believe she had enough energy to move, but somehow she must have had, because she felt the soft prickle of his stubbled jaw under her palm.

Then she experienced all the energy in the world.

It suffused her, pouring into her skin and bones and blood when he turned his head against her hand and inscribed a circle with his tongue.

She thought again of the odd buoyancy of weightlessness as her arms rose, seemingly of their own accord, to his shoulders. He moved in front of her, so the light cut a path across his face, half-bright, half-dark. She could see nothing other than his face before her. There was nothing else she wanted to see.

He leaned into her, so she felt the weight of his body against hers.

"You have the most amazing upper lip," he murmured as he took it between his own, pulling slightly, then testing it with his teeth.

"Family trait," she finally got out when her lungs had produced enough oxygen to fuel the words.

He shook his head slightly, and since he still had his mouth on hers, she felt it as a change of texture, a sliding and melding. "No. I think it's a sign of great hidden sensuality."

He kissed her, not hard, not deeply, but thoroughly. A kiss that seemed to muffle every sound in the world except their breathing and their heartbeats, that seemed to stifle every thought in her head except the urge to get closer, to give more to him.

Lifting his head at last on a low, quiet groan, he rested his forehead against hers.

"That's something else," she told him when she could once again control the motor skills necessary to form the words.

"Hmm?"

"The sign of hidden sensuality—that's something else."

He ran the back of his knuckles down her throat once more, this time beyond the hollow at its base, across the edge of her collarbone and softly along the rise of her breast. "It sure is."

It took three deep breaths to regulate her lungs into some order, but when she did, she doggedly finished. "It's a gap between the two front teeth." For emphasis, she tapped her own closely spaced front teeth. "Like Terry-Thomas, the actor, had. A gap—" another tap "—is supposed to be the sign of great sensuality." And another tap.

She wouldn't have thought he could move so fast, but before she finished the final tap, he swooped in as if to kiss her and instead caught her finger in his mouth and pulled it gently in. Her eyes drifted closed. Her heartbeat skittered. Her breathing stopped.

His tormenting mouth released her finger and she tried to straighten herself. "Paul, I—"

He simply shifted his torment from her finger to her mouth, slipping his tongue through her parted lips, and drawing a moan that vibrated in her throat. His palm went to her neck, as if to absorb that vibration, then skimmed the sensitive skin, following the path his knuckles had traced.

As he had before, he ended the caress with a fleeting brush to the first swell of her breast. She felt an ache there, an ache of deprivation, and it brought a sound to her lips that she was grateful his mouth muffled.

But he must have heard it, or sensed the frustration, because his hand returned to that spot, pressing lightly, then circling until he cupped the weight of her breast in his palm. Through the folds of cotton and the slide of lace, she felt the rub of his thumb. His touch fueled her ache the way someone tends a fire, keeping it burning steadily yet brighter and hotter.

She felt her own hands dispensing with the buttons of his shirt. When she reached the waistband of his jeans and paused, he jerked the tails out with one impatient hand, and she finished the task.

She didn't have a chance to hesitate. He brought her hands to his chest, spread them wide against his taut skin, then pressed them tight by trapping them between their bodies as he leaned into her. His fingertips stroked a path from her collarbone down, across the smooth skin where it curved, and lower. Then he turned his hands and skimmed the backs of his fingers over the same tingling territory, only to start again. The draped folds of the V neck retreated a little farther with each movement. She felt her breast swelling and rising against the lace of her bra. She shifted restlessly. He stroked down, his fingertips easily sliding under the lace, not quite grazing where she most wanted the touch, then skimmed up. And started again.

Under the lace, his fingertips tempted and teased. If he didn't touch her— Her breath came in on a gasp and released on a moan. His fingers had found the peak, already pebbled and proud. They lingered, stroking and circling.

He muttered something, then twisted, turning their bodies so she no longer rested against the seat, but across him, in the circle formed by his right arm and his body.

"Paul, I don't think...I don't think this is a good idea." The habits of a lifetime formed the words, though she felt unconnected to them and knew herself incapable of backing them with action.

"We're well beyond the idea stage, Bette. Don't you think?"

He gave her no chance to answer as he returned to her mouth, but she must have been well beyond thinking, because she found her arm straying from his back to his shoulder, and some part of her knew it was to allow him greater access.

Her bra strap slid over her shoulder. She didn't know if it was her movement or his that was responsible, but she knew the result immediately. His hand curved around her inside the loosened lace, treasuring the weight of her breast, his thumb caressing her nipple. She heard his moan mingled with her own.

He wrenched his mouth from hers, and their breathing came in oxygen-depleted gasps. But he couldn't seem to bear to be away from the taste of her skin as his lips formed wet, openmouthed kisses to her jaw, her throat, her collarbone. She knew what would happen and she wanted it. Oh Lord, she wanted it.

Sensation was all that was left in the world. The sensation of his mouth on her breast, his hand sliding across the curve of her thigh. The pull on her nipple, the feathering touches near the juncture of her thighs, were promises of the rhythm, of the touches she most desired. The desire rose in her throat, escaping as his name, a soft moan of a syllable.

"Paul."

He raised his head, and she felt the force of his look, demanding that she meet it.

No teasing, no amusement in those eyes. Just intent desire.

But he had reined that all in. Barely. For the moment. For long enough to ask her. For that was the other thing she saw in his eyes: a question. He left it up to her. She could say no and he would abide by that, but he wanted her. Now.

The weight of the decision crushed her with something like disappointment. If he hadn't stopped, if he hadn't left her to answer— But he had.

They had to stop.

But she'd hesitated too long. His mouth met hers, his tongue passing the restraints of her lips with bold certainty. The exploring was past. His tongue set up a rhythm that echoed in the brush of his fingers against her. The stroking, thrusting excitement of it foretold of how their bodies would match in another union. And that thought pushed her closer to him, tightened her fingers on him until her nails pressed into the hard flesh. But it also let the future slip back into her mind, to voice its demands and expectations.

This single moment couldn't be separated from what could follow—*would* follow—if they didn't stop.

They had to stop.

The union her body craved would mean a blending of lives to her. But to him? How could someone who refused to look beyond the moment give her the permanence she needed?

He couldn't. She knew that. As she knew that if they made love, in the end, she would feel so much pain.

Ah, but first there would be such pleasure. Under her touch, his muscles contracted, and she shivered at the controlled power. Such a delicious aching pleasure she would feel....

If they didn't stop...soon...

He groaned and shifted, so he could slip his hands beneath the lace edge of her panties.

No. No, she had to stop it—now.

"Paul." She broke away from his lips and gasped the name. "No."

She had to stop.... She had to stop before...

"No." She pulled away from him and reached for the car door handle.

...before she couldn't stop.

* * *

She refused to hide just inside the door as she had the other times. In the living room she gathered the real estate listings, straightening them inefficiently with hands that trembled and shoving them haphazardly into a folder.

When she heard a sound at the door, she froze. He was just outside. She could practically feel him there, standing and looking at the solid wood door with its rectangles of high windows.

He hadn't said anything, done anything when she had wrenched away, hurriedly straightened her clothes and snatched the keys from the ignition, barely pausing to say, "I have to go, Paul. Good night." As a farewell it wasn't much. If he rang the bell—demanding an explanation— would she have the strength not to answer?

But he didn't ring. And in another endless moment or two she heard his car pull away from in front of her house. When that faded to silence, she let out a deep, long breath and went to the door. She opened it cautiously.

There on the step sat a trio of pumpkins, a round one, a tall one and a squat one. When she started laughing she knew she was in trouble.

Oh, she was in a *lot* of trouble.

Chapter Five

Bette Wharton was everything Paul could ask for in a business associate. Polite, professional, cordial, accommodating. She was also elusive, unattainable and distant. She was driving him crazy.

She managed to be tied up on another line each of the four times he called Monday. Each time her assistant, Darla, asked if she could be of help. Finally, Darla pointed out they needed his decision on which secretary he wanted as his permanent temporary. With less than his usual good humor, he muttered that they should send him whomever they felt like.

So, starting Tuesday morning, he had Janine Taylor to place his calls to Bette Wharton several times a day. And he had Janine Taylor to tell him with polite indifference that Ms. Wharton was not available at the moment, several times a day.

Wednesday, he had an appraisal to do for a gregarious Lionel train collector in a small city about two hours away, but he called three times with the same results. The fourth time, when he'd finally pried himself clear of the collector and was on his way back, he got the recording that said her office had closed for the day. After quick calculations of train schedules, he took a chance and called Bette's home number, acquired from information.

On the fifth ring, he heard her breathless "Hello," and his blood started moving as if it had been dammed up for the past three days.

"Bette, it's Paul. How about some dinner tonight?"

The pause was long and telling. He thought he could hear her resolve hardening. "No, thank you, Paul."

That was all. No explanation, no nothing. She left him nothing to grasp on to.

"You have plans?" He tried to make it sound understanding.

"I'm sorry, Paul. I don't think it's a good idea—" She broke off so abruptly, he knew she remembered Sunday night and what else she hadn't considered a good idea. That gave him renewed hope, which he needed after her next sentence. "I don't care to see you, Paul. Good night."

The click was nearly as soft as her voice.

He stayed irked all that night and the following day. Irked enough not to get much sleep and irked enough to resist the temptation to call her office again the next day. But not irked enough to kill the urge to see her.

Part of him wondered at that. But it was a small part, easily drowned out by the parts that wanted to discover the secrets in her eyes, to make her laugh when she thought she should frown, to feel the heat of her passion so it fueled his own desire like a race car's high-octane. He'd be damned if he'd meekly fade out of her life.

It was the challenge that attracted him, he reminded himself.

When he arrived at Top-Line's office a few minutes after six Thursday evening, he was told Ms. Wharton had left for a meeting with a client.

He looked from Darla's bland brown eyes to the closed door of Bette's office, and back. He pivoted on one heel and walked out. Marching out the blocks with punishing steps, he reached the broad sidewalk of Michigan Avenue and turned right toward Mama Artemis's with some vague intention of finding a spot where people would be glad to see him.

A client. A meeting with a client. A client like him? A meeting like the one they'd had a week ago, full of laughter and exchanged glances and the implicit possibility of more?

He startled a few people by stopping abruptly in the middle of the sidewalk and swearing vehemently. "A client? She's meeting with a *client?*" Most of the people kept walking, parting and passing him like a rock in a stream, although he thought he noticed a few trying to hide smiles. They were all women.

"You can come out now. It's safe, he's gone."

Darla clearly intended irony, but Bette had a nasty feeling in the pit of her stomach that if Paul Monroe had stuck around, she wouldn't have been safe.

"I don't know why you don't just go out and have some fun with the guy."

"I told you I—"

"Have a schedule to keep." Darla completed the sentence in unison with her.

Bette frowned. "Besides, Darla, you were the one saying just a few days ago that all Paul Monroe looked fit for was funny business."

"I didn't say that's *all* he was fit for, unless you include certain other activities under the heading of funny business." Heat swept into Bette's cheeks, more in memory than embarrassment. "A woman would have to be blind to miss that man's potential in that area, and I may be married, but I'm not blind. Besides," Darla added with a pugnacious tilt to her chin, "I've never seen anyone in more need of funny business than you."

"Really, Darla, I—"

"Really, Bette," she mimicked. "You work too hard. You schedule your life down to the minute and you don't leave any time for fun."

"That's not true. How about this weekend? I'm going on a trip—"

"Only because your mother made you feel guilty when you first said you couldn't go." True, but Bette wasn't about to admit it out loud. "And if you can look me in the eye and tell me you haven't already packed three days' worth of work and arranged a couple business meetings up in Minnesota, I'll eat my hat. Better yet, I'll promise to keep quiet about the whole matter."

Bette said nothing. Did the Fifth Amendment hold in dealing with scolding assistants?

"Humph." Darla produced a sound somewhere between disgust and triumph. "All I have to say, young woman, is you better start penciling in time on that schedule of yours for exactly the kind of funny business Paul Monroe can provide, or you're going to be old before your time."

Darla opened the door, then added a parting shot over her shoulder. "And while you're at it, schedule in some hanky-panky, too."

"I'm sorry, Mr. Monroe, the office informs me that Ms. Wharton has left for the weekend."

Left for the weekend by ten o'clock on a Friday morning? Paul snarled at the voice on the intercom, but apparently Janine Taylor didn't hear, because when she went on, he noted for the first time all week a hint of humanity beneath the efficient exterior.

"I believe she flew out early this morning for a weekend trip." Janine hesitated, then added in her usual tone, "Can I put through another call for you, Mr. Monroe?"

Since she hadn't managed to "put through" the one call he'd wanted, he thought that bordered on sarcasm.

"No. Thanks. I have a call to make, but this one's private so I'll put it through myself."

Let her inform all her cronies at Top-Line that he didn't consider his calls to Bette Wharton as anything more than business. And let her also tell them that he had *private* calls to make.

"Grady, it's Paul," he said when he got through. "What do you think about taking the afternoon off for a last sail of the season?"

"I think it's too damn cold, for starters."

Actually, Paul thought so, too. The three-day rain that had washed away Indian summer had eased yesterday, making the lingering cold all the more noticeable. But he needed something to vent this restlessness, and the lake had always been good for that.

"And it's supposed to rain again," Grady added.

"Afraid your good looks will melt in the rain?" The taunt about his friend's blond, blue-eyed handsomeness was too old to hold much sting.

"I don't know, but I'm not going to risk it. Not now. I've got a big weekend planned with Cindi."

"Who's Cindi? No, never mind. I'll just get her confused with the two hundred other women you've dated this year whose names end in 'i.'" Paul leaned back in his wooden swivel chair and propped his feet on the edge of his desk. Maybe he wouldn't go sailing, but talking to Grady reminded Paul that some things in life don't change. "I'll bet you a pair of tickets to the Cubs' opener that Cindi spells her name with an 'i' on the end."

A slightly sheepish silence followed. "Yeah, she does. But it's no bet," Grady protested. "I didn't bet."

Paul grinned at a photograph of Grady, Michael, Tris and himself from their college days. "That's okay, Roberts. It was a sucker bet, anyway."

He hung up, feeling more like himself than he had all week.

The sense of well-being lasted less than twenty-three hours.

He couldn't find anything to do.

He called his cousin, but got her machine in D.C. Just as well, he decided as he paced his apartment. He didn't want Tris asking nosy questions, anyhow. She'd read too much into his answers, or lack of answers. The same went for his parents. Grady was otherwise occupied. Michael... He'd go see Michael.

He didn't bother to give the idea a second thought, or to call ahead. He headed southwest to Springfield, whisking between cornfields that hinted at next summer's fertile crop even with last summer's reduced to brown stubble. His mind followed its own track.

Unlike Grady, who often waged elaborate campaigns for his lady of the moment, Paul had always simply let relationships happen—or not happen—as the Fates decreed. And he'd always been honest about looking only to the moment. He made no promises, so none were broken. Obviously, he should follow that path with Bette Wharton and forget her. He depressed the accelerator another five-miles-per-hour's worth.

The outside of Michael's Victorian house looked great, the scars of renovation nearly healed; inside was still under reconstruction. Michael came to the door with a paintbrush in hand. His slight frown metamorphosed into a grin when he saw who stood outside the leaded glass.

"Boy, am I glad to see you."

Paul groaned. "Don't you think you got enough free labor out of me? How many walls did I help you knock down? Thirty? Forty? I don't think I'll ever breathe right again after all that plaster dust."

"Free, maybe, but definitely unskilled labor."

"You complaining?"

"Absolutely not. In fact, I'm offering you a chance to hone those skills. Painting's very marketable these days. And I need to get this done while I still have the time."

"Is that your way of telling me Joan's running for the U.S. Senate?" With Michael on state senator Joan Bradon's staff, Paul had paid close attention to the rumors.

"I'm not telling you anything, Monroe. Read your morning paper."

"Real nice. And then you expect my help? Oh, what the hell, lead me to that paint bucket."

As he outfitted Paul for painting, Michael probed for the reason for this visit. Paul evaded and, though he felt the weight of Michael's wondering, the questions ceased.

Spreading paint across the patched, multicolored surface was definitely preferable to breathing plaster dust. Windows, open to disperse the fumes, brought in the spicy air of fall. He could hear drums from a marching band at a high school football game in the distance, and an occasional roar from the onlookers. His perfect swipes covered the wall in a clean expanse of color.

The drawback was that his mind, free to wander, returned to the topic he'd tried to drive away from: Bette.

A sound reminded him of Michael, painting woodwork across the room. He could talk to Michael, tell him . . . tell him what? That he'd met a woman he found attractive. So? Big news flash.

He tried to divert his mind; the first topic he came up with was the woman Michael had been seeing for some months.

"So how's Laura these days?" He tossed the question over his shoulder, then turned for the answer. "How come you didn't rope *her* into this drudge work?"

The brush in Michael's hand went still. "I believe Laura's doing very well."

Paul pivoted to face him. "You believe?"

"She moved to California at the end of last month."

"Why?"

"She had an offer for a better position in a senator's office there. Joan gave her a great recommendation, so—"

"Don't give me that bull. What happened?"

At the rawness of the question, Michael rocked back on his haunches, turned his head. The surprise in his eyes quickly gave way to a delving, measuring look. That look had always bothered Paul, because he never knew what Michael Dickinson might pull out of him in such moments.

"We couldn't give each other what we both wanted." Michael spoke with measured reluctance.

"What was that?"

"Forever."

The word was like a spark to Paul's smoldering mood.

"What's so almighty wonderful about forever? Settling down, getting married, having a family, is that what you're talking about? Why does everybody harp on that? What—"

He snapped the words off when the look in Michael's eyes hit home. He should have remembered that Michael's past had given him a different view of this subject.

"Paul, you take it for granted, and you shouldn't. Family and stability—that's pretty damn rare, you know."

"Stability," Paul repeated with disdain. "Yeah, so stable that at the age of twelve your life's mapped out for you. Just follow the step-by-step instructions and you'll turn out to be the perfect family clone."

"You haven't done so badly in the individualism department, Monroe."

Paul dropped the roller into the pan, not caring about the spatters on the drop cloth, and took a deep breath of the cool air. "I'm not going to let my life be run by somebody else's rules, Michael. Not ever."

Michael said nothing. After a while, Paul heard him return to painting and Paul took up the roller, though he found less pleasure in it. The silence had changed.

"Who is she, Paul?"

"Who's who?" Michael didn't bother to answer that, and Paul felt foolish for the evasion. "Bette. Bette Wharton."

"And?" Michael prompted.

"And not much. Grand total of three dinners and a few kisses." He felt no guilt at the understatement. "We went out last Wednesday, Thursday and Sunday. Things seemed to click. Then she avoided me Monday and Tuesday, said no Wednesday and resumed avoiding me Thursday."

"What about Friday and today?"

"She wasn't around Friday and today."

"Ah."

"Ah what? What's 'ah' mean?" Irritation spurted sharp and hot.

"What do you do when a woman turns down a date?"

"Forget her, because..." He broke off the familiar words. He'd said them to Michael and Grady maybe two thousand times over the past fifteen years. Forget her, because there're plenty who'll say yes.

"Yet, *this* woman you keep asking. That's why 'ah.'"

Paul loaded paint on the roller and slapped it against the wall, then had to roll like crazy to remedy the drips, splotches and spatters. He was short on breath by the time he re-wetted the roller, this time more cautiously.

"You've got another session at the Smithsonian coming up, don't you?" Michael asked from behind him. From the sound of it, he'd continued painting, too.

"Yeah."

"Made any decision about taking up the offer to be a regular consultant?"

They were all after him about the damn museum—Jan, his father, Michael. Bette would join them if she found out about the opportunity. It was the sort of thing that would appeal to her plan-ahead mind. Probably tell him what a step forward this could be. If he were stupid enough to invite the lectures by telling her... if he ever had the opportunity to be that stupid, if he ever saw her again.

"No."

"All right, all right, don't bark at me. I'm not the one inconsiderate enough to give you a flattering offer."

"Shut up, Dickinson."

"All right."

That was one of the most annoying things about Michael—he shut up when you told him to shut up. By the time Michael spoke next, Paul had turned the corner to the next wall, and his mood had subsided to low-level hostility.

"So, you're leaving for D.C. a week from Wednesday and will be back the next Sunday?"

"Something like that. How'd you know?"

"The same way I ever know anything about your plans—I hear it from your mother, your sister or your secretary. This time it was Jan. I called her to congratulate her on the baby, and asked when you'd be around."

"Why'd you want to know? You want to come with me? I'm staying with Tris. I'm sure there'd be room for you, too."

He regretted the words instantly. To Paul's knowledge, Michael had never told anyone of his feelings for Tris. Maybe never even admitted them to himself. But Paul knew him very well, and the stillness betrayed him. "I was kidding, Dickinson. Why'd you want to know those dates?"

"I'll have to spend some time up in Chicago. I thought I'd make it coincide with you being in town if I could."

"Before Thanksgiving?" Since the first year of college, both Michael and Grady had spent most of their holidays with the Monroes.

"Yes. I've just decided to make it the first full week of November. Right after you get back from D.C."

Paul twisted around, but Michael remained bent over the woodwork and the back of his head revealed nothing. "Why?"

Michael kept painting with even, steady strokes.

"I think I should meet this Bette Wharton."

The rest of the weekend passed without another mention of Bette.

Paul wished his mind had been as cooperative.

Driving home Sunday night, he found himself on I-55 instead of his usual meandering back roads, almost as if he were in a hurry. When he swung north on the Tri-State, he justified it as trying a new way back to his apartment. That excuse held until he got off at the Elmhurst exit. In front of Bette's house, he was out of excuses.

Also out of luck, he thought wryly as he considered the dark windows. Either she wasn't home or she was in bed.

In bed. The image appeared instantly, hot and heady behind his eyes. The sheets cool and serene like her voice, but with that promise under them of smooth heat.

He shifted. Too abruptly. His right thigh jammed against the steering wheel. He closed his eyes against the thoughts, then opened them immediately. Closing his eyes made it worse.

She probably wasn't home. Common sense said ten o'clock on a Sunday night was a little early to go to bed, unless . . . unless you weren't alone.

Sense drowned in unfamiliar jealousy. A meeting with a client Thursday night. A Friday morning departure for an out-of-town trip. Could one have extended into the other? Could she be away with someone? Could she . . . ?

No. Bette wouldn't have kissed him the way she had if she'd been involved with someone else. The certainty in his

gut was stronger than common sense or jealousy. He relaxed.

So she wasn't home yet.

He could leave a note . . . and say, what?

A snatch of lyric from an old song entered his head,
something about the singer's determination to get his girl,
and his lips curved. Yup, that was exactly what he wanted
to say. But some things were better left unsaid—and simply acted upon.

She might think she'd shaken him loose. She might think
he'd forget the laughter and teasing, the kissing and the
holding. She might think his ego would forget all that after a week's worth of refusals. She thought wrong.

He turned the key in the ignition and pulled away from
the curb in front of Bette's house, still smiling and softly
singing to himself.

Bette pushed open her front door and automatically
checked her watch. Nearly eleven o'clock, and she had to
unpack and go through files she hadn't finished reviewing
this weekend at her brother's house in Minneapolis.

It was a lovely house, and it had been wonderful to see
the whole family, with her parents up from Arizona for
two weeks to visit their new baby granddaughter—although Bette didn't envy her sister-in-law a fortnight of
houseguests on top of a rambunctious two-year-old and a
new baby. Still, Clara had seemed to greet the chaos with
equanimity.

Bette frowned as she maneuvered her suitcase down the
hall and around the corner to her bedroom. Perhaps there
would have been less chaos if there'd been less equanimity. It only required some planning, some forethought. She
knew that wasn't Clara's strong point, but surely Ron had
learned that at home, as she had.

As it was, her decision to rent a car had been wise. Otherwise she never would have made those business appointments she'd set up.

She slipped off her coat and rubbed her forehead, pushing against muscles tightened by the frown. The odd thing was, her parents had seemed perfectly content to go with the flow, no matter how undirected. She didn't remember them as being that relaxed when she'd been growing up.

She remembered them following the precepts her mother had learned from her own parents—selecting a goal, working toward it step by careful step and never wavering until you reached it. That made for a very organized life. That was how she'd always viewed her parents. Maybe they'd changed in the relaxed atmosphere of her father's early retirement.

She pressed her fingertips harder against the frown. Or could her memories be skewed?

Her hand went from her forehead to her mouth to cover a huge yawn. She should go to bed.

Instead, she returned to the front table where her neighbor had stacked her mail and newspapers. She flipped through quickly, checking each envelope but opening only those she couldn't immediately identify. Nothing. Nothing of interest, anyhow.

Hitting the play button on her answering machine, she listened to the neighbor who'd checked her mail ask her to care for her cat the following weekend. A longtime friend passing through the area called to say hello. Then came two real estate brokers confirming appointments she'd made to interview them. And Darla suggesting she take Monday morning off since her return flight was so late.

The tape ended, the machine clicked and whirred, resetting itself, and Bette sighed deep and long.

She'd been looking for something from Paul Monroe.

The realization didn't startle her; she'd been too busy all weekend trying not to think of him to be surprised that she was thinking about him. But it did irk her.

She'd had relationships with men before. A few. Each as carefully constructed as the rest of her life. She set the parameters; she guided the pace. She knew when the first kiss was coming, and she was prepared to stem or accept greater intimacy, depending on her feelings for the man. But this... this was something different. There was no predicting Paul Monroe, so there was no preparing for him. Nor for her response. That frightened her. No, disturbed her. Yes, disturbed was a better word.

She wasn't accustomed to it, she didn't understand it. Not that she was in danger of really falling for the guy. She saw his flaws too clearly. She didn't view him the way, say, her sister-in-law saw Ronald's faults as somehow endearing, or the way her mother took her father's worst habits in unblinking stride.

But what kind of namby-pamby person spent several days giving a man every clear signal she could to keep things strictly business, then turned around and hoped he'd call or write? She'd made her decision, and it was the right one. Paul Monroe was not her kind of man.

A tingle along her spine shivered her skin. Her lips parted in memory. Not your kind of man? Oh, really?

All right, in the realm of moonlit kisses on urban beaches or embraces in a darkened car, he was most definitely her kind of man. That made it worse.

The blank red stare of the answering machine reminded her that he'd listened to her signals. He'd taken his moonlight kisses, darkened embraces and their accompanying danger and, for all intents and purposes, disappeared from her life. Other than sending him bills from Top-Line Temporaries, she'd finished with Paul Monroe.

She sighed again, then slapped down the pile of mail and headed along the hall with firm steps. It was good that he hadn't tried to call or write. In fact, perfect. She'd get her life back to normal. All her spare time this week would be devoted to searching for the right house. She had gotten behind on her timetable, what with unexpected dinners, unscheduled pumpkin buying and a full week of avoiding the telephone when it rang, then listening for it to ring when it didn't.

She might actually get some work done tomorrow with him out of her life.

At fifteen minutes before four o'clock the next afternoon, he reentered Bette's life, if somewhat obliquely, when Janine Taylor walked into her office and announced she would rather quit Top-Line than spend another second as Paul Monroe's temporary secretary.

Chapter Six

"I can't work for that man. Bette, you know I have handled every assignment you've given me. I have worked with demanding bosses, with disorganized bosses, even with sexist bosses. But I can't and won't work for Paul Monroe."

"I don't understand, Janine. You seemed to be getting along fine last week."

Janine Taylor shook her head, and if Bette thought there was confusion in the gesture she also recognized rock-solid determination. Janine Taylor would not spend another minute as Paul Monroe's temporary secretary.

That was one characteristic Bette had considered when she'd assigned this particular secretary. She figured it would take someone determined to keep a rein on Paul. She had told herself Janine's plainness had not been a factor in selecting her.

"From the beginning, I knew he was a little different. After all, look at all those calls to you." Bette felt her cheeks sting. "But today...today! He was..." Janine hesitated. "Odd. Very *odd,*" she repeated, putting great emphasis on the word. She seemed to be trying to communicate some greater meaning with her eyes, like the player in a TV quiz game hoping to get her point across without giving away the clue.

Bette stared across the desk at the woman who'd been among her most reliable employees, and tried to reconcile Janine's reaction with the man she'd come to know. Perhaps Paul was not the run-of-the-mill Chicago businessman, but she couldn't imagine him doing anything to elicit such an extreme reaction from a woman...unless it involved the feel of his lips on hers, the rasp of his skin against hers, the draw of his mouth...and then the woman's response would be very different from Janine's.

"Can you tell me what, specifically, he did that made you walk out before the end of your assignment, before, even the end of a *day?*" She couldn't prevent the astonishment from creeping into her voice. The whole thing was so unlike Janine.

"No schedule," Janine jerked out. "He wouldn't give me a schedule, even when I practically *begged.* And a curator from the Smithsonian—the Smithsonian!—called, and Mr. Monroe said, no, he wouldn't take the call right then. He didn't feel like talking...he just didn't *feel* like it. And that's what he said to tell them. I didn't, of course, but... And he said— He didn't..."

Her fluttering hands, which seemed to be trying to finish sentences her mouth couldn't accommodate, floated back to her lap and she set her jaw pugnaciously, allowing just one word to escape. "No."

"No?"

"No, I won't try to tell you any more. Because if I tell you, you'll think I'm crazy, too. Because it's not what he did, it's how he did it."

There seemed to be no answer to that.

"I'm sorry, Bette. I'm truly sorry." Janine stood and slung the strap of her oversize handbag over her shoulder. "And if you want to fire me or put me on suspension, I'll understand. But I won't go back there."

The door hadn't even clicked closed behind her before it opened again to admit Darla.

"Paul Monroe's on line one," she announced, then gave a sympathetic frown when Bette cursed emphatically. "You want to take it or shall I?"

"I'll take the call."

"Okay, but you know, I don't think that man's nearly as harmless as he might seem on the surface. I saw his face Thursday when you made me tell him that you'd already left for an appointment with another client, and that's a stick of dynamite I wouldn't go playing around with too much."

Bette grimaced her understanding. She knew. She knew all too well. Defusing the dynamite was exactly the point.

She had her hand on the phone when she stopped, with something tingling along the nerves of her arm, something ringing cheerfully in her head. Uh-oh. She *wanted* to take this call. She looked forward to hearing his voice. And that was dangerous. Very, very dangerous. Lighting a dynamite fuse required only a spark.

"Wait a minute."

Darla turned from the door, and waited for Bette to continue.

"On second thought, you take the call. Tell him we'll have a replacement secretary in his office first thing tomorrow morning. And tell him . . . well, you know what to tell him. Then come back in and we'll have to adjust the schedule to free up Norma Schaff to go there for the rest of the week.''

Norma Schaff, in her mid-fifties and razor-sharp of mind and wit, was made of sterner stuff than Janine Taylor. At least Bette would have sworn to that before Norma Schaff had to face Paul Monroe. She lasted two-and-a-half days.

To finish out the week, Bette tried a new approach, sending Jonathan Roiter. He finished out the day, which Darla termed a moral victory, and then said he'd rather swab toilets than go back Monday morning.

''Paul Monroe's on line three,'' Darla announced as she held open the door for Jonathan's departure. ''And before you tell me to take this call, too, I think you should know that he said he wants to talk to you this time.''

Bette stared at the phone a moment, then looked up at her assistant and friend.

''I don't understand it, Darla.''

''Me either, but I think the only way we're ever going to have a shot at understanding it is if you get an explanation from him. You know the odd thing is, he sounds perfectly charming on the telephone. I wonder what he's doing to these people.''

Bette waited until the door closed, took a deep breath that should have steadied her more than it did, then picked up the phone.

''Hello?''

''Hi, Bette. How are you? It's good to hear your voice. Have you had a nice week?''

Darla was right. He sounded perfectly charming. Pure irritation swept aside uncertainty.

"I've had an absolutely miserable week, as you well know since you are directly and solely responsible for it. What have you been doing to those people we send to your office?"

"Me? Nothing. I haven't laid a hand on a single one of them. Why?"

Nobody could sound that innocent and really be innocent. "Why! Because we've had three of our best people come back this week—three people in one week!—saying they would never work for you again."

"Oh, that."

"Yes, that!"

"It's just that I've been feeling sort of crazy this week—"

"The feeling's mutual."

She knew he heard her, but he ignored it.

"But that's easy enough to fix."

"Oh, really. How do you suggest we fix it?"

No, no, no, Bette! Her brain listened, aghast, at the opening her mouth had given him, and she braced to be run over by the Mack truck he would surely drive through it. She could have sworn the phone line hummed with his glee.

"Go out with me."

As Mack trucks went, that wasn't so bad. A mere four-ton—or four-word—model. But he didn't fool her. This truck was just the lead vehicle in a caravan. Because after going out, there would be talking and laughing, then holding hands, kissing in the moonlight, embracing in the dark and who knew what else.... Only she *did* know what else. Just the thought of it changed the pattern of her breathing and heartbeat. And that was the problem. If she went out with Paul Monroe, the man most likely to be named least likely to be her type of man, she could fall for him hard. More than she already had.

She had to be firm. "No!"

"You don't have to shout."

She might have overdone the firmness, but she hadn't actually shouted. "I didn't shout."

"Could have fooled me," he grumbled, and to her dismay she felt her lips quirk up in a smile.

"No," she repeated, definitely not a shout this time, perhaps because the word was mostly aimed at herself.

"I heard you the first time." Something in his voice made Bette put a hand to her throat, made her want to take all the words back and erase that—was it pain?—from his voice. "All right, so you don't want to go out with me." Yes, I do want to go out with you, she thought, but I won't. I can't. "Then I guess you'll just have to send another temporary secretary Monday morning."

Whatever she'd heard in his voice had disappeared. His last words were almost cheerful. She swallowed, hard. "Yes, we'll send you another new secretary Monday morning."

"Fine."

"Fine."

"Have a nice weekend, Bette."

"You, too, Paul. Goodbye."

She hung up, but left her hand on the receiver. She knew she'd have an absolutely miserable weekend—for the same reason she'd had a miserable week.

She wasn't even surprised when Karen Van Ryland came in Tuesday at 11:30 and announced she wouldn't work for Paul Monroe.

"That's it. I'm mad as hell and I'm not going to take any more of this, Darla." Bette pressed her hands on the desktop and rose slowly from her chair.

"What are you going to do?"

Do? Yes, she had to do something. The weekend had turned out worse than miserable—it had been unproductive. She hadn't caught up with the paperwork from Top-Line the way she'd wanted to. She hadn't investigated the two prospective neighborhoods she'd had on her agenda and she hadn't attended the real estate open houses she'd targeted.

In fact, all she had accomplished was carving jack-o'-lantern faces into the three pumpkins that had taken up residence on her front steps. Oddly, they all bore a striking resemblance to the mask of Tragedy. Her neighbor had remarked that she had the most depressing doorstep in town. She had added that only seemed fitting since Bette's expression matched that of the jack-o'-lanterns.

Yes, she had to do something. She had to at least try to stop this.

"I'm going to face that maniac on his own turf and tell him he can't get away with this!"

"Do you think that's wise?"

She hadn't told Darla what Paul's condition for behaving normally was, but she had an uncomfortable feeling the older woman had her suspicions.

"No, I don't think it's wise, but I think it's inevitable." As inevitable as it had been that those three pumpkins would get faces.

The phone rang and they looked at the instrument, then at each other. Bette swung her coat on as it rang a second time, grabbed her purse and was to the door by ring three.

"Tell him I will be in his office in fifteen minutes, and then we'll just see about this nonsense."

* * *

"This is ridiculous, Paul."

Paul's gaze followed Bette as she prowled across his inner office for the third time. Her dark green dress was made of some heavy material with just enough swing to caress her curves with each move. Loose sleeves were gathered into tight cuffs that made her wrists look impossibly small. He could hold both her wrists in one hand with no problem. He would hold them behind her, encouraging her to arch, while he explored the white slender throat that rose from the circle of a scarf tied at the neckline of that green dress.

The warmth gathering in his groin made him grateful he'd assumed his habitual pose when Bette first came in—feet propped against the edge of his desk, knees bent, slouched a bit so the back of his neck rested on the high back of the old-fashioned wooden swivel chair. He'd done it deliberately, emphasizing his calm casualness as a contrast to her high-wired agitation. Sitting like this was also comfortable, and luckily in this case, it masked certain realities of male human anatomy.

For a week and half, he'd found such fantasies involving a certain dark-haired, blue-eyed woman had become increasingly frequent. They'd also become disturbingly realistic. And the trouble was, the fantasies also seemed to be producing increasingly realistic reactions.

It was as bad as being a teenager again. No, worse. As a teenager he'd had no thought of fulfilling the fantasies. Now he had a fairly good idea how incredible it would be if he did.

Just one stumbling block—Bette Wharton.

He watched her slim fingers pick up a framed photograph from the bookshelves to the right of his desk. He'd wager she wasn't aware it was the second time she'd picked up that particular photograph, a shot taken his senior year in college, with Grady, Michael and Tris on the front steps of the university library. And he'd up the bet to any amount anyone cared to name that she'd deny ever letting the tip of her finger stroke the image of his youthful face the way she'd just done.

If it wouldn't have raised her hackles, he would have grinned at her. She was weakening.

He wondered if a tiger on the hunt felt this way as it watched a particularly graceful gazelle graze closer and closer to being within the predator's grasp—a little sorry for the creature about to become lunch, but at the same time hungry, so very hungry. Maybe he'd missed something by never pursuing a woman before. Or did it only work this way with Bette?

She put down the photo with a bit of a thunk and swung back to face him, and he thought maybe the gazelle wasn't as defenseless as it looked. It certainly had the speed to escape, no matter how delicate its limbs.

"Did you hear me?" Her exasperated tone informed him he'd missed something.

"No."

She let out a short, irritated spurt of breath that made it harder for him to restrain a grin. It also had the effect of drawing his attention to her mouth, and rekindling memories of the way it had felt against his lips, his teeth, his tongue.

"This has got to stop, Paul."

"My not listening?" Or my fantasizing?

"Your scaring off my secretaries!"

"I told you that was easy enough to remedy. Go out with me."

"Paul—"

The warning sounded clearly, but he didn't heed it. He'd dismissed the possibility that she was involved with someone ten days ago as he sat in his car contemplating her dark house, but the thought came again now. Maybe that was why...

His feet hit the floor with a thud and the old chair creaked upright. "Is there a special reason you won't go out with me?"

"What do you mean, a special reason?" He could almost see her caution.

"Another man," he rapped out. "Are you involved with somebody else?"

"No." The word came too fast, and she was too flustered, for the answer to be anything but automatically honest. But then she faced him, hands on hips, and glared full force. "There's no 'somebody else' about it. I'm not involved with you, either."

"Yet." He let himself smile a little as he said the word, more because the tension had eased than anything else.

"Not at all."

"Why not, Bette?"

"Why not?" she repeated. She sounded more uncertain than outraged. He took that as a good sign.

"Yeah. Why not? It's not like you could be suspecting I have some horrible secret in my past. You know pretty much all there is to know about my past. You've even met my parents. You seemed to like them."

He let the last sentence linger, forcing her to say something or be rude.

"Yes, I liked them."

Who would have thought that getting her to agree with him would be such a kick? He had a feeling his fantasies might start including the word *yes*. "You must have been able to tell that most of the time they think I'm a pretty good guy. I could give you affidavits from a couple friends, maybe even Judi. Surely you'd take a younger sister's word for it that I'm not a monster."

"I don't think you're a monster." She sounded almost sullen. The signs were better and better.

Abruptly, he didn't want to play the game of reading signs anymore. He wanted to know. He wanted her to tell him. "Then what *do* you think? Why won't you go out with me?"

For a long, tenuous moment he thought she wouldn't respond. Willing her to answer, he kept his eyes on her.

"It's too... You're too—" she darted a look at him, then off to the side "—dangerous."

"What do you mean, dangerous?" An extraordinary relief surged through him, and he couldn't stop the grin this time—dangerous was a whole lot better than her just not wanting to spend time with him. But when she stiffened, he knew he'd done exactly the wrong thing.

She took a deep, backbone-steadying breath, walked over to the black leather couch under the windows and sat down with dignified composure. If he'd rattled her, she'd recouped. The gazelle had not only escaped, it was prepared to face down its pursuer. He felt absurdly deflated, shut out.

"Paul, I have a business to run. Running it well is important to me. I've worked very long, and very hard to build it up."

"And you'd hate to lose this 'in' with Centurian." He'd accepted that from the beginning, known how she must view that opportunity. It made sense for someone with a master plan. Still, part of him hoped she'd deny it, to say he was more important to her.

She met his eyes. "An account with Centurian would mean a great deal to Top-Line."

"I already told them I highly recommend Top-Line. So that's not an issue."

"Thank you."

He was the one who broke the look. He was being an ass. Of course her business was important to her. He understood that. He thought about telling her how long and hard he'd worked building his business. But then he remembered the things he'd told her that first night at Mama Artemis's; she wouldn't take his protests too seriously. He didn't generally care to have people know that satisfying his clients, and more important, his own standards, was an issue of self-respect. But he wondered if, this time, he'd made a mistake in passing off the demands of his profession so blithely.

"But you are making it very difficult for me to run my business well. This sort of turnover in staffing with one client makes it nearly impossible to schedule so we can meet all our clients' needs fully—"

She'd exaggerated his impact on her business. Not only was the sight of her hands twisting in her lap a telltale signal that she was fibbing, but Darla—who was clearly encouraging his pursuit of Bette—had told him that to this point he'd been merely a nuisance, not a roadblock.

His instincts, honed by twelve days of focusing all too intently on this woman, told him it was her own hide more than her business that felt threatened. Perhaps in more ways than one.

"—and since that is what Top-Line has built its reputation on, your performance this past week has been dangerous to my business."

"That doesn't explain why you won't go out with me."

She ignored that. "So if you will tell me exactly what your needs are—" She paused, but when he opened his mouth to tell her exactly what his needs were and what he

was just arrogant enough to believe *her* needs were, her
eyes widened in recognition of the opening she'd left and
she rushed on without any additional oxygen. Her voice
came as a whispery spurt that did something strange to the
nerves down his backbone. "In a *secretary.* If you will just
tell me, I will make every effort to see that Top-Line fills
those requirements."

His nerves settled, and he sighed deeply, the disappointment unfeigned. She wouldn't be budged. At least
not today. He considered her, sitting there on the couch.
The dark green dress covered her from below her knees to
her neck. Yet he only had to see the way the fabric draped
across the slope of her breast to remember the feel of her
amazingly soft skin under his fingertips, and then to re-
live the clenching, cramping pleasure in his gut at the sensation of her beaded nipple in his mouth.

Swallowing a curse, he stifled the urge to put his feet
back up on the edge of the desk.

"All right, if you won't change your mind today, there's
always tomorrow. And the day after that."

"My, my, Paul Monroe thinking as far ahead as tomorrow?"

"If I have to get through to you," he shot back.

Twisting to face him squarely, she leaned forward and
met his look, apparently reading the determination in it.
"Why don't you just give up this silliness, Paul?"

"Because I want to go out with you."

"Why?" The question swirled with exasperation and
doubt and perhaps a bit of wonder.

"Because..." Because? Did he know? He'd never indulged in much self-analysis and he wasn't comfortable
doing it now. So what if he acted a little out of character.
So what if his family and friends had taken to allowing
oddly knowing silences to creep into recent telephone

conversations. So what if he didn't know why it was so all-fired important that this particular woman be convinced to change "no" to "yes."

He looked at her. Her dress glowed like green jade against her ivory skin. Her hair shone glossier than the smooth black leather of the couch. He could answer her question by doing what he wanted most to do at that moment. He wanted to go to her, to let his lips reacquaint her with what they could do to each other, to touch her in ways that earned those small, secret sounds of hers, to stretch her out on that couch, to press her body into the soft leather with the weight of his own and to feel her desire.

He said the words that came easiest. "Because I want you."

For a moment, both too long and too short to measure by a clock, she remained still. Then she slowly straightened and stood, her composure complete.

"Goodbye, Paul. I'll send you a new secretary tomorrow morning."

"Bette—"

She gave him a palm-out gesture with one hand that stopped him. Just as well. He didn't have a clue what he would have said, what he could have said.

"Paul, I enjoyed our dinners. I enjoyed meeting your parents. I've enjoyed our conversation and—" She flashed him a look, and he wondered if she was thinking of the kisses and caresses. If so, the thought didn't crack her calm. "But we're very different. We have different attitudes, approaches..." She let the words wind down, then turned and put on her coat, meticulously adjusting the collar before looking at him again.

A smile tried to turn up the corners of her mouth. "There's no future in this, Paul. So let's just leave it at that, okay? For both our sakes. We're best being business associates. That's all. Cordial business associates.''

She closed the door behind her, then he heard the click of the outer door.

She was gone.

Anger filled the emptiness.

Who the hell had said anything about a future, anyway? All he wanted was the present. To have fun while there was fun to be had, to explore this strangely powerful attraction. That was all. No big deal.

He jammed his feet back against the edge of the desk, but there was no relief for this new ache he felt. The ache of an opportunity lost.

Six days. One hundred forty-four hours. Eight thousand six-hundred and forty minutes.

Bette punched numbers into the calculator on her desk as if jabbing the keys would cure what ailed her, then wiped out the total before it could come up on the tiny screen. She didn't want to know how many seconds. That would only make it seem longer—if that were possible. It was bad enough expressed as six days. And six nights.

The days she could fill with all the busyness of running Top-Line Temporaries. Even the weekend had been crammed with duties and responsibilities, plans and projections. After the havoc Paul Monroe had wreaked on her life, she'd needed time to catch up.

They had sent Heather Carlini off to Paul's office Wednesday morning, and held their breath—though Bette was honest enough with herself to admit her feelings and Darla's were not identical in this situation.

Heather Carlini was a knockout. Dark hair, huge brown eyes, petite but blessed with an abundance of the right curves, and an apparently innate sense of how best to use them to her advantage. Bette had assigned her the job with deliberate intentions, and almost immediate regrets. What if Paul fell for her? Well, wasn't that the best solution? Yes. No!

Bette felt as if the rumbling in her head might let loose any second with an explosion to rival Mount St. Helens.

But there had been no eruptions of any kind. Not from inside her, not from Paul Monroe. Not Wednesday, not Thursday, not Friday. Nothing.

"All quiet on the Monroe front," Darla had said as they closed up Friday night, leaving the words to echo in Bette's head all weekend. And now it was nearing five o'clock Monday and all was still peace and quiet.

At least until nighttime came.

Even with all the effort she'd put into work over the past six days, Bette discovered she still had energy for tossing and turning each and every one of six nights.

She'd rerun the scene in Paul's office so many times that the mental tape should have worn out. Instead, in some ways, it seemed to have become clearer and clearer.

Crystal clear that she'd assessed him correctly that first night. Intelligent, warm, charming, wry, sexy, endearingly funny and open. And truly a kid at heart.

He'd practically flinched at the word *future*. In his vocabulary any synonym for forethought was a bad word. The man ran from plans and schedules as if they came from the same litter as Godzilla. He looked no farther ahead than the moment. She'd always wanted—needed—to know that this moment, added to the next moment and the one following that, was building toward something.

He'd made no bones about what he looked for from her. He'd said it right out: *I want you.* Not that he cared for her, not that he was interested in the potential of a long-term relationship with her.

Not that she expected a relationship immediately. They'd known each other such a short time, and relationships—lasting relationships—took time to build, to mature. It took a lot of small steps to reach a goal. But, just as she had known there was the potential for success before she started Top-Line Temporaries, she wanted to know that the *possibility* of a long-term relationship existed with a man. That after getting to know each other gradually, step by step, they might think about a more permanent future.

But that wasn't how Paul Monroe operated. He wanted her. Right now, for this moment, and let tomorrow be hanged.

That wasn't her approach to life, so it couldn't be her approach to—to— The word *love* leaped to mind, but she shied away from that and substituted one less volatile. To relationships.

Limiting their contact to a strictly business association was the right thing to do. And surely the only sane thing.

So why was sanity driving her crazy?

Six days, six nights. One hundred forty-four hours. Eight thousand six-hundred and forty minutes. And for every one of them, she'd thought of him.

Worse even than the memories was the way her body reacted to them. Her heartbeat skittered, her breathing turned jagged, her skin pulsed, her insides heated. Six days without seeing, smelling, touching or tasting Paul Monroe, and he still filled her with sensation every one of those six nights.

And, yes, she admitted, sitting in the rational atmosphere of her office at 4:47 of an ordinary Monday afternoon, she had wondered if he would ever again try to make those sensations real. Would he ever call her? Show up at her office? Arrive at her front door?

Would she ever stop wishing he'd do one of those things, any of those things, as long as it meant she saw his dancing eyes, heard his amused voice? She wouldn't tempt the Fates and her heart with anything more than seeing and hearing him. She'd only risk enough exposure to him to break this pervasive ache of isolation.

She shook her head once, emphatically, more than a little disgusted. Who was she kidding? Did she really think just seeing and hearing Paul Monroe a *little* would satisfy her?

Something had to give. She had to either learn to control these longings and get on with her life or—

Darla pushed open the door, slipped inside and leaned against the closed panel.

"What is it, Darla?" The grimace drawing her assistant's face seemed to be the result of trying to stifle some extreme emotion. Laughter or tears?

"I have some news for you, Bette." Darla spoke as if trying to prepare her for a shock, to soften a blow.

"Yes?"

"Heather Carlini is here."

"Oh?" It took a moment for that to sink in. Six days and six nights can dull the wits. "Oh, no! Not again!"

But even as she said the words, something inside her exulted. He hadn't fallen for Heather Carlini, long wavy hair, huge dark eyes, petite curves and all. And he hadn't given up. Paul Monroe was back in her life. She wanted to shout. She wanted to sing.

"Yes, again."

She wanted to cry. The urge to grin died of its own accord. Paul Monroe was back in her life, and she had some questions to consider. What was Top-Line Temporaries going to do? What was *she* going to do?

"But...but it seemed to be going so well. We hadn't heard a peep out of Heather for six days. Six days! That was twice as long as Norma."

Darla shook her head, and the laughter she'd fought so hard it contorted her face escaped at last. "There's a reason for that."

"Well?" The demand was none too patient.

"I asked her if she'd had any trouble last week, and she said no. So I asked how it could be so terrible to work for Paul Monroe if she'd breezed through the last three days of last week with no problems. And Heather said— Heather said..." Darla gulped twice and finally seemed to get her voice back in order, although tears leaked from the corners of her eyes and left a shiny trail on her cheeks. "She said there was a simple explanation for that. He wasn't—he wasn't there last week."

"What?"

Darla nodded hard, and expelled a sigh that shimmered with laughter. "That's right. Out of town. In Washington, D.C. All those days we sat here congratulating ourselves that we'd finally licked the Paul Monroe Problem, he wasn't even there!"

Bette watched Darla feel for a chair to lower her laughter-weakened body into, and she tried to take it all in, tried to assess what it all meant and what she should do next.

Standing, she carefully closed the folder on her desk, returned her pencil to its holder and the calculator to its drawer. Moving automatically, dreamily, she felt as if her muscles functioned with no direction from her mind. But underneath she felt a glow of energy such as she had never before felt.

She couldn't consider this feeling too closely or, like looking directly into the sun, it might blind her. Instead, she concentrated on accomplishing the mundane. She pulled her coat on and took up her purse, some portion of her recognizing the actions as slow-motion reruns from last Tuesday.

The phone rang, as it had last Tuesday.

She looked at Darla, and saw her dark eyes widening with recognition of the repetitions. The phone rang again.

"Tell him I'll be there in a few minutes, and we'll settle this," Bette said, knowing that that, too, was a near repeat of Tuesday.

Only it wasn't like Tuesday at all, because Tuesday she hadn't felt this gush of joy, this flooding of relief and fear and anticipation.

Tuesday, she thought as she elected to walk the nine wind-whipped blocks that separated her office from his, she had concentrated only on what his presence was doing to Top-Line Temporaries. Now she knew what Paul Monroe's absence could do to Bette Wharton.

He'd been out of town. He'd stepped out of her life, stopped harassing her for six days because he was out of town. Not because he no longer wanted to be with her. Not because he'd given up on her.

The relief of it stung her eyes as much as the wind. She might extract some small compensation, some payment for the toll he'd taken on her emotions the past six days. And she had to remember that this situation could have some bearing on her business, though anything to do with business seemed a remote and misty concept right now. She had more immediate concerns.

Like knowing that at the end of this confrontation she would not walk out of his old-fashioned office the way she had Tuesday. She could not turn her back on the fact that he wanted her. On the fact that she wanted him.

Even though it meant, this once, accepting the moment, and letting the future be hanged.

She knew now that Paul Monroe hadn't given up. And now she knew that neither could she. Whatever happened next.

Chapter Seven

Bette walked through the outer office, devoid once more of a secretary, then hesitated at the door to the inner office. She stared, unfocused, at the wood panels, before giving a small shake to her head.

Don't be an idiot. What is there to be nervous about? You're going to go in there to straighten out Paul Monroe, once and for all. Make him see he can't tie Top-Line Temporaries into knots this way. Make him see he can't tie Bette Wharton into knots this way.

Methodically, she peeled off her leather gloves.

Who are you kidding? He *did* tie you in knots.

Maybe.

Maybe? You were a pretzel! Not an hour ago you were wishing for just this chance to see him, to hear him and—let's be honest—to touch him. So here it is, now take it.

The hand she stretched out toward the door trembled a little, but she commanded it to grasp the knob and turn it slowly, smoothly. She must have succeeded because the door opened without a sound, and she was inside without betraying her presence to Paul.

He stood in front of the shelves to the left of his desk, consulting a volume so big he'd propped its open spine on the edge of a shelf. He was bending a little to study the page, his light blue shirt molded across his shoulders and upper back, emphasizing their strength. The rolled-back sleeves showed forearms toughened with muscle and sinew under a fuzz of hair the same glinting color that rode over the collar of his shirt. The khaki slacks were conservative, well-fitted and yet hinted at the power beneath them.

Uh-oh. Bette could hear the blood pounding in her ears, almost like a warning. *Facing* Paul Monroe was one thing; by now she was almost accustomed to the danger of his dancing eyes and humor-quirked mouth. But from the back he gave a different impression, a view of his strength and sexiness she didn't think she'd recognized half so clearly before. The sensations she'd experienced in his arms resulted from her reacting to this aspect of him. And it would happen again, she knew, if she gave it half a chance.

She'd told herself she wouldn't consider "what next." She'd be impulsive. She'd follow this craving for Paul Monroe without considering where it might lead. She could handle it, wherever it led. She *would* handle it, when the time came. She'd told herself all those things.

But now, catching a hazy glimpse of where her craving might lead, she wasn't so sure. Maybe she should forget this. Maybe she should back away as silently as she'd entered and let Darla take over. Maybe she should run.

"Bette?" he said.

He had looked over his shoulder and was staring directly into her eyes.

It felt as if a weight had landed suddenly on her chest, so that every breath burned. He was looking at her the same way he had two weeks ago in a moonlight-sliced car in her garage. His eyes held the same intent, the same desire . . . and the same question.

Only a concerted effort kept her next breath from becoming a gasp, but at least the added air fueled her muscles to movement. Three jerky steps took her to a spot directly in front of his desk. Without looking at him—she couldn't risk it—she slapped her gloves down on the wooden surface. If she tried her damnedest maybe she could divert some of this emotional energy into anger.

"What in the hell do you think you're up to, Paul?"

From the corner of her eye she tracked the way he turned back toward the shelves, his head bowed over the book once more. Then the two halves of the book came together in a thud that made her jump. He spun around and strode behind his desk to face her across it.

"The 400E," he said.

She gaped at him. She tried not to, but she knew she did. What was the man talking about?

"The Blue Comet 400E locomotive from Lionel. That's what I think I'm up to." He tapped a sheaf of papers spread out on his desk. "That's how far I've gotten with this appraisal."

"Oh."

"It's not as rare as the Black Diamond 400E locomotive he's got, but the Blue Comet set's complete, all four passenger cars plus the locomotive. And it looks to be in great condition, so—"

"Paul!" She slapped her palms on his desk, then spread them wide to lean forward belligerently. "Stop it."

He mimicked her posture, right down to the thunk of his hands on the desktop as he brought his nose a foot from hers.

"Stop what, Bette?" No laughter in his eyes now, only demand. "Tell me."

"Stop the whole thing! Stop sending back secretaries. Stop messing up my schedules. Stop making me—" She bit it off before she could tell him to stop making her want him, but she wondered if he'd still divined the thought.

"We both know how you can make me stop sending back secretaries. And stop messing up your schedule." Were his eyes informing her he wasn't about to stop the issue neither of them was mentioning?

"Yes." An acknowledgment that she knew what he was talking about, not an agreement.

"Yes." An acknowledgment, perhaps slightly disappointed, that no agreement had been given.

She stared at Paul Monroe across the twelve inches that separated them, and she knew. She'd take the moment he offered, and for once she wouldn't think of the future. Even though she had a darn good idea that if she did look ahead, she'd see she was building toward heartache. Maybe that was *why* she wouldn't look this time. If a plane never takes off, it won't ever crash. But it won't fly, either. Dammit, this time, she had to try her wings.

"All right, I'll go out with you." To her own ears, her tone sounded more appropriate to accepting a dare than a date, but she figured they both knew that might be closer to the truth.

Under his stare, the moment drew out with the heart-stopping, stomach-dropping sensation of hitting an air pocket. What if her plane crashed on takeoff?

"Fine." The word was just this side of pugnacious.

"Fine," she shot back.

"Great," he said, then before she had a chance to continue the cycle, he hurried on. "We'll start right now."

"Right now?" she repeated a little numbly. She figured her voice sounded so flat because her emotions were busy pooling deep inside of her: panic, desire, anticipation, fear, affection, wariness, liking, lust and anger, all roiling into a bubbling mass.

"Right now. With dinner tonight."

"Dinner?" What did dinner have to do with what she was thinking about? *I want you,* he'd said, right here in this office six days ago, sitting behind this very desk, looking at her in a way that made her know he meant it.

"Yeah. You know, eat? Usually done sometime in the evening? We've done it a few times together. Fairly successfully, too. I'm meeting a couple friends for drinks— Michael and Grady, the guys I told you about—then we're going to dinner and I—" His light, wry tone slipped and he stopped, paused and started again, but she hardly noticed. Her mind was on other things. "I'd like you to meet them."

"But..."

"But what?"

She couldn't tell him. She couldn't tell him how she'd been expecting him to react. She couldn't tell him what she'd been expecting him to do. She couldn't let him guess how part of her had been anticipating—certainly since he'd kissed her in a moonlit garage and possibly since he'd first sat in her office with his dancing eyes inviting her to join him in a jig—what she'd been expecting him to do.

Although she feared from the way he was watching her, like a cat with its target mouse well in sight, that he suspected what she'd been thinking. She fumbled mentally for an acceptable end to a sentence that started with "but."

"But you still need a secretary." Not bad. Short on originality, maybe, but logical.

He eased back, his eyes never leaving hers.

"Then send back Norma Schaff. She was a great secretary."

Bette stood straight so quickly she thought she could hear her backbone click into place. "If she was so great, why'd you scare her off like all the others?" she demanded indignantly.

He slowly levered himself completely upright before answering.

"It was the only way to get to you," he said with a nonchalant shrug that left her speechless. "Besides, I didn't scare Norma off like all the others. She's the only one I finally had to resort to bribing in order to get her to leave. Ever since, she's been my ally."

Meeting his friends should have eased her nerves. Fat chance.

In one way it did, of course. At least it temporarily delayed the consummation of the step she'd taken today.

Her wayward mind's production of the word *consummation* coincided with Paul shifting next to her in the booth of the tiny bar. The simple brushing of his leg against her set off sparklers along her skin that translated into something brighter and hotter deep inside. Maybe relief wasn't her only reaction to the delay.

This introduction to his friends unsettled her in another way. Somehow it seemed Paul was allowing her to see a side of himself he had previously kept hidden. But she couldn't let herself fall into the trap of hoping for things like that. She knew what Paul was, what he'd offered. And what she'd accepted.

He'd said it—he wanted her. Not a relationship, certainly not a future. The moment. And when the moment was over... Well, she'd be better off then if she didn't delude herself now.

She glanced up to find Michael Dickinson's observant eyes on her. Paul had said he had a law degree and worked on the staff of State Senator Joan Bradon. She found herself pitying his political opponents.

He shifted his gaze to Paul.

"You're the one who keeps track of everybody, Paul. How's Judi doing?" Paul had told her both Michael and Grady viewed Judi as a kid sister. A sophomore at Northwestern, where they'd also gone to school, she lived in a dorm a mile from Paul's Evanston apartment.

"Classes, she's doing great. Socially, she's always complaining that the right guys don't go for her."

"They will," declared Michael. Michael Dickinson, Bette decided, would be a very good friend to have.

"She comes by sometimes. Claims she needs to use my computer, but it's really to raid the fridge. She's always complaining I don't have anything to eat in the place."

"Aw, Judi's Judi," said Grady with undisputable logic and affectionate acceptance. "Remember how she could pack it away when she was a kid, and she still stayed scrawny."

"Maybe so, but she's not scrawny anymore and she's still eating me out of house and home."

They all smiled at the plaintive note in Paul's voice.

"I heard you were out in D.C. last week, Paul. How's Tris? She's not pining after that jerk ex-husband, is she?"

Grady asked the question, but Bette had the impression Paul didn't direct his answer to him, but rather to Michael. "If she ever pined for him at all, she's not now. It was a pretty friendly divorce, really, and she's long past it. Years ago. She's grown up, like we all have."

"No way," objected Grady with a chuckle. "Maybe Michael's grown up, but you and I are as crazy as ever, Monroe."

Bette thought she felt Paul's gaze on her, but she'd discovered a fascination for her nearly empty wineglass.

Grady's words didn't express anything she hadn't thought. So why should it bother her to hear someone else say it? Paul could deny it. He could say he wasn't a kid anymore. He could say he'd grown up.

The silence continued.

"Hey, how about another round?" Grady's attempt to turn the conversation was unsubtle, but effective. Without waiting for an answer, he eased out of the booth.

"I'll go with him," said Paul, with another glance at Bette. She felt the awkwardness from the moment before lingering, and wondered if he wanted to escape. "Another white wine, Bette?" When she nodded, he, too, rose, following Grady toward the jammed bar.

"So you've gone and done it."

Paul stilled at Grady's words. "Gone and done what?"

Grady placed their order with the harried bartender, then tipped his head back toward the table. "Found someone worth bringing into the family."

"I don't know what you're talking about."

He wished he didn't know what the clutching panic in his gut was about. It was the same fear that had kept his heart from soaring right now out the window, past the Hancock Center and beyond Sears Tower, when Bette said she'd go out with him.

Go out with him? She'd agreed to more than that. They'd both acknowledged it in the heated exchange of looks and desire across his desk. So why postpone the moment? He'd dealt with other women this way, no promises made or expected. Why not now?

"Whoa, don't take my head off, Monroe." Grady pretended to back away. "I meant the family of your close friends—you know, Michael and me. Tris."

"Stuff it, Roberts," he growled, but his tension eased. It seemed the most natural thing in the world to bring Bette together with the other people he— He stumbled on the mental phrasing, realizing he was including Bette in the group. That he cared for, he finally supplied.

"You've got to admit this is a novel experience. I can't remember ever bringing a woman to meet us before."

Paul scowled at the echo of his father's words from a few weeks before. Why was everyone making such a big flaming deal of this? "So? You think everybody's like you, with the passion of the second? You've introduced us to so many women you must have a revolving door."

The blue of Grady's eyes seemed to flicker. Paul wanted to kick himself. As he had with Michael not so long ago, he'd lashed out and hit his friend where it hurt worst. What the hell was the matter with him? He knew Grady wasn't proud of his track record with women.

"No, that's just it, Paul. I don't think you're like me. I think you've always recognized what I'm just starting to figure out: quality beats the hell out of quantity."

"Look, Grady, I'm sorry for that crack. I didn't mean it. It's just . . . let's just forget the whole thing, okay?"

Grady's impatient shrug dismissed both the apology and the effort to turn the conversation. "She seems like a nice woman, Paul. A good person. Try not to be as stupid as the rest of us. Try to make it work."

Paul stared, astonished by Grady's intensity. They'd been friends since grade school, and he couldn't remember if they'd ever had a conversation like this.

Handing money to the bartender, Paul felt grateful for the mundane occupation. At least something remained normal in a world developing more and more unfamiliar corners.

Bette watched Paul weave through the crowd, and considered this trio. Michael Dickinson, perceptive and rather intense. Grady Roberts, accepting and trading on his charm. And Paul. The man who said he believed in no strings and keeping his options open, yet clearly the glue that held the three of them together.

"They're great guys," Michael said, appearing not to notice when her hand jerked, dragging the wineglass an inch across the table. With an offhand directness that belied the scrutiny he focused on her, he added, "Of course, Grady's a bit spoiled from having things go his way so much."

She smiled. Michael clearly liked Grady, yet had no delusions. "Probably understandable when you grow up good-looking, wealthy and smart and then add your own success."

"Yeah, that'd do it." She liked his dryness.

He looked over to Paul and Grady at the bar. "I guess it's understandable, too, that Paul's the way he is."

She felt her lips stiffen. "What way is that?"

"Oh, sort of a fly-by-night character. Not willing to be tied down long enough so anyone else can rely on him."

"He is not." She tried to keep the hostility out of her voice, but heard her own indignation.

"Isn't he?" His quietness didn't soothe her.

"He definitely is not." What sort of idiot could be his friend for fifteen years and not see the truth about Paul? Why are you so angry at him for saying exactly the same things you've said to yourself? she wondered. "He's devoted to his family and friends. Who's the one who keeps all of you in touch? He's a well-respected professional, who gives his clients honesty and impartiality. Plus he has the loyalty of the people who've worked for him." At least the ones he wasn't trying to drive crazy. "Look at Jan Robson. You don't have that sort of relationship with an employee when you're a 'fly-by-night character!'"

"Don't you?"

"No!"

"No," he agreed.

The mildness finally reached her. The adrenaline surge faded and she examined Michael. His lips twitched and a dimple appeared high on his left cheek.

"You're a rat," she informed him. "A tricky, wily political rat."

The grin completed its escape. "I just wanted to know if you'd seen through the Paul Monroe facade."

"Facade?"

"Mmm-hmm." He grew serious. "Not that he doesn't believe in it—at least parts. That's what's such a shame."

A skittering of panic trembled through her and settled in the pit of her stomach. Michael reached across the table to put his hand over hers. "He's not always the free spirit he pretends to be."

She thought she understood what he was saying: Paul did look beyond the moment—with people and responsibilities—but he didn't want to admit it. And that frightened her, because it gave her hope.

"Hey, Dickinson, get your hands off my date." Paul clunked down two glasses with a mock glare, but in his eyes, she saw something flare to life. A hint of possessiveness, of claiming? "Find yourself your own woman."

Paul Monroe was everything Bette could ask for in a date. Funny, attentive, entertaining. He was also elusive, unattainable and distant. He was driving her crazy.

They joked and laughed and talked. They had long conversations on the phone when she should have been working. He called to say nothing more complex than good-morning. He brought Chinese food to her office for lunch. They met Grady and Michael twice more that week for dinner. They pored over real estate listings she had compiled, with Paul volunteering plenty of opinions, most of which involved the idea that she shouldn't live so far away—whether from him or her work, he never quite specified. They saw a movie.

He never touched her.

Well, that wasn't quite true, she admitted to herself. He touched her just enough to drive her mad. Just enough to make her consider raking her fingernails along a brick wall to get rid of the frustration of envisioning circumstances when she would press them into his back, but never having the satisfaction of doing it.

He looped an arm around her shoulders at the movies, then never drew her closer. He brushed his fingers across her collarbone while helping her with her coat, then never ventured lower. He touched his lips to hers each night when he drove her home, then never pressed the kiss deeper.

Tuesday. Wednesday. Thursday.

Now it was Friday. In frustration she'd told him she needed to work late to catch up, hoping to escape his tormenting presence for one night, just long enough to regain some control. He'd appeared at the office shortly after five and sat patiently waiting for her, until she wanted to scream. Instead, she'd given up and gone for a sandwich with him, and they'd come out of the tiny deli to find the sky streaming a combination of rain and snow.

"I don't think it's safe to drive tonight."

"Paul, it's not even really snowing. Look at the roads. It's more like slush." Spending dinner trying not to fantasize every time she looked across at his mouth had left her more than a little irritable.

"Slush," he repeated, shaking his head as if verifying his worst suspicions. "Slush can be very dangerous. You know, they don't even make slush tires. That's because no tire in the world can help you in slush."

"You're right," she agreed, abruptly changing tacks. Maybe she could at least cut the evening short. Go home now, spend a few hours alone, try to regain some sanity. "You've been driving way too much. I've tried to tell you it wasn't necessary to take me home every night, and I'm glad you're finally being sensible about this."

He grinned, but she saw that his eyes were heating in a most dangerous way. She needed to get away from him. She needed a respite from this constant arousing of her desire with never any satisfaction.

"I'll take the train."

"The train!" He looked thwarted for a moment, but quickly gathered himself. He gave her a long, considering look. "The train's the very worst thing you can do. Do you know what slush can do to train tracks?"

"No, what?"

"Make them a veritable death slide."

"Really? I've never heard that before."

He made a scoffing sound. "Of course not. You think the railroads would let you know a thing like that? They'd lose all their commuters for the whole winter." He perked up, as if seeing the possibilities in the vision he'd created, and she wondered again at his ability to make her see humor even while he was making her lose her mind. "In fact, commuters by the droves would stay home all winter. No more driving, no more taking the train, just settling in for the winter at home in front of the fireplace and next to a good woman."

"Or man."

He tilted an eyebrow at her. "That's kind of liberal for my taste."

"I meant," she explained severely, "that a lot of the commuters are women."

"Oh. Yeah, of course. I guess I was just speaking from a personal point of view."

"Uh-huh," she said with disapproval. But it hadn't been such a bad point of view at that. In fact, it definitely had its attractions. Yes, with a little imagination, she could visualize herself snuggled next to Paul Monroe in front of a fire, maybe with soft music in the background, a glass of wine, and without too many clothes. Settling in for the winter.

Tipping her chin up, she looked at him more closely in the eerie glow of streetlights diffused by sleet.

Four days ago, she'd reopened the door she'd earlier tried to close. But it hadn't led into a new stage in their relationship the way she'd expected it to. On Monday, the day she crossed that emotional threshold, she'd been braced for the consequences. She wouldn't have been particularly surprised if he actually had taken her right then and there in his office. When he invited her to dinner with his friends instead, and left her at her front door with a near-chaste kiss, she'd thought he was showing an unsuspected tenderness, almost a delicacy.

But after Tuesday and Wednesday and Thursday, she was inclined to say the hell with delicacy.

She'd made her decision. Why wait for winter? Waiting wouldn't change who he was, and it wouldn't give her any guarantee of safety for her heart. Nor would it change how much she wanted him. It was time to fly. Now.

"So where shall we stay?"

"What?" His eyes met hers. Confusion showed for half a second, then only a blaze of instant fire. Like being struck by a bolt of lightning, one moment there was nothing, the next unadulterated sizzle.

She'd never been so happy to be singed. As much as she'd tried not to, she'd wondered about the reluctance she'd detected in him. But that look, that one flash in his eyes, vaporized her doubts.

"Since you're not going to drive me home tonight, and taking the train would be such a reckless thing to do, what are we going to do for accommodations tonight?"

"I know just the place," he said. She figured that now he'd explain how his apartment in Evanston would be a safe choice, since it wouldn't mean as long a drive in the "treacherous" slush. "There's a great little hotel not far from here. You hardly notice it from the street, but inside, the lobby's all polished wood and plush furniture. The rooms look like a spread from some magazine on English country homes. The perfect place to wait out a slush storm."

Surprise opened her mouth to the first thing in her mind. "How do you know about this place?"

The glint in his eyes looked positively devilish in the eerie light.

"Not how you're thinking, you suspicious woman, you. I can tell you with a totally clear conscience that I have never waited out a storm, slush or otherwise, with a woman at that hotel. In fact, the only times I've been there have been with a man— Michael. It's where he stays when he's got business downtown."

"I wasn't asking for explanations. I didn't think—"

He cut off her protest with a kiss on her nose. "No, of course you didn't." He looped his arm more securely around her shoulders and guided her footsteps. "It's not too far away," he said, mentioning an address not far off Michigan Avenue.

"What if they don't have a vacancy?" she offered half-heartedly.

"They should. Michael said they cater mostly to businessmen, so weekends should be pretty quiet."

"Oh."

They'd gone almost two blocks—in a direct route this time, she noticed with some satisfaction—when she stopped short. "Wait a minute. We can't go to a hotel, Paul. We don't have any luggage. It'll look like...like..."

Her voice wound down. It would look like exactly what it was—two adults deciding to spend an impromptu night together at a downtown hotel. He would surely tell her it didn't matter what anyone else thought. And deep down, she really *didn't* care what anyone else thought; being with Paul was right for her. Still...she cringed at the idea of going into a hotel without luggage. It seemed such a blatant announcement of something that should be private.

"All right."

"All right?" Just that easily, he was willing to let the opportunity to spend the night together go—willing to let *her* go?

"Yep. We'll go to Water Tower Place first."

"Water Tower Place? Why?"

"We have some shopping to do."

Chapter Eight

Bette mentally checked the contents of the shopping bags she'd accumulated, then looked at her watch. Nine minutes left before she was to meet Paul. Unexpectedly, a bubble of laughter rose in her. Who would have guessed how much fun this would be, this rather sexy kind of scavenger hunt?

They'd started off together, buying tote bags after a long, intricate discussion of exactly which ones they should get. Paul had wanted to buy matching ones because, he said, it was a visual symbol to any astute bellboy that this was an established couple. She had opted for different ones because it might look less like just-bought goods. Paul had prevailed, and for a moment as the clerk rang up the purchase, she'd considered how odd it was for Mr. For the Moment Only to be the one to want them to appear as a couple. But then there'd been no time to give the matter further thought.

She had shopping to do.

They'd agreed to meet in forty-five minutes at the front entrance to Water Tower Place. She'd gone directly to a drugstore, tossing into the mesh basket a toothbrush and toothpaste, a disposable razor for her legs, deodorant and a small perfume vial, plus trial-size shampoo and moisturizer in case the hotel didn't provide them. Then, trying to tell herself not to blush like an idiot, she added a foil packet to her collection.

She'd spent most of her time in Marshall Field's, buying a change of clothing for the morning: jeans and a white oxford-cloth shirt, which weren't extravagant since she could always use spares. With her tweed suit jacket and flat pumps, she at least wouldn't look blatantly like a woman wearing her Friday night clothes on Saturday morning.

Her last stop was lingerie, for a change of underwear. Now, with nine minutes left, she glanced across the aisle that separated the lingerie basics from the frivolous and saw a royal-blue froth of lace and sheerness. She knew she had to have it. She was woman enough to know it would draw lights to her eyes, and practical enough never to have owned anything like it.

Stifling the habit of checking the price first, she found the right size and headed for the counter.

Oh, she'd been with men before. A couple. But she couldn't imagine having had the nerve to wear something like this for them. This was a gown to wear for a man who could make her laugh, but never laughed at her. She felt a swelling in her heart as she accepted the bag with the gown. She'd wear this for Paul, and she'd have no shyness about it. He would see her vulnerability, and he would honor it.

With her final few minutes, she found a rest room and transferred the contents of her shopping bags to the tote.

As she hurried through the heavy glass doors, she caught sight of Paul immediately. Grinning, he held up his bag to show off its packed state. She thought his looked lumpier than hers, and there was definitely a sharp edge poking against the soft fabric. She felt it against her calf as it dangled from his hand when he wrapped her into a tight embrace and kissed her hungrily, right there on Michigan Avenue.

"C'mon, let's get a cab," he said a little huskily.

She'd have been lucky to achieve even husky if she tried to talk, so she settled for nodding. She didn't care that it was impractical to take a cab the few blocks to the hotel. It was faster, and it gave them an excuse to sit cuddled together in one corner and share another, long, lingering kiss. He seduced her mouth, luring her upper lip between his, tempting her with forays of his tongue and teeth. Kissing her in a way that left her feeling a little vague all through the process of paying off the driver, checking in and finding their room.

If Paul had kissed her like that earlier, she might never have noticed that they didn't have luggage. And then she wouldn't have had any excuse to funnel this shivery feeling of anticipation and trepidation into a show of great curiosity about what he'd bought.

They stood side by side just inside the door, before slowly moving in. Thick carpeting and drapes shut out the city's noise, making the drumming of her blood louder in Bette's ears. Soft lights she knew wouldn't hide the flush heating her cheeks, a flush of awareness. Before them the room stood, plush and cozy. All it needed to complete the country-house look was a fireplace.

But no fire was needed to provide heat. Her imagination was taking care of that. From where she stood at the foot of the bed, her eyes traveled up the wide and generously pillowed expanse. Oh, Lord, the bed . . .

"So what do you have in your bag?" she asked in a brightly forced voice. She gave his tote's strap a tug, but he held tight.

"Uh-unh. Let's see yours, too." His voice sounded huskier than before.

"Okay. We'll take turns. But you go first."

He gave her a sideways glance, then rested his tote on the edge of the bed and unzipped it. "Okay, first item." Humor overlaid the deeper note in his voice. He produced a chrysanthemum stem with three perfect yellow blooms on it and held it out to her.

"Flowers! Where in the world did you find flowers?"

"That wasn't so hard. The hard part was packing it."

She giggled a little, and inexplicably, her nervousness eased.

"I tried for roses, but there must have been a run on them. Some sort of romantic epidemic hitting the city."

"This is lovely. I love yellow chrysanthemums."

"I know. I remember the flowers by your front walk."

She couldn't say anything to that, so she leaned across the corner of the bed and kissed him lightly. She heard his quick intake of breath, and backed up hastily.

"Your turn," he ordered.

Opening the bag, she gave a quick laugh. "Nothing so frivolous as flowers."

"Jeans? Is this something kinky I should know about?"

Despite his teasing note, she felt her cheeks warming. "No. They're for tomorrow."

"Tomorrow. Ah, I see." He said that as if thinking of tomorrow somehow betrayed today—or tonight. "I suppose you're planning to be incognito when we leave in the morning."

"At least inconspicuous," she said more sharply than she'd intended.

He gave her an unreadable look, then reached into his bag. It was a clear nonverbal change of subject.

"Next, we have one bottle of white wine. Chilled to perfection, thanks to its recent sojourn in the Chicago night air."

Back to teasing. She was glad. Tonight she wanted to forget the differences between them. Tonight, at least this one night, was to explore this other thing between them.

"One blouse, to match the jeans," she responded, keeping her voice light. She caught an expression in his eyes she couldn't interpret, then it was gone and he was pulling out his next item.

As their respective piles of purchases grew on the bed, a trend developed. To her deodorant, toothbrush and toothpaste, new underwear and socks, he answered with a pair of wineglasses, a pillar candle, a tape player and two moody instrumental cassettes, a box of chocolates and a fluffy bath sheet she could easily imagine would accommodate two. It was almost as if he'd read her mind back on that sidewalk when she'd imagined a winter's night with him.

"Geeze, aren't you ever romantic, Bette?"

Even with his eyes glinting at her and his voice rough with the combination of laughter and desire, she found herself chafing at the comment. So she'd considered tomorrow morning. So she'd given some forethought to the practicalities of staying overnight in a hotel. So she wasn't the kind who thought only of the moment.... So she wasn't what Paul, with his music and wine and flowers, considered romantic.

Unthinkingly, she reached into her nearly empty bag and yanked out the small foil package.

Even before Paul's eyes went to what was in her hand, then came back to meet hers, she knew what she held. Everything else between them, the humor, the irritation and the tension, flowed away in a wash of awareness. The need that had brought them to this place surged through her, and, she knew from the sudden tautness of his stance, through him, also. "On second thought, I withdraw that question."

She couldn't help but react to the low note in his voice. Hers shook a little, but she got the words out. "I believe in being prepared."

She couldn't believe that with all the heat of desire flaring between them, amusement still lingered in his eyes.

Without a word, he reached into his bag and withdrew something, which he then held out for her inspection. Four packets just like hers.

"Four? Four!" And she understood now how he mixed the humor and the desire, because she simultaneously wanted the release of laughter and craved the tormenting pleasure of his hands.

"I believe in being prepared, too."

"For what, a harem?"

He made a sound deep in his throat, only half a chuckle. The other half was declaration and question, rolled into one. One corner of her mouth lifted, as she let her eyes answer the rest.

Tossing the packets haphazardly toward the nightstand behind him, he reached across the corner of the bed for her, pulling her to him.

They'd been so careful not to touch, and now, in kiss after kiss, she knew why. The lightning she'd imagined in his eyes outside the deli was in their bodies, jolting from one to the other at each point of contact, intensifying each time their lips came together, drawing power when his mouth roamed across her throat, her shoulders, her abdomen. Releasing energy in a line of fire through her when his tongue plunged into her mouth with deep, instinctive significance. She arched beneath him, hardly knowing how they'd come to be on the bed instead of beside it.

Fingers fretted with buttons. His shirt was jerked off and tossed aside. Her blouse opened and skimmed away by urgent hands. He cupped her breasts, his gentleness straining against ungentle desires. She felt the delicious rasp of lace and his hand against her flesh, and knew how right this was.

She wanted more. She wanted his mouth on her, as it had been that moonlit night in her garage. It was almost as if the weeks between had disappeared, and this was a simple, natural continuation of the desire they'd felt then. Or maybe it was an unending desire, always there, a lightning waiting only to be tapped.

Then his mouth was around her, open, wetting the lace and hardening her nipple to an exquisite ache, and she had no mind for thought, no room for remembered sensation because there was only now. This moment.

She stroked his shoulders, wanting to imprint the smooth, strong feel of them into her hands. He suckled, and she gasped with the pleasure. Then he added to it with fingers that stroked and circled her other breast.

Air came in gasps for both of them when he trailed his mouth lower, tracing the curve of her ribs, taking a nibbling bite at the side of her waist.

The tickling made her want to laugh, but she didn't have the breath for it. She'd never realized laughter and lust could be so closely allied; they certainly never had been for her before. No, it took Paul to show her this, to show her that the lightness of laughter didn't have to be eclipsed by the dark passion pulling at them. Not when the laughter was such an integral part of what they had together, not when the passion was strong enough.

Oh, Lord, it *was* strong enough. He flicked open the waist of her skirt, and hauled down the zipper so the material rode over her hips. Not satisfied, he slid one hand lower, under the hem, and skimmed up her thigh and beyond to the top of her pantyhose, then immediately started back, dragging the hosiery along. She'd barely helped free her legs from the encumbrance when he was tugging at her panties and slip all at once. He clearly intended her to be naked as quickly as possible... *Naked.* The word sparked an image of blue froth, carefully saved for last in their game of show-and-tell.

"Wait." She gasped the demand, so it sounded more of a plea. Only a small part of her recognized the way he froze.

"Wait?"

Fighting the weight of desire, her eyes opened wide as she understood he was questioning more than the word. As he had in her garage, he let her see the desire and longing in his eyes, but also the question. He was leaving it up to her. She could stop it . . .

"No." She shook her head quickly, hoping to make him see he'd misunderstood; she'd made her decision. "I have one more thing to show you."

"To show me?" His question was followed by a grumbling curse that didn't entirely mask his relief. But he let her remove herself from his hold, and she dived for the tote at the end of the bed, extracting the negligee. As she stood, her loosened skirt slid lower on her hips and with an impatient twist, she sent it to the floor. Feeling a little shy, yet not really self-conscious, she held the floating material up to her, resting the straps at her shoulders.

"See?"

Oh, yes, he saw. Oh, God, yes, he saw. He swore to himself that he would never again make the mistake of thinking Bette was not romantic. She was romantic enough to just about kill him, and all she had to do was stand two feet in front of him holding up a bit of filmy material.

Through the sheer fabric he saw the lace of her bra, he saw the wetness he'd added to it, he saw the straining points he'd felt against his hands and mouth. And he could see her, smooth and pale beneath it. Lower, the draping skirt of the gown revealed the paleness of her simple, straight slip. Despite the layers of material he knew what he would find there, too: heated silk. If she put on that blue torment now, so that he caught glimpses of her with more than his imagination, he'd want to rip it off her. But he also saw her eyes. The gown meant something to her.

"I, uh, I could put it on."

He swallowed hard. "I'd like to see it."

"Now?"

What was she saying? He knew damn well he wanted to delay seeing her in that material seduction, at least delay to some moment when he might stand half a chance of appreciating it. But what did she want? He'd thought he knew, and he'd been prepared to give it to her, no matter what it cost him. But from that last question and from the heated look in her eyes, he wasn't so sure.

"What?"

She glanced down at the blue sheerness she still held then back at him. "Do you have to see it right now or could it maybe wait until...uh...later? I mean, if you really want to see it now of course I could put it on, but—"

He ground out something he wasn't sure made any sense and yanked down the rumpled bedspread, far enough that it slid slowly off the foot of the bed along with most of their purchases.

"Later's fine," he got out as he reached for her. With a smile that managed to melt his bones and harden his muscles, she sent the gown spinning in the same general direction.

"Later," she agreed on a breath shivered against his neck.

They stripped each other of their remaining clothes with fervent, unsubtle movements.

Her hands were cold at first, with the lingering chill of outdoors and perhaps a bit of nervousness. Don't rush her, he reminded himself. Then gasped at her fingers' contact against his stomach, his abdomen, his hips. But it was a gasp of pleasured torture. Who was rushing whom? He figured it was only fair her hands and her feet were cold, because the rest of her was burning up. He could feel the heat of her under his hands, like waves off a sunstruck sidewalk in July. And he craved it, absorbed it, matched it with his own.

With her hands and feet like small, smooth slips of ice being dragged along his skin, he relished the contrast to his own temperature. Told himself that maybe this way he'd slow down enough to have some control. And when her hands and feet passed the comfortable stage and became coals, stoking the fire that already raged in his flesh, he knew he'd never needed anything the way he needed that stoking.

Still, he wasn't fool enough to have her help with the contents of the packets spilled on the nightstand. A fire stoked too high could burn itself out.

They tumbled across the bed, a tangle of arms and legs that drew a dual chuckle reverberating into a groan of need. A hip grinding into a hip, an elbow catching across a shoulder, a knee digging into a thigh. But then, somehow, amid the sounds of frustration, amusement and passion, the parts came into alignment. It wasn't the slow, tender introduction he'd envisioned in aching detail for days, weeks on end. But it was right. Utterly, undeniably right.

He thrust into her welcoming warmth, faster than he'd intended, slower than he wanted. He went still, his eyes squeezing tight in an exultation he'd never known. Then the pressure inside forced him to move. He felt her body adjust, accept, and another wave of sensation struck him. It flashed across his mind that this sensation flowed not from his nerve endings to his brain, but from somewhere deep inside him to where his skin met hers. He opened his eyes and locked with hers.

They were deep, deep blue. Bottomless and soft. The way they tugged at him took him off balance. No way to hold back against them...no way. He could fall into those eyes and keep falling. He was falling.

"Bette." He whispered the name as his hips surged against hers, the pull of the rhythm too strong to resist, the beat that guided them too insistent to ignore. It rocked them when they strained together, it echoed through them as they slipped away from each other, it amplified as they rushed together once more, closer, ever closer. They pulsed with it. It might have been a heartbeat of something alive, magnified to roar in their ears.

He heard other sounds added to it. Her voice, stripped of the crisp coolness, only the spice and fire remaining. Cries to him, for him. His own call of her name, encouraging, invoking. He cupped her buttocks, drawing her closer, straining to have her take all he had, to fill her ever more completely. Her cry turned sharp and triumphant. The thundering beat shuddered again through his taut-strung muscles one last, frenzied time.

* * *

It was quiet. Except for their breathing. He heard his own harsh intake and her no steadier exhalation. She'd have an easier time if he took all his weight off her instead of remaining half-covering her the way he'd collapsed. He didn't move. Not sure if he could, and certain he didn't want to. Macho, maybe, but even after what they'd just experienced, he relished the continued sense of possession from being connected this way.

What was this feeling, this draw to her, this need for her? It frightened him—he admitted that—but it also attracted him, a magnet bringing him nearer to something he'd always avoided. Now, too weak with satisfaction and contentment to fight the idea, the suspicion floated into his mind that as much as he might try to dig his heels in against it, he wouldn't be able to stop his progress toward the pole she represented. Right now, he couldn't even find it in himself to care.

Soft and even, her breathing soothed him. She was asleep. A powerful sense of protectiveness swept into him; she trusted him enough to give herself up to him, then to give herself up to sleep in his arms.

He recognized the dangerous, sharp edges of this emotion. He even knew, at some level, how it could shred his independent life.

So where shall we stay? One question, five words. That was all it had taken to blow his control to hell. So much for waiting until he knew what he was getting into. He was in, and he still didn't know.

He shifted slightly. Not away, but freeing her ribs of all but the weight of his arm. He thought that under the sigh of skin against sheets, he detected a breath from her. Perhaps relief, but he wanted to think it was also regret at even this minute distance. He pulled the rumpled covers over their cooling bodies.

The emotion he'd reined in from the time she'd said yes in his office was loose. He might soar with it, for now, but could he haul it back under control later?

Bette woke up with no confusion. She didn't even need to open her eyes to know where she was or whose arms held her, whose legs weighed hers down, whose breath stirred her hair and whose shoulder pillowed her cheek.

She knew.

A powerful, potent drug this lust could be. It lulled her from the tenets of a lifetime, so that as she rested in the circle of Paul's arms, she found herself thinking not of the future, but of the past. The immediate, incredible past.

She felt her cheeks warming under the heat of the memories, not in embarrassment but in renewed desire. He wasn't a smooth lover, or particularly gentle. But he was thorough. And powerful. The glimpses she'd had of his sensuality hadn't prepared her for the whole. She was honest enough with herself to admit that if they had, she might still be running.

Although he'd given her chances to run. She thought of the moments he'd hesitated long enough to let his eyes ask her if she wanted to back out. Not once, but twice.

A slight frown of concentration tightened muscles in her forehead. She had the impression a pattern was there somewhere, a pattern she hadn't recognized yet. What was it?

Still sleeping, Paul shifted against her, drawing her closer and making a low sound against her hair. Her eyes opened, the frown disappearing as her mouth curved.

Patterns and contemplation could wait. If she'd learned one thing tonight, it was the power of the moment. Under

Paul Monroe's touch, now was the only time that existed for her.

The room was softly aglow from a single shaded lamp on the nightstand. Sometime while she slept, he must have gotten up and switched off the other lights. How long had she slept? She really didn't care. Still night, she thought. The drapes showed no crack of morning light and the city seemed hushed beyond them.

The light burnished his skin and the blaze of hair, darker than on his head and arms but still with a glint no one would confuse with brown. It trailed the valley between his ribs only to disappear under a tangle of covers at his waist. Their earlier urgency had left no time to contemplate and explore his body. Her fingers lightly dusted along the tickling cover of hair. She lifted her head, and considered the form that had pillowed hers.

He was beautiful.

His eyes still closed in sleep, his personality for once stood second to his physical presence. His shoulders were broad, his torso narrowed to taut waist and slim hips, though she knew the power those sleek lines could produce. A swimmer's body, rather than a weight lifter's, she thought. Strength without bulk, hardness without display.

A body that could make the past no more than a memory of the joy it had given her before, the future no more than a hope for more.

She bent, putting her lips to the flat brown disk where the dusting of hair grew thinner. She let her tongue taste it, taste him, and felt the response—in him, and in herself.

He muttered something she chose to take as encouragement. When her stronger ministrations brought his hands to her hair, holding her tightly against him, she knew she'd been right. Tension hummed along his skin, a vibration that communicated itself to her through her tongue and lips.

"Bette."

His hands tugged at her, drawing her over his body, holding her shoulders above him.

"Bette, let me kiss you. Open your mouth to me."

The kiss started as a gentle one, then deepened and quickened to pulse with a beat she recognized and welcomed. Paul's hands clenched hard around her upper arms, then purposefully loosened, and the kiss eased back to tenderness.

He parted their mouths, and hitched himself to a sitting position against the padded headboard. Still lost in the kiss and her sense of loss that it had ended, she allowed herself to be twisted and adjusted until she sat back against his chest with his arms around her, the covers up to her shoulders.

"Are you okay?" His lips followed the question with a whispery touch to her temple.

The question and the concern of voice and touch surprised her. "Fine."

"Fine?"

"Wonderful," she amended, turning to kiss his chin.

"Wonderful? Really?" She tilted her head so she could see his eyes. "I was rather rough. And in a hurry."

She understood. He wasn't searching for reassurance on his performance, but was truly concerned.

"Yes, you were," she answered slowly, remembering. "And it was wonderful."

The concern in his eyes lessened, but didn't leave. "You're sure you're okay?"

She kissed his throat, just under his jaw, then nipped at it before kissing the spot once more. "I'm sure. Though I might be a little sore..."

He grinned. "You know what they say is the best cure for sore muscles?"

"What's that?"

"Use them."

"Ah, why'd I have a feeling you'd say that?"

"Because great minds think alike?"

"I don't think that was it."

"Because you'd heard that wisdom before?"

"Not that, either."

"Because you've known that I've been fantasizing about you for nearly a month now?"

It was odd the things that could catch you off guard. "Fantasizing? About me?" She wasn't a woman to spark fantasies. Respect, yes. Maybe even admiration. But fantasies?

He must have heard the disbelief in her voices. He placed a hand on each side of her head and turned her so she had to see the utter conviction in his eyes. "You better believe it, Bette Wharton. Fantasizing hot and heavy."

Feeling part of him harden against her hip lent credence to his statement.

"Like what?" She could feel her cheeks burning under his hands, and this time there was embarrassment mixed with the desire. She couldn't believe she'd asked the question, but she sure as hell wasn't going to stop the answer.

"I have one where you come to my office...." His voice sounded unusually husky, but his eyes didn't leave hers. He cleared his throat. "It's late. The building's empty. And you walk in the door, unexpectedly and ..." His hesitation let her heated imagination fill in details that gathered her blood, hot and heavy, in her breasts and loins. "And we make love on the couch. Long, slow, lingering love."

"I have one too," she murmured. "A fantasy." She didn't know where she got the bravery. Unless it was from him.

"Tell me."

"There's a boathouse where my parents live. They bought the house years ago to retire to. We used to go there for vacations, even when I was a girl." She was explaining too much, she knew, but she couldn't help it. She wasn't accustomed to this. "I've fantasized about making love in this tiny, private boathouse. It would be warm and dark, and so beautiful. But I never could see the man's face." Still, she'd known it would be the face of the man she'd love for all her life.

"Can you see the man's face now?"

He had needs, too. If she hadn't known it before, if he'd tried to hide it before, it was there between them now. Could she say no, and hurt him that way? Could she say yes, and hurt herself?

"I..." Paul's face swam before her in a shimmer of tears. "I think maybe I can."

Their lips met. This time he wasn't rough. Or in a hurry, though she witnessed the cost of his patience in muscles that quivered and tendons gone tense. She would have spared him that, in fact tried to tempt him beyond it, rolling her hips in invitation. But he resisted, tempting her instead. His mouth and hands and skin were a sensual abrasion, traveling lower and deeper across her sensitized skin. And in the end, she succumbed, falling first and fast as he found her moist warmth and brought there the beat they'd perfected before. She fell a second time when he joined her, but this was slower and deeper, and all the more wonderful because she watched him, his face rapt and taut, follow her to the ascent, and then over.

They lay as they had collapsed, too exhausted, too sated to move. When his voice came, it seemed to float between them.

"I have one question."

"Hmm?" Forming a word took too much energy.

"Don't your parents live outside Phoenix?"

"Uh-huh."

"A boathouse? In Arizona?"

She poked at his ribs and got a muffled chuckle in reward. "Shows all you know. Yes, a boathouse in Arizona. There's a lake with sailing and swimming and everything. Mom and Dad have lakefront property, and a little, enclosed boathouse."

He seemed to accept that. After a minute or two, he mentioned in an offhand way, "You know I have this other fantasy, too." He stroked his palm over her skin, from hip, over fanny, waist, back, shoulder and neck, then back down. "And for this one we don't have to go all the way to Arizona, or even leave the hotel. We only have to move about ten feet to accomplish it."

He drew her up, disregarding her halfhearted protests, and she saw they were heading for the bathroom.

"It has to do with being hot and wet and close," he murmured into her ear before stooping to snag the bath sheet from the tumble of objects at the foot of the bed. A froth of royal blue wove in among the other items.

"Are you ever going to show me this nightgown?"

She stifled a throaty chuckle. "I did show it to you, remember?"

"I meant on you, this time."

"I thought you had a fantasy you wanted to show me first."

He looked from her to the gown swirled at their feet, then back to her.

"Will you promise to show it to me later?"

"Later," she promised. "Much later."

Chapter Nine

Since his purchases hadn't run to such necessities as a clean shirt or a change of underwear, their first stop late Saturday morning was Paul's Evanston apartment.

Bette immediately liked the four-story red-brick building with the general air of solidity. At this time of year, with the leaves gone from the neighborhood's many trees, his top-floor apartment's bay window gave a glimpse of the lake a few blocks away.

But the view was one of the few things that could be said for the near-barren living room. A door topping a pair of file cabinets that supported a personal computer and accoutrements. Brick-and-board shelves for books, an old TV and mismatched stereo equipment. A rugged old couch and one side chair. That was it.

The landing place of someone who wanted to be prepared to take off again. A leaden mass formed in her stomach. It was all too clearly a reflection of the resident.

"Not quite as homey as your place, huh?"

He sounded almost defensive as he stood just inside the door and waved her in, and she didn't have the heart to agree as wholeheartedly as she might have otherwise. "No." Searching for something else to say, she added, "It's a nice neighborhood, Paul."

"Yeah," he agreed, brightening a little. "It is. Here's the kitchen." His gesture took in a cubicle as Spartan as the living room, although its 1940s-style appliances looked considerably less used than the living room furniture. "I eat out a lot," he explained.

"And the bath." It was mostly screened from view by towels and shirts hanging from door corners, shower curtain rod and doorknobs, but it appeared to be the same vintage as the kitchen.

"And the bedroom." A king-size mattress and box spring sat directly on the bare wooden floor with the pillows and comforter rumpled from the last time he'd used them. A canvas-covered director's chair at one side held a clock radio and a stack of books on its seat. She suspected that under the pile of clothes on the opposite side of the bed resided the chair's twin. A tiny dresser stood next to a closed closet door. "Not much storage space," he muttered. "Closet barely holds the suits and stuff, so the other things..." He shrugged.

"That's the tour, complete in thirty-four seconds, no need to tip the tour conductor." He smiled a little lopsidedly at her, and she couldn't resist leaning over as they stood in the doorway of his bedroom and kissing the corner of his mouth. Immediately, she felt embarrassed by the gesture. They'd shared a night of passion, but affection was something else.

"I'll...I'll just wait out here while you get your things," she said, trying to make her retreat to the living room seem less like scuttling than it felt.

"I kind of thought—" He broke off, but she saw him glance from his rumpled bed to her and back, and she had a pretty good idea what he'd thought. She didn't mind the thought, but hadn't a clue how to express that. But he obviously took her hesitation as a no. "Okay. This shouldn't take long. I've just got to find some clean things." He turned into the bedroom, then back. "I ought to stop by the cleaners and take some of this stuff in, too."

She hid a smile. The cleaners were going to make a small fortune. "Okay."

She wandered around the living room, looking at his eclectic mix of books and tapes, absently noting that the papers spread out by the computer dealt with his business, and looked professional and detailed.

The sounds from the bedroom finally drew her back. She'd pretended not to notice when he swept the bathroom clean by heaping clothes and towels into his arms. Now he'd formed a pile in the middle of the bedroom floor, and with his back to her, was busy searching out additions for it.

The search entailed digging through the layers on the chair with as much care as an archaeologist. He apparently hadn't found a shirt to his liking yet, because he wore none. But he'd put on a pair of jeans. Snug jeans that curved tautly over his fanny.

Bette swallowed. Heat ran through her system with deliberate speed, melting away the awkward shyness and the quiet protests of sore muscles.

She could slip into the room, sneak up behind him, mold her palms to the shape of the seat of those jeans, then rub up to the bare skin of his back, across the muscled width of his shoulders, and down again. Her fingers would snag in the waistband of his jeans on the return trip, maybe delve inside a bit, enough to feel the smooth hard skin.

Just before she pushed him too hard with her teasing touch, the split second before he would have to turn and tumble her into the bed, she would pull her fingers away and send her hands once more on their downward path to where they had begun. Only this time they'd go farther, across his fanny and around to—

Bette gasped and jerked at the shrill bleat just over her head, but Paul didn't even turn around.

"Get the buzzer, will you? Michael said something about stopping by today."

She did, holding one steadying hand over her heart as she used the other to press the button that released the ground-floor door. She opened the apartment door. Quick footsteps echoed up the stairs, along with a grim mutter about people stupid enough to live on the fourth floor without an elevator, then a young woman's head topped the stair railing. As soon as she made the turn and spotted Bette, she started talking.

"Who are you?" She asked the question with open curiosity.

Bette didn't need to ask the return question. The crown of chestnut hair, the sparkle in gray-green eyes and the energetic grace of her casually clad body proclaimed the young woman to be Paul Monroe's sister.

When she grinned, abruptly and blindingly, the likeness was startling. "Never mind," she instructed, just as Bette opened her mouth for a neutral reply. "I know who you are. Mom told me all about you. *And* the pumpkins."

She managed to make the latter sound wicked and depraved, or maybe that was just Bette's conscience. Here she had been thinking lascivious thoughts about a man when his kid sister must have been less than a block away. It made her feel illogically guilty. Had her sister-in-law, Clara, ever had such thoughts about her brother, Ronald? Oh, she knew they had two kids and all, but did Clara really have *those* kinds of thoughts about Ronald?

A giggle tickled at her throat, and that made her feel guiltier. Get hold of yourself, Bette, she told herself firmly.

"Hello, I'm Bette Wharton, a friend of Paul's. You must be Judi."

Judi shook her extended hand with enthusiasm and studied her. They stood just about eye to eye. Judi Monroe had a lithe athlete's body encased in sweatpants and three layers of shirts, a free-fall tumble of hair and a mobile, restless face. She looked very, very young, and Bette experienced a renewed wash of guilt. What interpretation would this girl put on the situation, finding her here in her brother's apartment?

"Geez, count on Paul to bring you here for a rendezvous!"

Bette gasped as if she'd just been kicked in the stomach. "No—"

Judi went on, pitching her voice to reach the brother she obviously expected to be in the other room. "Paul, couldn't you have taken her someplace better than this! You should have a little more class." She shook her head in disgust as she swung a heavily loaded backpack off her shoulders and onto the desk, then called out again. "And some imagination!"

"No. You don't understand. He didn't— This isn't—"

Bette caught herself in time from adding the "what it seems" cliché, but still couldn't find much of an explanation. Perhaps because part of her cried out to defend Paul, to tell his sister just how classy and imaginative and romantic and downright passionate he could be. Only that was the very last thing she ought to be telling his younger sister.

"We stopped by to pick up some, uh, papers. That's all. We weren't—"

Judi glanced back from the desk with one eyebrow raised. "You weren't?"

The wild thought occurred to Bette that the younger woman sounded disappointed. Through some sense beyond the normal five, she became aware of Paul. Turning, she found him lounging in the doorway to his bedroom not far behind her, and she had to fight the urge to go to him and put her head on his shoulder and let him deal with this whole awkward situation.

"Damn! Why not? What the hell's the matter with you, Paul?"

"Judith Marie." Paul's voice held censure, but his next words rocked Bette even more than his sister's had. "Stop swearing. You know how Mom feels about that."

Bette looked from brother to sister in amazement.

"Sorry," his sister apologized absently. "Dorm talk. But how about this other stuff? Why aren't you—"

"Shut up, Judi." It was mild but effective. "It's none of your business. Quit embarrassing Bette."

Judi Monroe looked stricken for an instant, then contrite. She turned wide eyes on Bette. "Did I? Embarrass you? I didn't mean to. Sometimes my mouth just gets away from me. I'm sorry."

Bette met her look and started to formulate routine words of denial to smooth over the situation. Instead, she found herself telling the truth. "You did embarrass me a little. Maybe startled me is more accurate."

Judi nodded. "I do that to people sometimes. I forget what I'm saying, and what I'm thinking just comes out. I really am sorry."

Bette smiled at her. "I know. And it's fine. Don't worry about it."

Judi's returning smile seemed to light the room. "Thanks!"

Paul cleared his throat in a way that made Bette flick a look at him. Did those changeable eyes of his hold an added emotion? "So, Judi, what brings you here today?"

"I came to use your computer. I've got a Russian history paper due Monday, and it's lots faster on the computer than a typewriter. Especially the way I type."

Her eyes slid past her brother. Bette wondered if she could see the bed and would draw incorrect conclusions from its state. With Judi's next words, Bette knew she could and she had.

"But if I'm in the way here..." Judi let it hang.

Bette knew Paul was looking at her. All she had to do was make the smallest sign and he'd get rid of his sister. She knew that. An afternoon spent the way they'd spent the previous night had definite appeal, but someone who balked at checking into a hotel without luggage wasn't about to make such a clear declaration in front of Paul's younger sister.

"Of course not," Bette supplied. It wasn't exactly her place to issue the invitation, but it was clear Paul wasn't about to. "Your brother was going to show me some real estate in the area. We just stopped off here to get some clothes—" she ignored the choked sound of laughter from behind her "—that he has to take to the cleaners," she added with emphasis.

Paul sighed gustily enough that Bette thought she could feel his breath stir her hair. She glared at him, but he ignored it, telling his sister with some disgust, "All right, you can stay here and use the computer. I guess we're going to be leaving soon."

Judi's face lit with the smile that was so like Paul's. "Thanks. That's great. It's a killer paper, so this will really help." She widened her eyes in a soulful look. "In fact, I'll probably be here well into the night, so—"

"Don't you have a date tonight?" Paul interrupted sternly.

"Nope. This paper's really important, so I decided to work all weekend on it. I won't even go back to the dorm for dinner, so—"

"No. Absolutely not." Paul was adamant.

"No, what?" Bette asked, confused.

"This human vacuum cleaner in the guise of my sister intends to sit around my apartment eating all day, and then she was going to try to wheedle us into bringing back some dinner tonight," he explained, all the while frowning at Judi, who appeared not a bit abashed. Even if his comments to Michael and Grady hadn't forewarned her, she would have known that this fencing between brother and sister was some sort of sibling routine. She and Ronald had had enough of their own verbal tugs-of-war for her to spot the similarity. "How many meals did you get out of Michael while he was in the area this week?"

"Two. But I just thought tonight maybe a pizza or some Chinese, if you had a chance—"

"No!"

"That doesn't seem so unreasonable, Paul," objected Bette. "Remember how it was when you were in school and you had to eat the horrible stuff served in the cafeteria and there was never enough money to buy real food? It hasn't been so long ago that you've forgotten, has it?"

The sound she heard might have been him grinding his teeth, but Judi's look was radiant. Feeling like a successful conspirator, she flashed the young woman a grin before turning an innocent face to Paul. He wasn't fooled.

"All right, you two. All right! The two of you make it sound as if I'm a hundred-and-seventy-year-old miser," he said with mock grouchiness. Bette had to admire his performance, though his eyes gave him away. "I know I can't win when the two of you gang up on me. Women!"

He lounged back into the bedroom, grumbling about women and being eaten out of house and home.

"C'mon," Judi invited Bette. "Let's see what he's got to eat."

Bette wasn't hungry after the elaborate room service breakfast Paul had ordered, but she couldn't resist Judi's grin. Soon Judi was perched on the counter eating graham crackers and Bette was leaning against the refrigerator with a soft drink, listening to the younger woman's account of her recent dating travails.

Despite the somber note of the tale, Bette found herself wanting to smile. She'd missed this, the exchanging of confidences between women. She'd lost touch with so many of her friends because of the demands of school and then her business. Even with Darla, most of the conversation and confidences centered around business. It was refreshing to talk about something else. For a moment she even had the uncharacteristic urge to start exchanging opinions on clothes or hair.

"This is nice," Judi said with a satisfied sigh, almost as if her mind had been running along the same lines. "It's hard to talk to most of my friends because we all hang out in the same group and you never know when one of them is going to turn around and start dating some guy you've been talking about. I've always wished I had a sister."

"Me, too," Bette admitted with a smile. "Although I've got a pretty good brother."

"Oh, I do, too," said Judi, leaving no doubt she meant it. "He puts on a big front, but he's a marshmallow underneath. He and his friends— Have you met Michael and Grady? Yes? They were great to me growing up. It was like having three older brothers. But sometimes you just don't want to be 'one of the guys.' It might have been different if Tris had been around more, even though she's seven years older. But her family moved away when I was about seven, and when she came back for college the three guys were always around, too, so that meant no girl talk. Sometimes I thought I'd go nuts if I heard one more word about sports." She sighed gustily. "You're lucky you met Paul in October."

"Am I?"

"Yeah, the baseball season's over—at least for the Cubs—otherwise he'd have you out at Wrigley Field every day. You do know that about him, don't you? He's a baseball fanatic."

"He seems to come by it honestly, since your father loves the game so much."

Judi looked at her a little strangely. "Yeah, Dad likes baseball, too, but..." Bette saw the moment Judi decided to trust her. "But I think Walter Mulholland hating it might have more to do with Paul's feelings."

"Walter Mulholland? That's your grandfather?"

How strange, and how cold-sounding to refer to your grandfather that way. Paul had done the same thing that night at Mama Artemis's.

"Yeah. Mom's father. Hard to believe they were related. He didn't pay much attention to me, since I was just a kid—I was only ten when he died—and a girl on top of it. But he and Paul..." She grimaced. "I can remember them going round and round. Walter Mulholland storming and laying down the law, and Paul standing there, not saying much except an occasional no."

She shifted position as though the counter had grown harder. "I remember sitting on the steps, listening to Walter Mulholland shouting at Paul that he would do what he was supposed to or he would no longer be a member of the family. I must have been about six, and I thought he really could make it so Paul wasn't my brother. I was sitting there crying when Paul found me. He took me up and tucked me into bed, and he told me that nothing could make him not be my brother anymore—unless I broke another of his clipper ship models."

Judi's chuckle sounded as if it had slipped past a lump in her throat. "He said Walter Mulholland wanted to plot out his life, and he wasn't going to let that happen. He said he'd be damned if he'd go to Walter Mulholland's Ivy League alma mater. And if the old man wanted to disinherit him for that, fine."

"But your parents . . ." The sentence trailed off because Bette didn't know how to finish it. She ached for the young Paul, yet her relationship with her own grandfather had been so warm and loving, how could she understand this?

"They pretty much stayed out of it. They stood their ground sometimes—like refusing to send Paul to military school—but Dad especially never understood why Paul said no to all those things. Ivy League schools and law school, joining the firm, making lots of money and buying a big house. He still doesn't understand. He was awfully poor growing up, and I guess that's the life he'd dreamed of, so he thought for sure Paul would want it, too. Does that make sense?"

Bette wasn't sure.

"Hey, are you ready?" Paul's voice, a bit muffled, came from the living room.

When they came out of the kitchen, they saw the cause: a stack of clothing that loaded his arms down to below waist level and reached as high as his nose.

Bette met Judi's sparkling eyes and they both broke up, perhaps partly as a release from the serious turn of their conversation. If they'd started to form a bond during the talk in the kitchen, the shared laughter now strengthened it.

"All right, you two, quit giggling and somebody open the door. Before I drop this stuff." He raised his eyebrows over the top of the stack in a way that brought on renewed laughter from the two women. "You know, Judi, the sooner we leave, the sooner we can come back with some dinner."

Judi promptly opened the door with exaggerated solic-itude, declaring solemnly, "Never let it be said I was im-mune to bribery."

All the way down the stairs, they could hear the echo of her chuckles. When a small sound escaped Bette, Paul muttered, "Traitor" and glared over the top of the pile. But she wasn't fooled, and the clothing didn't muffle all of his laughter.

"Hey, I like this one," Paul said as he pulled up to the curb in front of a Dutch Colonial. The front lawn sported an open-house sign decorated with yellow balloons. "Looks like we saved the best for last."

"Mmm."

He grinned to himself at the small sound Bette made as they headed up the front walk.

Earlier, when she'd talked about having a house-searching schedule, he'd persuaded her to spend the afternoon looking in suburbs strung north along the lake. Thoughts of why it was important for her to consider living nearer him were pushed away, just as he'd done with last night's questions about what he'd gotten himself into. Instead, he focused on overcoming her arguments about this not being her target area. When he finally resorted to asking what harm it could do and she gave in, he'd wondered if he'd gone crazy to actually instigate spending his Saturday looking at houses. The surprise came when he enjoyed himself.

With no intentions of ever buying, he'd never considered what he would want in a house. But this afternoon he discovered opinions he'd had no idea he harbored. Also, he found pleasure in watching Bette at each house, analyzing and weighing. It wasn't his way. But on her it looked good.

As they wandered through the Dutch Colonial's rooms, he felt something expanding in his chest until, standing in the otherwise deserted basement watching Bette frown at the monster-shaped furnace, he pulled her into his arms.

"Paul!" Her small squawk of protest sounded breathless enough to be encouraging.

He lowered his mouth to hers and felt a sunburst of pleasure when she immediately parted her lips in welcome. Backing her up, a slow, kissing step at a time, he pressed her against the smooth surface of the washing machine. She was gripping him, letting him know she wanted more closeness, too. God, how could anything feel so good? Rubbing against her, he marveled how her softness hardened him.

"Paul!" This gasp held enough true urgency that he lifted his head from where he'd been following the open collar of her shirt. "Somebody's coming!"

At her words, the world beyond the two of them returned, and he heard footsteps on the basement stairs. Together they shifted their clothes into order before the people coming down the stairs reached the bottom. Another matter, however, required more time to adjust.

The newcomers nodded a greeting, casting them doubtful looks as they started their survey of the basement. Keeping his back to the room, Paul pretended great interest in the washer and dryer. Hoping it would help, he changed position as if to see behind the appliances.

"I don't know about this venting system," he told Bette, trying to sound knowledgeable.

"Maybe," she started, with a chuckle underlying her words, "it's the coupling that's causing the problem."

He tried to glare, but couldn't hold in the laughter. The other house hunters stayed strictly on the opposite side of the basement before leaving hurriedly.

"C'mon, you troublemaker, let's go upstairs before you get me in real trouble," Paul ordered.

They accomplished the rest of the tour in companionable silence, thanking the real estate agent as they headed out.

"The hardwood floors are great, aren't they?" he said as they reached the car.

"They need refinishing."

"It has a terrific yard."

"The taxes are high and they're scheduled to go up next year in this neighborhood."

"Look at all the big old trees."

"The furnace is awfully old."

"And that screened porch is wonderful. You could put up a hammock in the corner and—"

"I think the roof would need replacing in a couple years."

"You could practically live out there all summer."

"The kitchen is crying out for updating, and the second bathroom shows sign of moisture damage."

"So you didn't like it?" He felt oddly deflated by her reaction. What was the matter with him? It wasn't as if he had a stake in this. It wasn't as if it affected him what kind of house she bought. He turned the engine on and pulled away.

"Of course I liked it. It's a charming, warm home. But it's much bigger than I'd need living alone. And looking ahead, there would be a lot of expenses keeping that kind of place up, Paul. Besides, I can't afford a house like that. I couldn't even afford a garage in these neighborhoods. Nobody can."

"Well, somebody's buying in these neighborhoods, because the houses are getting sold."

"Yes, but to two-income families. I'm buying on my own. And with one income, I need to look farther out, and in very specific neighborhoods."

Why did she keep emphasizing that she was buying the house on her own, going to be living in it alone? Wasn't he supposed to show any interest? Was she trying to remind him it was none of his business?

He accelerated from a stop sign with more force than necessary. He just wasn't wild about her moving farther out. It was a long enough trip as it was from his place to hers. Not that he had any expectation one way or the other about still seeing each other by the time she found a place and moved. But she'd certainly be farther from her work, and chances were she'd be farther from whomever she might be dating by then.

He ignored the gnaw of acid in his stomach that came with that thought. Hungry, that was all. He was hungry.

"So what do you want to get my ravenous sister for dinner?"

"What?" Bette blinked at him as if her mind had been very far away. "Oh, dinner. I don't know. What does Judi like?"

"Everything," he said with feeling.

She laughed, and he felt his mood lightening.

"Surely she demonstrated that while the two of you were in the kitchen."

"Well . . . she did nibble on a thing or two."

He snorted in disbelief. "Nibble? She eats with as much abandon as she talks—which reminds me, what were you two talking about so earnestly in the kitchen?"

"Oh, girl stuff."

"Like?" he pursued.

"Dating. Clothes. Uh, men. Baseball. Families."

"An interesting collection."

Suddenly serious, she turned to face him. "She told me about your arguing with your grandfather about where you were going to school."

He slanted a look at her, surprised at her intensity.

"Does that bother you?"

"It seems so sad. I loved my grandfather. He was a wonderful man. He had such dreams for me, for the whole family. He was always telling me how we would do wonderful things in this country, building our lives, our successes. I learned so much from him. He could see the family's success unfolding, step by step."

If the steering wheel hadn't required both his hands right then, he might have taken her by the shoulders and shaken her. Yeah, she'd learned a lot from her grandfather, all right. She'd learned to sacrifice happiness today in hopes of success tomorrow.

"I guess you could say the same thing for Walter Mulholland," he ground out. "Only I didn't fall for the indoctrination."

"Indoctrination? It wasn't like that with my—"

"As far as rebellions go," he cut off her protest, "it wasn't much, but the episode Judi told you about was my formal declaration of independence."

She seemed to forget her earlier objection in concern for him. That shouldn't have warmed him so.

"What happened, Paul?" she asked.

"Not much, really. He had it all mapped out. Where I'd go to school. What I'd study. Where I'd get my law degree. How I'd fit into the firm. When and where I'd buy a house in the right neighborhood and memberships to the proper clubs. Who I'd marry—at least that she'd be 'our kind.' Hell, he probably had a schedule for our sex lives so he'd have a great-grandchild produced on order."

Without looking at her, he could feel her eyes on him. Strange, he felt understanding in them, too.

"I refused to go along. My senior year in high school, I turned down admission to his Ivy League choice and signed up to enroll at Northwestern instead. Not exactly a felony. But you would have thought so to hear Walter Mulholland. The old fool actually threatened to disinherit me, as if I gave a damn about his money." His laugh died abruptly. "I found Judi huddled on the stairs, crying her eyes out. She was just a baby, all skinny arms and skinned knees, and she thought he was kicking me out of the family or something."

It sounded foolish spoken out loud after all these years. But the feelings were still raw and powerful. The anger. The determination. The triumph. Walking out as the old man ranted futilely. Then finding Judi, and knowing he was fighting for more than himself. He had to break free, so he could prevent her from being caught in Walter Mulholland's straitjacket.

A staccato horn reminded him he'd been sitting at a stop sign too long for the patience of the driver behind them.

He drove. And waited, wary of what Bette would say next. He didn't want questions. He wouldn't be able to take sympathy. He couldn't abide platitudes.

The touch on his arm was light, fleeting. Perfect. He glanced at her and saw the smile she tried to produce. He felt a closeness to her that went beyond the physical.

"You know, she still has skinny arms," Bette said.

"What?"

"Judi. She still has skinny arms. We should be thinking about what to feed her tonight."

He slid the car into a parking spot amid Evanston shops and restaurants. Turning off the ignition, he twisted to face her, his knee touching hers. He wanted to kiss her. To take her face between his palms and let his tongue sink into the warmth and sweetness of her mouth. But he knew that would be only the start of what he wanted—and couldn't have, here on this downtown street.

He contented himself with brushing the side of his thumb along the slant of her cheekbone, the tilt of her upper lip, the rounded point of her chin.

"Okay, what shall we feed my ravenous sister?"

They decided on pizza, after a survey of the neighborhood where he'd parked. Just before they got out of the car in front of his apartment, he pulled her close for a quick, hungry kiss.

"One thing, let's agree now that we'll go back to your place tonight," he told her. "That way we don't have to worry about getting Judi out of the way."

She gave him a quizzical look, as if he'd said something surprising, and he wondered if he'd presumed too much.

He sure as hell knew he wanted to be with her, but maybe she didn't feel the same. Maybe she wanted time away from him. Maybe...

"Okay."

The word had never sounded so good. It carried him through a dinner surrounded by laughter, easy conversation and the certainty that Judi and Bette had hit it off. He felt oddly touched by that. Especially when Judi admitted to feeling she'd never gotten over the tomboy stage. He'd known his sister wasn't sure yet of her attractiveness as a woman, but he'd never heard her refer as openly to it as she did to Bette. She clearly felt her vulnerability would be safe with this woman.

Bette tentatively suggested she and Judi could go shopping together sometime.

Judi pounced on the offer. "Really? When?"

"Uh, I don't know. Any time, I guess."

"Really? Like maybe this week? Maybe Thursday? I have early classes, so I could take the El downtown and look around first, then get your opinion. Do you think?"

"Uh, yeah, I guess so."

"Are you sure? That wouldn't be an imposition?"

Bette hesitated and Paul wondered if she would plead the demands of her schedule. She might have wondered, too, because her smile held some surprise. "I'm sure. It would not be an imposition."

"Great! There's this holiday formal coming up, and I want the absolutely perfect dress. I just know you've got great taste and you won't try to make me buy something that makes me look fourteen, like Mom always does." Judi smiled glowingly at both Bette and Paul. "You might be good for something after all, Paul," she added.

He grinned, but grumbled, "Yeah? I was good enough to teach you how to sail, and to play basketball and tennis."

"Yes, but there are other things in the world, you know. I've always wanted a sister, and maybe you're finally going to get around to providing me with one."

Paul felt as if a prison door were being slammed in his face. The only way he could give Judi a sister was by marriage. Even the word conjured up prison bar images. And the man closing the door on him was his mother's father.

The "right" marriage was another link Walter Mulholland had planned to chain his grandson to the "right" life. He would have approved of Bette Wharton as a hostess, as a helpmate, as a mother to his great-grandchildren. The old man would have seen Bette's business sense, her ambition, her dedication and her dignity as business assets.

Paul didn't give a damn about that. But the idea that he might be moving in a direction Walter Mulholland would have ordered, even for different reasons, left an uneasy feeling.

The odd thing was that neither the uneasiness nor the reflexive 180-degree change of subject could dilute the warm feeling that had settled somewhere deep in his chest. Very odd.

He'd looked as if he'd just been informed he owed ten years' back taxes and the IRS was at the door. Or, worse yet, that baseball historians had discovered a grave error and they were taking away the Cubs' last World Series championship, even if it was back in 1908.

She'd read too much into the smallest things, things like his planning ahead how they would spend the night together at her place. Then his sister had mentioned the m-word and she'd seen that look on his face.

Horrified. Numbed. Panicked.

Over the next two weeks, as Paul Monroe wove himself deeper and deeper into her life, Bette reminded herself of that look.

It was as much a part of him as the way he loved to tease her, as the way he liked her home, as the way he appreciated her warmth to his sister, as the way he held her and made her crazy. She had to remember that.

When he took her to dinner most nights, when he drove her home every night and sometimes to work the next morning, she reminded herself of that look.

When his voice turned mellow as he confided in her, when his hands turned sultry even as he made her laugh, when his eyes turned soft as he smiled at her, she reminded herself of that look.

But it kept getting harder.

Chapter Ten

Bette stood in front of a filing cabinet Wednesday evening, returning a folder—the Centurian file. In their cautious way, they'd asked for a proposal on the services her firm could offer, and she'd sent it off that morning.

But when her office door swung open, the Centurian account was forgotten. Almost before the door clicked shut, Paul had his arms around her from behind and his mouth on her neck.

"Mmm. Lord, you taste good." He nipped at her skin. "You should have quit work hours ago."

"There's a lot to do—"

"You've always got a lot to do. Too much. But this time I forgive you, because it means you're still here. I've missed you."

"I saw you last night," she pointed out, trying valiantly to maintain a reasonable tone when her hormones were doing the samba.

"Mmm-hmm. But not this morning. Or yesterday morning."

He had a point. After they spent all their time together from Friday evening until Monday morning, he'd started the week with an appraisal of the stock of a north suburban collectibles shop being liquidated. She'd been the one to point out it made more sense for him to commute there from his Evanston apartment than from her house. She'd felt a momentary stab when a look flashed across his eyes that might have been relief. Maybe he'd been trying to figure out how to ease away already. But he'd made sure to see her each day. Besides, she'd thought with something between a mental grimace and a grin, he probably wouldn't have thought far enough ahead to see they were setting a pattern.

It had been left to her to be the practical one, and practical she'd been.

But practicality had its price. After three days of waking up in his arms, the last two mornings had felt surprisingly empty.

"We had dinner together both nights." Was she reminding him or herself?

"Not the same thing. Not the same thing at all." His mouth traveled lower on her neck. The openmouthed kisses carried the veiled hint of his teeth, reminding her of the power behind his tenderness. "Some things you just can't do at a restaurant."

His hands slid up her ribs, opening to capture the weight of her breasts, then curving to press warm palms against quickly tightening nipples. His movement had drawn her tighter against his chest. She felt the melting warmth inside her, the warmth that needed the heat of his body. She arched more firmly into his hands and dropped her head back to his shoulder.

Shifting, he brought her even closer as he circled and molded and teased her breasts.

He knew how to pleasure her. In such a short time, he knew her body, her responses, so well. She wanted nothing more than to sink to the floor right here, right now, and to have him display that knowledge in the most intimate way imaginable.

What would she do when he left her? She squeezed her eyes shut against the fear.

This moment. Take this moment, but build no expectations that there will be others. She'd made her choice, to take her moments with Paul and deal with life without him when that came. But she hadn't known the moments would be so wonderful or the prospect of living without them so terrifying.

"Paul..." She planned to lift her hand, to gain that much control over herself, but the muscles wouldn't obey and she felt hot stinging tears at the corners of her eyes. After a lifetime of using the present to build toward a clearly foreseen future, she didn't even know how her muscles would react in the next second.

And yet it felt so right to be in his arms.

By her ear, his breath rasped harsh and irregular. It was a sound of pleasurable torment, and it flashed across her mind to wonder if she was not alone in this drowning pool of jumbled emotions.

She covered his hands with hers, and slowly lowered them to her waist. He didn't fight it, but circled her tightly, squeezing the breath and some of the tension out of her.

"Paul."

Her murmur was distracted, at best, as he bent and touched his tongue to the point of her collarbone just inside her blouse's neckline. Her moan was involuntary. If he kept that up, in another second they'd be right back where they'd been....

Abruptly, he raised his head without letting her go. "Bette, how about spending Thanksgiving at my folks' house?"

She was surprised. Maybe stunned. She twisted around to get a better view of his face.

"Are you serious? Thanksgiving's more than two weeks away."

"So?"

So? So, the man she'd come to know quite well over the past month would rather not plan an hour ahead, much less two weeks. A tremor vibrated at the base of her stomach.

"Your mother might not appreciate your inviting people to a holiday dinner like that without letting her know," she said.

"She knows."

"She does?" Bette feared her voice squeaked unbecomingly. The tremor in her stomach intensified and spread.

"Sure. So will you come?"

"I'm sorry, Paul," she said. "I usually spend Thanksgiving with Darla's family, and I've already accepted her invitation this year."

She wouldn't be able to avoid wondering what it might have been like to be with him. She had no lingering concerns about being with his family, so what caused this odd sensation? If this had been any other man than Paul Monroe, she might have thought it was nerves over an invitation some could view as significant, perhaps even a statement of serious intentions.

But this was Paul, and she knew better.

"That's all right, Bette. You go right ahead and go to the Monroes for Thanksgiving."

The disembodied voice of Darla Clarence floated into the office. Bette spun around in Paul's arms and they stared at each other. His look of astonishment quickly gave way to amusement.

"Darla?" Bette called out.

"Go on, girl, you say yes to that invitation right this second."

"Darla, where are you? How did you hear that?"

"I'm in my office, and I can always hear what you're doing in there."

Bette's mouth worked, but her vocal cords didn't, so she only mouthed the words: "Oh, my God."

"And I say you should go right ahead and take the boy up on his invitation," Darla continued. "You've spent the past three Thanksgivings with us, you probably want something different for a change. Maybe their turkey won't dry out like mine. I've been hoping he'd get around to asking."

Bette studiously ignored the quirked eyebrow Paul directed at her. "But, Darla—"

She wasn't sure what she was going to say, but it didn't matter, because Darla wasn't listening. "But, nothing. Just say, 'Thank you very much, Paul, I'd love to come to your parents' house for Thanksgiving.'"

Paul looked a hairbreadth short of laughing as he prompted her, "You heard the lady."

Bette knew when she was licked. Even with the unsettled sensation back in full force, she found it impossible not to smile as she followed orders. "Thank you very much, Paul, I'd love to come to your parents' house for Thanksgiving."

"You're welcome, Bette." He pitched his voice slightly louder. "And thank you, Darla."

"You're welcome," came back the reply.

Paul grinned at Bette, then kissed her hard. Her heart swelled, but so did the trembling in her stomach. And now she knew what she feared: hope.

That Saturday she went shopping with Judi for the second time. Paul groused, "You spent the morning working and the afternoon with my kid sister." The first was a familiar complaint, but she suspected her growing friendship with his sister pleased him.

She and Judi found a wonderful dress for the upcoming college formal, and after Judi returned to campus, Bette and Paul occupied the evening by making up for the time apart.

She finally got around to wearing the royal-blue negligee. He took it off her without ripping it. Barely.

The next day, he surprised her by insisting she accompany him to dinner at Mama Artemis's home. Surely he had to realize how people like Ardith and her family would construe his bringing her along....

If he hadn't before, he must now, she thought as she headed into the huge, old-fashioned kitchen to volunteer to help. The greeting had been warm, interested and arch. In the few minutes from their entrance until Ardith's nephews snared Paul to look at something in the basement, Ardith, her mother, her sister-in-law and even her teenage niece had made it clear they considered Bette and Paul an "item." Their bluntness had made her feel a little uncomfortable. Since she'd been too chicken to look at him, she could only imagine how it had made Paul feel— probably like running.

Mama Artemis—a grayer, rounder, no less forceful version of Ardith—and the others shooed her out of the kitchen, where bustling seemed to be the only mode of movement. She was a guest, she was told, she was not to work. It was just as well. Not only wouldn't she have known what to do; she didn't think she could have kept up.

She tracked down Paul and Ardith's two young nephews in the basement. They were making enough noise that they didn't hear her coming down the wooden stairs. When she got far enough to see them, she sat on the steps and watched.

Taking up nearly half the neat basement, they had a huge, complicated track circling the edges of the biggest piece of plywood she'd ever seen, raised to waist-level by several sawhorses. In addition to the main route, there were smaller loops and shunts. Around the tangle of tracks grew a tidy, thriving community. The downtown sported a railroad station, of course, along with houses, shops, churches and schools. On the outskirts she spotted a few farms.

Amid this imaginary world, Paul Monroe played with as much verve as the two young boys.

Her lips lifted into a smile, but she denied the simultaneous urge to cry. He truly was a kid at heart.

She was very quiet the rest of the night.

Bette had found a house she wanted to buy, and Paul hated it.

He hated the house.

It wasn't a bad-looking building, but it was all wrong for her. It didn't have character, or charm. And, most of all, it was several towns west of Elmhurst. Another twenty minutes of driving wasn't going to stop him from making the trip, but this distance couldn't be counted in miles.

He hated the process.

Bette worked too damn much as it was, and now she spent all her spare time talking to loan officers and house inspectors. Since he'd made his feelings clear about this house right away, she didn't talk of her progress to him. He should have felt grateful; instead he felt left out.

He hated the idea.

And that was what really bothered him because he wasn't sure why he hated it.

Now he was driving her to the real estate office to make a bid on the house. It was the last thing he wanted to do, but the alternative was letting her go alone. At least this way, she was in the car next to him, a foot or so away.

He wished he could delay the moment she'd walk into that real estate office and make the move farther away from him. If there were some way...

"I think we should go see Jan and Ed."

"Jan and Ed?"

"Robson. And the baby. I haven't seen the kid since the christening. It'd be fun. We'll go pick up some Chinese and take them lunch. It's a perfect day for Chinese."

"Today? *Now?* I want to be at the real estate office at noon to make the bid."

They had pulled up at a stoplight. He turned to her, reached out to outline that tempting upper lip with his fingertips. "You could call them. From the way you explained it, it's not a firm appointment. Is it?"

"Well, no, not really."

He heard the uncertainty in her voice, and pressed his advantage. "Besides, when I talked to Jan earlier this week, she sounded pretty down. You know, new mother sort of stuff. Feeling like she didn't have any contact with the adult world anymore."

"I guess that can happen when you have a newborn baby."

"She practically begged me to come see her soon," he added.

"I don't know...."

"We'll just stop in and say hello."

It didn't take much more for him to persuade her to call the real estate office and tell them she would be in later in the afternoon, although she did give him a pointed look when they arrived nearly an hour later at Jan's with Chinese food in hand to discover the new parents in obviously fine spirits.

"This is great!" Jan said for about the eighth time since they'd settled around the dining room table. The sideboard sported a baby carrier flanked by an oversize box of disposable diapers and a stack of neatly folded terry sleepers. The food had long since been disposed of, and the conversation had proceeded in comfortable fits and starts, with Edward Robson, Jr. the recurring theme.

"We really should be going now," Bette said for the second time, but with enough regret in her voice that Paul didn't feel guilty for ignoring it.

"You can't leave yet," Jan said. "You have to wait and see Eddy. He should wake up any moment."

She proved a prophet. Practically on the heels of her words came the dissatisfied sounds of a baby waking.

"I'll get him," volunteered Ed before anyone else could react.

Jan's eyes followed the direction her burly husband had gone, then she grinned at Paul and Bette. "He does dote, doesn't he?"

As background to Jan's tales of her husband as a father, the baby's noise intensified, then changed to neutral commentary and finally to small sounds of pleasure.

"Here he is," she announced as Ed appeared at the doorway with the baby, dressed in a minute version of a Chicago Cubs uniform. The baby puckered his brow and smiled at the same time.

"I figured I'd put him in the Cubs uniform in honor of your visit, Paul," Ed explained.

"You gave a newborn baby a baseball uniform?" Bette pretended disgust, but he caught the amusement underneath.

"Sure. Got to start him out right."

Jan nodded as she took the baby. "The Cubs outfit is from Paul and the Bears is from Ed. It's amazing how early the brainwashing starts, and it's so unfair. There's no cute little outfit for brain surgeon or engineer."

Counterpointing their laughter, Ed, Jr. expressed a request.

"Oops, I think it's lunchtime," said Jan. "We're about to find out how Eddy feels about Chinese."

Somehow, as Jan and Bette moved into the living room to be more comfortable, it turned out that this was the best time for Ed to show Paul the deck he'd added to the house. Paul was relieved. As the two groups parted, he saw Ed cup a tender hand around his son's head, then stroke his wife's cheek, and envy pierced him. Would he ever know that fierce peace he saw in Ed? Would he and Bette ever exchange a look so full of love and understanding? Would he ever watch Bette nurture their child?

It wasn't until they'd exhausted the details of deck construction and returned to the living room to find Jan coaxing bubbles from the baby that one level of his mind bothered to wonder why he'd focused his questions on Bette.

He didn't know the answer; he didn't like the question.

Avoiding the couch where he could have sat next to
Bette, he chose an easy chair across from her. Too much
family, that was his problem. Too much happy family and
cute baby. A guy could take only so much.

"Here, hold him a minute."

Jan plunked Ed, Jr. into Paul's arms as she walked past
where he sat.

"Hey! I don't know how to—"

"Of course you know how to hold a baby. You must be
a natural," said Jan with a sly smile as she kept going out
of the room, "because you're doing it exactly right."

He glared in the direction she'd headed, but the muscles of his face rearranged as he looked down at the small
person dressed in Cubs colors in his arms. A bottom well
padded with diapers drooped between where his left arm
propped the baby's shoulders and head and his right arm
rested under the knees. In his hands, Ed, Jr. wriggled and
smiled and felt incredibly alive.

Paul met Bette's deep blue eyes, and felt something slam
into him. Not the gentle warmth that so often seeped into
him when they were together, and not the fierce flow of
passion she could stir so easily. Something more visceral.
Something as deep as the warmth and as powerful as the
passion. And a hell of a lot more disorienting.

A scene from some movie he'd seen flashed into his
mind, the vision of an earthquake caught at its peak right
along the fault line, where the ground heaved, trembled,
then resettled itself into a new, unfamiliar landscape.

And from the look in Bette's eyes, he thought she'd felt
it, too. Somehow that was both less—and more—fright-
ening.

Blinking, he looked at his hands and was surprised to see
Eddy, still grinning owlishly up at him. Apparently earthquakes didn't rattle the younger set. Jan came back into

the room, and Bette moved restlessly on the couch as if in preparation for leaving; he took all that in, but it seemed distant, not quite real.

Not knowing why, he grinned at the baby in his arms.

"Paul, we really have to leave. Now. Before it's too late."

He caught Jan giving Bette an indecipherable look. At least it was indecipherable to him, but maybe Bette got some meaning out of it, because she flushed, a warm, bright color that made him both more irritable and more eager to have her entirely to himself. And—remembering what came next—without some damn real estate appointment hanging over their heads.

"Oh, I was hoping you could stay for dinner," said Jan. "Nothing fancy, but it would be fun."

"You heard the lady," said Paul. He couldn't prevent harshness from entering his voice, even if it wasn't entirely fair. He couldn't have explained it, but he didn't give a damn about fairness right now. "She has a schedule to keep."

Bette glared at him, but said the right, pleasant words of leave-taking to Jan and Ed, with promises to call. He knew she'd keep those promises. To him, she said absolutely nothing.

In fact, he realized forty minutes later as they neared the real estate office, she still hadn't said anything to him. He hadn't noticed because he'd been sunk in a dark mood he would have labeled brooding in someone else.

"Turn right at the corner." Her first words since they'd left the Robsons.

He did, and saw the sign for the real estate company. He pulled in to the parking lot and turned off the engine, but made no move to pull the keys from the ignition.

"I'll wait here."

"It may take a while." Her voice was distant and cool, devoid of underlying spice. He wanted to shake her.

"Fine."

"Fine."

She seemed totally unaffected by his mood, getting out of the car and walking into the office with her usual calm. For some reason, that irked him more, and he couldn't for the life of him figure out why.

He turned on the car radio, picking up a college football game, then failing to make sense of a single word.

Why did it bug him so much that she was in there buying a house? He didn't want one himself, but he'd thought it was great when Michael bought the place in Springfield. Despite the long hours and traveling required by his job, Michael was the kind of guy who needed a home.

A thought pricked at him. Did it bother him that Bette was the kind of woman who needed a home? Because he wouldn't give her one?

He didn't even have to bother pushing aside the idea, because the real estate office door flew open, and a woman stalked out. Jerky, angry strides brought her to the car almost before he comprehended that this walking emotional storm was Bette.

If her earlier calm had irritated him, her agitation amazed him. She got in the car, pulling the door closed with enough force to shudder the frame.

"Don't you ever say anything about my schedules again." She practically hissed the words, but didn't look at him. "Four hours and forty-five minutes late. I was four hours and forty-five minutes late. I have never been that late in my life."

"Bette..." He reached for her, but she hitched her shoulder away and he lowered his hand.

She took a deep, slow breath that for a terrifying moment he thought might turn into a sob. The thought of Bette crying turned something sharp and painful inside him.

"They sold the house to someone else."

The words didn't connect in his mind immediately. "Your house?"

"Yeah, *my* house." The bitter sarcasm was worse than her earlier calm. "A couple looked at the house this morning, and put in an offer at two-thirty—two and a half hours after I had planned to be here making my offer. No inspection, no research, they just sailed in and made an offer. Thirty minutes later, the seller accepted. It's all done. The house is off the market."

Reaction jumbled on top of reaction. He wanted to celebrate. She wouldn't be moving farther away, at least not yet. He wanted to console her. Disappointment slumped her shoulders, and he knew he was largely at fault. But he couldn't regret it.

"I'm sorry I got you here late." He knew he should stop with the apology, but he couldn't stem the next, belligerent words. "But it wasn't the right house for you."

"Oh, really? When did you become an expert on real estate?"

"It doesn't take an expert to see anything so obvious. It's not the right house for you," he repeated stubbornly.

"Why not?" she challenged, her voice this time shorn of the sarcasm.

What could he tell her, when he wasn't sure himself? "It was too far away."

"From what?"

"From your work, from downtown, from—" *From me.* The words were nearly through his lips before he stopped them. He could have said them; she would have taken them as he meant them. Only how *did* he mean them? Was he talking about geographic distance? So what if it would be a fifty-five-minute drive instead of thirty-five? Twenty more minutes wasn't going to keep him away.

But in some indefinable, unalterable way he felt that buying this house, maybe any house, would take her away from him.

It was stupid. He wasn't making any sense. If she'd already owned a house when they met he wouldn't be feeling this way, so what was the big deal?

He shook his head, and watched her frown deepen.

"From everything," he finished flatly.

They looked at each other. He thought perhaps they both regretted the isolation that surrounded each of them. He wished he could reach out, hold her in his arms. But a crowded parking lot didn't offer the privacy for delivering an apology. He had to satisfy himself with touching her hair, pushing the silky black cloud back behind her shoulder and cupping her cheek with his palm.

"I'm sorry, Bette. I'm sorry you're disappointed. I'm sorry I disappointed you."

Tears pooled immediately in her eyes, her lips parted, but no words came. She gave a futile gesture with her hands. He had never had an apology so eloquently accepted.

"You'll find another house. A better one," he promised. "I'll help you." No matter how he felt, if that was what she wanted, he'd do his damnedest to help her.

"Thank you," she mumbled in a tear-clogged voice.

He dredged up a smile and switched on the ignition.

Bette stared at her gloved hands as they twisted in her lap, but the tears threatened to fall, so she faced the side window. She'd seen the confusion in Paul's eyes, and she couldn't blame him. She'd lashed out at him, and it was herself she should have been berating.

She owed him an apology at least equal to the one he'd given her. But how could she apologize without betraying herself?

She'd been trapped by her own good sense and organization. She'd set up the criteria, the checklists, the measurements, and then, when she'd found the house that fit them all, she didn't want it. It didn't feel right.

But she'd ignored that. She'd planned so carefully that following each step *had* to take her to the right place. That was the lesson she'd learned from her grandfather, it was the tenet she'd followed through life.

She'd arranged to put the bid on the house. But when she realized Paul's schedule-be-damned attitude had cost her the house, the spurt of relief had been so strong it had terrified her. So she'd put all her confusion and anxiety on Paul's shoulders.

Now she had another problem.

She didn't want to find another house—at least not one to live in alone.

Watching Jan and Ed, she'd finally admitted to herself how tempted she was to look to a future with Paul. She wanted what the Robsons had—a marriage, a child, a home—and she was having a harder and harder time not thinking of those things in connection with Paul.

Jan, she feared, had seen her longing. If she wasn't careful, she'd give herself away to Paul. She didn't know how much longer she could fight off the wanting before the sorrow of knowing it wouldn't happen would poison the present he *could* give her.

Paul eased his chair back from the table still laden with Thanksgiving dinner, even after seven people had spent the better part of two hours depleting its bounty, and let the conversation flow over him.

He'd started it off with a comment to Grady about the blonde he and Bette had seen him escorting the previous Friday night. Now he was content to listen to Grady try to explain his relationship with Randi, which with Grady consisted of the chase, one big weekend and a goodbye ranging from pleasant to sticky, depending on the woman.

Since Judi and Michael also knew Grady's habits, the questions aimed at him were pointed enough to have him shifting in his seat and darting occasional looks at Nancy and James Monroe. Paul could practically read his mind; it was one thing for his friends to tease him about being a lady-killer, it was another to have the couple who'd been more like parents to him than his own get that impression.

It was an old game among them, and Paul usually served as ringleader, but today... today he felt too peaceful and too restless, to comfortable and too discontent.

He looked around the table, his mother at one end, Judi and Grady side by side, his father at the other end, then Michael, Bette and himself. His gaze lingered on Bette.

Elbows on the edge of the table, she rested her chin on her laced fingers, her eyes glinting blue humor as she listened to the interplay among the others. The urge to touch her pulled at him. If her hands had been free, he'd have taken one of them. Instead, he placed his palm, fingers spread wide, against the soft jade wool of her dress at the small of her back, remembering the sensation he'd experienced from the same gesture when he'd introduced her to his parents. He felt that now, and so much more.

She lifted her chin from her hands and turned to him, a half smile, half question in her eyes. He shook his head slightly, telling her he hadn't been trying to draw her attention; he'd just needed to touch her.

But now, meeting her eyes, the need was for more than physical contact. It hit him often these days. The urge to give in to it was nearly as strong as the urge to yank back against it. Sometimes when he wanted to give in the most, he yanked back the hardest.

"Want to go for a walk?" he asked in a voice low enough that only Bette would hear.

"All right."

He gave a brief excuse to the others as he and Bette rose. He thought the look his parents exchanged down the length of the table held a significance he wasn't sure of, but all his mother said was to wear warm coats and not go far, since she'd be serving dessert a little later.

They walked in silence, covering blocks of his parents' neighborhood, scuffing the final, sodden leaves out of their way and holding hands. They got by, just barely, without gloves by holding hands tightly, feeding off the warmth of where they joined.

"How'd you like to see my secret hideaway?"

She looked at him, with the gleam in her eyes he liked to tell himself he'd put there. "What self-respecting person could say no to a question like that?"

"Is that a yes?"

"Yes, that's a yes."

He started off at a jog, pulling her along. By the time they reached the driveway clogged with the cars belonging to him, Michael and Grady, they were both breathless with exertion and stifled laughter.

"Aren't we going in?" she protested around gasps.

He continued leading her along the driveway, around the house. "Nope. My hideaway's not in the house."

At the garage, he drew her up an exterior stairway to a second story, then slipped a key into the heavy wooden door at the top, all without letting go of her hand.

"This is it," he announced. He shut the door against the chilling wind, and glanced at the sheet-draped forms of furniture. "When Walter Mulholland owned the house, it was servants' quarters. When I was a teenager, Mom and Dad let me make it my room most of the time. Now they close it up for the winter, drain the pipes and stuff. But back then, I'd stay here for all but the coldest nights of the year. It used to make me feel like I was independent, on my own."

She glanced at him, but in the deepening gloom he couldn't read the expression in her eyes. She wandered into the room, looking toward the kitchenette behind the counter that doubled as a table, taking in the wide bed, trailing fingers across the back of a love seat his mother had added when he took the old couch for his apartment. At the picture window, framing winter twilight, she turned. Her movement swirled the skirt of her dress, the same jade-green dress she'd worn to his office that first time when he'd fantasized about making love to her there, right on the black leather couch. He knew the reality now, and the fantasy seemed pale.

Against the light behind her, she was a shadowed outline. But, he realized with a sensation that was more pain than anything else he could identify, she was the most vital thing in his life.

"It must have been great for a teenager. Only in high school, and already the possessor of a wild bachelor pad."

He knew she was teasing, but for once he didn't want humor. He wanted her. Here and now, yes, but in other ways, too.

He crossed the room in quick, impatient strides and his mouth came down on hers with an urgency he still wasn't quite used to, even after the weeks of experiencing it every time he touched her. Her arms came around his neck and her lips parted, and that opening of herself sent emotion swimming into his blood. The kiss deepened, ripened, eased, then gave way to another, and another.

Breathing hard, he pulled back only enough to murmur against her lips, "No. No wild bachelor pad. All the time I was in high school, I think the only other person who slept here was Grady."

But he wanted *her* to. He wanted her beneath him in his bed—here, in his apartment, or wherever that bed was. Now. And tomorrow. And the day after.

His need for her. He could feel it reeling him in, drawing him closer. He dropped his hands from her hair, took a half step back.

He said the first words that came to mind. "Poor Grady."

"Poor Grady? Why? Because you all tease him unmercifully?" She seemed to speak automatically. Crossing her arms, she rubbed at her upper arms, as though the distance he'd put between them made her feel the cold.

He grinned, sure it didn't hold enough true humor to fool anyone, least of all Bette. "Hell, no, he brings that on himself. I say poor Grady because he's always running into these women who want to tie him down, when he just wants to have a good time."

Bette's hands stilled. "You think every woman has marriage in mind the minute she sees a man?"

"Some women. A certain type. They can't help it. They think in terms of husband material. They immediately assess and project." The same kind who always looked ahead. The kind who saw the present strictly as a training ground for the future. The kind who lived by five-year plans and appointment calendars. The kind who could get under your skin and inside your life until you wondered what you'd do if they ever left. The kind you chased even though you knew you shouldn't. The kind you pushed away with unfair cracks, then prayed they'd stay.

He moved his head just enough to watch her. She stared ahead a moment, then turned. "So, you think I'm that type?"

"How could I be talking about you when I was the cha—"

"You know one thing about types is they can change," she went on, not heeding his answer. "They can meet someone totally unsuitable as a husband and still—" her eyes flitted from his, returning only when she'd found a word, a *safe* word, he thought, and wondered what he meant by that "—enjoy him, learn from him. They can start learning to live for the moment, have fun while there's fun to be had and let the assessments project themselves right into oblivion."

She was saying that was what had happened to her. He wasn't sure he believed it. He wasn't sure he *wanted* to believe it. What did she mean, 'totally unsuitable as a husband'? And why the hell did that make him feel as if he wanted to ram a fist into the wall?

"And one other thing." She tapped a finger to his chest, with a strange half-sad smile on her lips. "You chased me, remember?"

"Yeah, I remember." He remembered too much, felt the need for her too strongly. "But you know what they say: the man chases the woman until she turns around and catches him."

He saw the hurt in her eyes immediately, and regretted it instantly and deeply. Some part of him also welcomed it, though, because he knew it would make her retreat from him. Some part of him grieved for it, because it would make her retreat from him.

She turned away, but from the movement of her shoulders he knew she drew in two deep breaths. When she whirled back, the attack was a relief. Better to face that than her hurt.

"And heaven knows you wouldn't want to be caught, would you, Paul? You wouldn't want to marry and have a family, because that would be too much like being a grown-up wouldn't it? And that would never do for Paul Monroe, the kid at heart."

He slashed across the last bit of sarcasm. "So you're saying I should follow in my parents' footsteps, become another—"

"I'm not saying—"

"—family clone. Just like you are, docilely fulfilling someone else's dreams—"

"I am *not*—"

"I won't live my life by somebody else's dreams, Bette. Not yours, not anybody's."

Silence stiffened around them, echoing with harsh words. The hurt was back in her eyes, dampening the anger. There was something else there, too, something that pulled at him at the same time he tried to hold it off.

"And what are your dreams, Paul?" Her soft voice didn't push him away with challenge, but drew him to her in a way he couldn't explain. "What dreams are you living your life by? What dreams, Paul?"

He stared at her. She drew her coat more tightly closed, then walked around him and headed for the door. He stood there a long time after it closed behind her.

He hadn't answered her questions because he didn't know the answers. Work? He liked it, but it wasn't the most important thing in his life. Certainly not his dream. So what was? He liked his life all right, but not enough to satisfy him the next fifty years, or even the next five.

What are your dreams, Paul?

What scared him as he stood soaking the cold into his body like a punishment, was the possibility he didn't have any.

What scared him even more was the idea that he did have one—the one he'd never wanted to have.

Michael found him there half an hour later.

"Your mom's serving dessert and coffee. You ready?"

Paul dug his hands into his pockets and shifted his weight, finding his shoulders tense and sore from maintaining one position so long. The awareness of time passing had penetrated his abstraction, but he couldn't have said what he was thinking of all that time.

"Sure. Let's go."

Turning, he was stopped by Michael's hand on his arm. "Wait a minute."

"Why? Don't want to miss dessert, do you?"

"There's time. And if you go in there now, looking like this, you'll make everybody think it's Halloween instead of Thanksgiving."

"Thanks."

Michael nodded, as if the word hadn't been loaded with sarcasm. "I thought Bette didn't look too happy when she came in, but you look a whole lot worse. What happened, Paul?"

He dismissed the possibility of ignoring the question as quickly as it occurred to him. They'd been friends too long. But he did try to laugh. "You know how it is. Just like you said while we were painting your place. Women want what you don't have to give—forever. They want commitment and families and houses, and the whole schmeer.''

"And you think you don't want the same thing?"

"I *know* I don't want the same thing."

"Ah."

"There you go with that damned 'ah' again. What the hell does it mean?"

Michael gave him a long, considering look he found even more discomfiting than usual. "It means you already are committed to Bette."

"The hell I am."

"The hell of it is, you are. It might scare you, but be honest with yourself. Bette's the only woman you've ever made the commitment of pursuing. You told me yourself, something about her 'just clicked.' You may not have known it then, and you may not like it now, but it looks to me as if your heart's been committed pretty much right from the start."

"You don't know what the hell you're talking about."

"Maybe not. But you know what I'm talking about."

Chapter Eleven

"Where are you going?"

Bette half sighed at the demanding note in Paul's voice. He'd been so odd lately. One minute the man she'd first met, full of humor and teasing. The next minute a brooding, belligerent stranger. And the minute after that the man who could make her blood simmer with something as simple as a look.

They'd gotten past the scene Thanksgiving Day by pretending it didn't happen. She knew the underlying tension remained, however, no matter how well buried it was.

"Down to State Street." She finished pulling on her coat. If he hadn't arrived before she left, she would have left him a note. Then he could have made the decision whether to come out to her place, as he did most nights, or not. She couldn't help but think his moods might be the result of feeling pressured, so she was conscious of giving him room. "I have some last-minute things to pick up for Christmas at Field's and Carson's."

"Last-minute? It's barely into December."

She relaxed at the lightness in his voice. But she repeated doggedly, "Last minute for me. Especially since Centurian is interested enough to want a more detailed proposal. I'll have to work extra hours to get it ready."

"I don't see how you can work extra hours when you're already working twenty-four a day," he grumbled. "Besides, they probably won't do anything until after the first of the year."

"I know, but I want to get it to them quickly, so if there's a delay, it's on their end, not mine. So I have to do it before I leave for Arizona next week for my parents' anniversary."

"Oh. Yeah. When's your flight?"

"Wednesday morning."

"And you won't be back until 7:45 the next Monday night?"

"That's right."

They'd gone through this routine of her telling him the date of her departure at least three times. As haphazard as he could be about times and dates, she was beginning to wonder if there was more to this than met the eye. Each time he seemed to have only the vaguest recollection of when she was leaving, but knew her return flight by heart.

Oh, how she wanted to believe it was because he didn't want to be apart. Just as she wanted to believe that there'd been more behind his getting her to the real estate office too late to make the bid. Maybe even as she wanted to believe there was more behind these odd behavior shifts than simple moodiness.

But then she would realize all over that Paul Monroe believed only in the moment. Not a future together.

"I'll go with you."

"Go with?" He *couldn't* mean to her parents', yet—

"Yeah, you know, as in accompany you to State Street."

"*Shopping?*"

"You don't have to sound so surprised. I have been known to enter a store now and then."

"But, as you said, it's barely December."

"I didn't say I was going to do Christmas shopping."

She knew she should say no, she knew that having Paul around would surely prevent her from finishing all the tasks she'd planned. But she couldn't resist.

"All right, let's go."

Shoppers teemed in the streets, and they decided walking the last few blocks would be faster. While Paul paid off the taxi driver, Bette noticed drifts of people piling up in front of the broad expanse of glass in front of one of the stores.

"Hey, the window decorations," said Paul, hooking an arm around her waist and drawing her in to his side as they started down the street.

"Uh-huh. They do that every year." The words were dismissive, and she knew she really should be starting on her errands, but her feet slowed as they neared the display of mechanized bears skating on a mirror pond.

She couldn't even pretend to be surprised when her own voice offered. "We could look at the decorations first, sort of get in the mood."

But Paul's amazement showed. "Are you sure? I thought you didn't have much time—"

She waved his caution away. "It hardly takes any time at all," she said. She wondered at her blitheness—for about half a second, the time it took for the smile to light his eyes. Then she was lost.

It did take time, but she found she didn't begrudge an instant of it. Hand in hand, they walked from window to window, oohing and aahing with the best of the kids, then moving on to the next department store to start all over. From a street vendor, Paul bought roasted chestnuts because Bette said she'd never had them.

"Don't you want any?" she asked after the third of the rather gamy-tasting morsels warmed her mouth as well as they had her hand.

"No thanks. I don't like them."

"Then why'd you buy so many?" She looked at the large paper container in dismay.

He shrugged. "I like the idea of them."

Her laugh seemed to catch him by surprise. But when she threw her arms around his neck, he showed no surprise in responding to her kiss, only desire. He turned her kiss from a brief, affectionate gesture to a caress of lips and tongue and teeth. Layers upon layers of cloth buffered their bodies, but their mouths met, naked and honest.

When the basic requirement for oxygen forced them apart, Bette was sure she wasn't the only one rocked by the intensity of that kiss at the State Street corner. Paul's eyes looked opaque, with bright flecks of green against polished pewter. With his hair flaring color in the glow of tiny fairy lights, he looked almost fierce, and very unfamiliar. Not at all like the man she'd come to know.

She pushed her hair back from her face in some futile instinct to reorder her thoughts along with her appearance. "I, uh, guess Dickens would be proud, huh?"

He stared at her. "Dickens?"

"The chestnuts," she supplied weakly.

"Oh. Yeah, I guess." He considered her a moment longer, then grinned, slowly and meaningfully, a movement of his lips unlike his usual quick humor. "I thought you might have meant something else."

"Something else?" She heard the breathlessness still in her voice, corroborating the information that her heartbeat had not slowed from its sprint.

"Yeah, I've always had the feeling that behind all those closed Victorian doors, old Charles knew a thing or two about passion."

He didn't wait for her answer, but tucked her back in by his side, and headed for the Marshall Field's entrance. She followed docilely, unable to remember a single thing on the list tucked in her purse, and too content to bother looking.

"I've got an idea," Paul announced. "Let's have dinner in the Walnut Room."

The restaurant was a Marshall Field's tradition, especially at Christmastime when an elaborately decorated tree rose from the center of the room to a point some two stories higher. She opened her mouth to say she'd love to eat there, but before she could get a word out, he jumped in.

"I know, I know. You have a lot of things to do. But there's always a line. I'll stand in line while you shop. So you won't be wasting any time." He slanted a look at her that reminded her of their first few dinners together. "After all, you do eat. That's one thing I have learned about you. Sometimes even lunch, despite the way you misled me at first." He shook his head disapprovingly. "Telling lies."

His reminder drew a grimace that turned to a smile. "Purely self-defense. I was trying to protect myself from this maniac who'd burst into my life."

He smiled into her eyes, and she knew his voice would be low and intimate even before he spoke. "Now aren't you glad your ploy didn't keep me away for good?"

Only the truth, she couldn't give him anything else. "Yes. I am glad."

And she was, she thought as she reached the department where she hoped to find a special calendar for her father. Though glad seemed entirely too mild.

As she ticked off items on her list, her mind kept drifting back to the man waiting in line, and waiting for her. Two months ago, she would have made this same shopping trip, have made the same purchases. In fact, without Paul distracting her, she probably would have accomplished more in the same amount of time. But she wouldn't have enjoyed it half as much.

She accepted another package from the salesclerk, exchanging wishes for happy holidays, and moved aside to consult her watch. She still had ten minutes before she was supposed to return to the Walnut Room. With four more items on her list, she should make use of every minute. She really should. . . . But she didn't want to wait another ten minutes to see Paul.

She stepped off the escalator at the Walnut Room's floor and scanned the line. There, at the front, she caught the glow of Paul's hair. He turned, and then she felt the impact of his smile.

She was in love with him.

She reached him as the hostess indicated they were to follow her, and he took her hand. "Perfect timing."

"Yes, perfect." *Perfect.*

She was in love with a man who gave her laughter and joy, but could never give her what she most wanted—the promise that they would spend every Christmas together.

If her plot had worked, Paul was waiting, just inside this door.

If he'd believed her, he thought she was home packing for her early-morning departure for Arizona. When she told him it would be better if he didn't come to her house until later because she needed time to get ready, he'd said exactly what she'd been hoping for—that he'd stay late at the office and use the time to catch up on some work. In fact, his ready acceptance had irked her at some level. So he thought she'd sacrifice a last evening with him in order to neatly fold slips and shirts?

At home her suitcase waited, already packed. She'd left work in midafternoon to do that, and to find exactly the right thing to wear. Now she stood, just outside his office door, trembling between nerves and anticipation.

It might not be the kind of spur-of-the-moment inspiration he'd have had, but he'd shown he appreciated her planning... at least in some areas of their relationship. Areas such as soft, clean sheets, fluffy bath sheets and scented candles. And her lingerie. Bette fought an urge to giggle. It used to be she only considered if something was clean and appropriate for wearing under a certain blouse or dress. But now she found that every morning her choices were affected not only by how she would look, but by what was easy to get into and out of... especially out of.

Maybe she wanted to give him something to remember her by while she was gone. Maybe she wanted to give herself a final memory... just in case it *was* a final memory.

She sucked in a breath and turned the door handle.

From behind the desk, tieless, first two buttons opened, cuffs rolled to midforearm, Paul looked up as she walked in, surprise heating immediately to pleasure, and beyond. It was the look she needed to keep going. "Bette! What are you..."

Perhaps he saw something in her face, because he let the words trail off as she closed the door and leaned against it.

Without taking her eyes from his, she let her coat slide off her shoulders and down to the floor in a heap.

She smoothed a nervous hand down the wrap-front knit dress and wondered if she'd lost her mind. Maybe. But the look in his eyes left her very sure she hadn't lost her senses. He knew why she'd come.

"If memory serves me, you're supposed to be on the couch, Paul." Nerves, and something rawer, made her voice low and breathy.

His look never wavered as he dropped his pen onto the pad on which he'd been writing, and rose from behind the desk. Slow and deliberate, he moved to the couch and, obeying her slight gesture, sat down.

Shaking knees didn't prevent her from taking the three steps that brought her in front of him. Trembling hands didn't stop her from undoing the dress's tie at her waist. The weight of the material swung the sides open, and she knew he could see what was underneath. She knew, because she'd tested it in front of her bedroom mirror, wondering all the time if she'd feel like a fool when she did it in front of Paul.

He swallowed sharply. She watched his Adam's apple drop and rise and she felt her own tension ease. She felt a lot of things, but none of them was foolish.

She eased one knee onto the couch near his thigh and supported herself with a hand on the cushion by his shoulder, as her blood pulsed hotly under the lace and satin of the midnight-blue bustier. If he didn't touch her... And damn soon.

"Uh, Bette?"

"Hmm?"

"I have a question."

Was he going to ask her what she thought she was doing? Oh, Lord, if it wasn't obvious, maybe she wasn't doing this as well as she thought.

"What?"

"Have you gotten me a Christmas present?" At least his voice sounded as strained as his face looked. She moved her free leg, and one side of the dress slipped behind it, revealing more of her body to him.

"A Christmas present?" She bent to touch her lips to his temple, and absorbed the hard, demanding beat there. His skin felt hot under her lips. This close, she could feel the heat of him, holding off the chill of her state of near-undress.

"Uh-huh." He went even stiller when she moved to the other temple, leaning across him, close enough that his breath teased the tops of her breasts. "I know you shop early, so I wondered if you'd already gotten my present."

She noted his assumption that she would get him a present, but felt too absorbed by the way his pulse first hesitated then sprinted to comment on that.

"No. Why?"

"I know you like to save time, and I can save you some time shopping."

"Oh?" She leaned back enough to see his eyes, and felt a deeper heat when she met his look.

"Yeah. I know exactly what I want."

"What's that?"

"This."

He pushed the dress off her shoulders and down her arms. His palm cupped her left breast possessively, weighing it, testing it, molding it. His thumb hooked over the bustier's edge, stroking the bare flesh and catching her nipple tauntingly.

"You like that, don't you, Bette?" he asked when the nipple hardened and peaked.

Swaying a little toward him, she gave him the answer they both knew, but he seemed to need to hear. "Yes."

"You feel so wonderful. And you look..." He pulled her forward sharply, so she fell against him while he buried his face between her breasts. She felt the rasping moistness of his tongue against her skin and shivered with it. Slowly, he eased her all the way down to his lap, and raised his head and looked at her.

She felt herself responding, her blood pooling deep in her body at the flame of desire in his look, her lips curving at the glint of humor. He'd pulled a tighter rein on his control. For now. They both knew what pleasure there'd be in testing how much longer it would last.

"You look like the most beautiful package I have ever seen," he said. He stroked her from hip to belly to waist to abdomen to breast, burning the feel of his touch into her through the thin fabric. He slid the narrow straps off her shoulders and freed her breasts, letting his fingers trail one by one over peaks already hard, until she wanted more, much more. He tongued each, briefly, tantalizingly. "A beautifully wrapped package, too. But you know what happens to wrapping paper Christmas morning."

Something blazed in her, but she wouldn't give in to it. Not yet. When he raised his head, she forced her fingers to move slowly, deliberately. Open one button of his shirt. Then the next. And the one after. Complete one task, then start on the next. "In my family," she told him, pulling out the tails of his shirt, and helping him slide it off before unlatching the waist of his slacks, "we carefully remove the tape and fold the paper neatly."

Her primness was marred only by a soft gasp at the end when he guided her hands under his loosened waistband and around him.

"You would," he groaned. Quickly, he shed the rest of his clothing and dragged the hosiery down her legs. "Not me. I rip."

One word, and he would. She knew it, and it thrilled her. But sense prevailed—this time, she thought with a wicked grin to herself and a defiant mental promise that there would be a next time. She bent her head, dipping her tongue into his ear, then whispering, "There's no need to rip in order to unwrap, Paul."

"No? Then there'd better be a fast way to undo this thing."

"There is."

"How?" She heard the break of control in his voice, felt it in his urgent hands. "How the hell do you—"

"There—"

"But, it doesn't—"

"Yes. It has—"

A growl reverberated against her skin in the vicinity of her breastbone, the sound a mixture of frustration eased and satisfaction anticipated. "Snaps."

Abruptly, she felt the couch's smooth cool leather against her back, the lace and satin bunched around her waist, the heat and weight of her man above her. Around her. Inside her.

"Ah, Bette . . ."

"Yes."

"God . . . so good. So damn good."

Then there were no words. But whispers. Warmth. Moist darkness. Movement. Moans. Fire. Wet lightning. Rhythm. Explosion.

* * *

She still breathed, her heart still beat, her body still felt the damp weight of him against her, so there had to be a basic resemblance to the woman she'd been before. But she knew...she knew she was different. She'd lost her heart. Somehow, when she flew apart in his arms just then, the piece of herself she'd been trying so hard to hold on to had slipped through her fingers and into his.

What am I going to do? The question arose from reflex. There was nothing to do. Too late, now.

"Bette?"

"Hmm?"

"Come spring, I want to take you sailing." He didn't move from her, but he turned his head so his words wouldn't be muffled against her skin. "You'd like it. Out on the lake. You can skim along the coast, watching the city. You know there's traffic, noise and people with problems, but you're far enough away that all you see is the beauty of the city, the strength of the skyline, the green of the parks. Or we can go way out, where there's nothing but us and the water and the sky. Out in the middle like that, it's a place to tell dreams and secrets."

"It sounds magical."

"It is." Her content ruptured as he raised his upper body from hers. "Well?"

"Well what?" He was nearly glaring at her, and without his body as a blanket, she felt the room's chill.

"Will you?"

His impatience fueled hers. "Will I what?"

"Will you go sailing with me next spring?"

The direct question surprised her, but also made her wary. She'd accepted his comments as vague daydreams in the afterglow of their lovemaking. Paul Monroe didn't make dates for spring when winter hadn't even started. If she pushed the point, he'd surely back off. That would hurt, but it wasn't as bad as the alternative. Because if she didn't push the point, she'd be seduced by the mist of hope, with nothing substantial behind it.

"When?"

"The first fine Saturday in May." No hesitation. Almost as if he'd been planning what to say before she asked the question.

"Yes, I'll go sailing with you the first fine Saturday in May."

The smile lit his eyes, setting the green-tinted flecks glinting against the gray. "Then it's a date," he promised, kissing her with intent.

What had she done? *What did it matter?* The hope was so woven into her life, her heart, that she had no choice of holding herself off from him. She loved him. Completely. Undeniably. And maybe, just maybe, her hope would pay off.

"You know, there was just one thing wrong with this."

She had a hard time taking in his words. "Wrong?"

"Uh-huh. You know, different from my fantasy."

She'd caught the gleam in his eye. "Oh? What was that?"

"We were supposed to make slow, lazy love."

"Hmm. You don't think that qualified?"

"Not a chance. Guess we'll just have to try again."

She made a move as if to get up, although with him sprawled atop her she couldn't budge. "Well, let me know when you want to give it another try, and I'll see if I can schedule you in."

He gave her an insolent look. "You don't look too busy to me right now, and I think—" he flexed his buttocks and rolled against her where they were still joined, grinning wickedly at the moan she couldn't suppress "—now would suit me just fine."

"I still don't think we've gotten that quite right. It doesn't quite match my fantasy."

Paul sat behind his desk, pulling on his socks, while she retied her dress. She gave a deeply martyred—and utterly fake—sigh. "You mean we'll have to do it *again?*"

"Afraid so. We'll just have to keep at it until we get it right."

"Maybe we're doing something wrong, Paul. Are you sure it was the couch?"

"Now there's a thought!" He snagged her wrist and pulled her down onto his lap. "Maybe we should try the desk."

Fighting the laughter, she twisted away from him. She spread her hands wide on the desk to try to regain some balance. A letter lay open in front of her, next to the legal pad he'd been making notes on when she came in. The letterhead and a few phrases in the letter caught her eye.

"What is this, Paul?"

"What's what?" He looked over her shoulder, but seemed rather uninterested. "That's a letter from the Smithsonian."

"The Smithsonian?"

"Uh-huh. They want me to be on this panel of consultants they're forming."

"They just asked you?" The letter was dated more than a week ago, but with the mails, maybe he hadn't had it long, maybe... Then she saw another phrase in the letter, and she knew this was not the first time the offer had been made.

"No. They've been asking for a while. Middle of September, I guess they made the official offer."

September. He'd known all fall. He'd been thinking about it all fall, and he hadn't told her. An opportunity like this, the chance of a career, a credential in his field that would look great on any résumé.

The trip to Washington, snippets of comments from his father, from Jan, from Michael all came together and told her what she'd been too involved to see before. He'd had this offer all along. All these weeks they'd been together, and he hadn't told her. She'd thought....

She pulled away and stood up, hardly noticing he didn't try to hold her.

She'd thought what? That he cared enough about her to truly share his life with her? Because he hadn't walked away from her yet, because he'd looked two weeks ahead to ask her to spend Thanksgiving with his family, or even months ahead for some vague date to go sailing, she'd thought he was changing his whole way of living, of existing? She was a fool. He'd shown all along how he operated. She straightened her back and lifted her chin.

"They made this offer nearly three months ago and you've been holding them off, delaying giving them an answer?"

"Sort of."

"What does 'sort of' mean?"

He picked up the pen from his desk, and let it slide through his fingers. "It means I told them I had several factors to consider, and I wouldn't be giving them an answer until I felt satisfied with the way things would work. It's not like they gave me a deadline and I've blown it. They said they don't mind waiting for my decision."

She watched an uncharacteristic shadow of defensiveness cross his face, and was sure he was thinking about the bid on the house. Maybe she still owed him an apology on that score, but not now. She wasn't going to be side-tracked.

"What is there to decide, Paul? Are there drawbacks?"

"Yeah, there are drawbacks," he shot back with something close to bitterness. "You sound just like my father, and he learned it from the master—Walter Mulholland. Just because it carries you one more step up that great career ladder doesn't make it automatically the right move." He paused. *Just like my father...learned it from the master.* A glimmer of understanding came, but slipped back as he continued, slow and controlled. "I'd have obligations to them. I'd have to be in D.C. a certain number of days each month. It would cut into my business here. I have obligations to clients here. Loyal clients."

"And of course," she started silkily, "it would entail having to look ahead enough to keep some sort of schedule. Even if only for a few days a month."

The smoothness of her tone didn't fool him. He flicked her a look, then made a sound that could have meant anything. A noncommittal sound. Under her breath, she swore.

"What?" His sharpness indicated he'd caught the drift of her sentiment, though she didn't bother to clarify.

She knew exactly how this situation with the Smithsonian had come about. He'd probably been all friendly and helpful at first, making them think he was exactly the sort of person they needed, leading them on to believe he'd be there when they needed him. Then, at the last minute, he'd backed off and left them to be the ones to make the final move.

Just the way he had with her.

She swore under her breath again, then turned to stare blindly at the bookcase in front of her.

Oh, he'd worked it perfectly. He had pulled her along. He'd pushed and prodded and chased—up to a point. Then he'd backed off and waited for her to make the next step. At each level, he'd forced her to make the final decision whether to go on to the next. Until there was only that final step to take toward him—to give her heart.

Well, she had. And now she'd just have to live with the resulting pain. But she wasn't going to live with it alone. He wouldn't take the step himself, but by God she wasn't going to let him pretend she hadn't.

Pivoting, she faced him.

"I love you, Paul."

For all the uncertain anger bubbling inside her, Bette knew her voice carried conviction. Heaven help her, she did love him. In a way she knew she'd never get over.

As she watched, his eyes lost their narrowed look of defense, then widened in astonishment. They stayed wide, but into them leaped a flame that seemed to add a glow to his entire face as he rose and started toward her.

She held him off with one outstretched arm. Desire wasn't enough this time. There was more to say. Words that desire couldn't burn away.

The glimmer of understanding grew brighter, bright enough to illuminate the connection between past and present, between father and son, grandfather and grandson.

"I love you, and that's my problem."

He frowned at the word *problem* but she went on. "You pretend you're a free and easy spirit who doesn't commit to anything, but we both know that's a lie. You're committed to your business and your friends and your family. And probably, in your own way, you're committed to me. But that's not the kind of commitment I want. I want the kind that doesn't wince at the word *marriage*, that makes plans for a home and a family, that arranges a life together. The kind that doesn't need options left open because loving each other is the best option there is. The kind that doesn't mind strings."

Looking at her, he imagined for a moment that he could feel the strings she said bound her to him breaking loose, snapping so hard and so fast that they rebounded back to whip at him. God, she was going to leave him.

"That's what I've wanted as long as I can remember, Paul. I knew from the beginning that you wouldn't—maybe couldn't—give that to me. You were totally honest about that. That's why I tried so hard to stay away from you. But you can be persistent. And charming."

Her mouth, still red and swollen from their passion, lifted on one side in a smile that squeezed his heart. And in his pain, he lashed out.

"Are you saying I seduced you? Sold you a bill of goods? Because I didn't. I never made you promises I didn't keep."

"No. You never made promises. You were honest. At least about that. But you haven't been honest with yourself."

"I don't know what you're talking about."

"No-o-o." She drew out the negative. "You probably don't. But I should have seen it before. That first night . . . you practically spelled it out. Your whole life has been spent opposing your grandfather. Whatever his expectations and goals were for you—school, career, attitude toward life, marriage, family—you did something different."

He didn't bother denying it. It was true. He'd been determined from the start not to do what Walter Mulholland ordered. "And what about you? Haven't you spent your whole life living up to your grandfather's expecta-

tions? No time for fun, only time for work and advancement. Life goals and schedules and step-by-step plans."

Her eyes opened wide and he saw the blue intensified by
pain, then they narrowed. "I see now. All this time, you've
thought I was just like your grandfather, haven't you?
That what *my* grandfather taught me was what your
grandfather tried to force on you. Maybe you've even
worried that I'd try to run your life, to remake you like
your grandfather did."

"That's bull—"

She didn't seem to hear. "I won't ask for anything from
you, Paul. I just want to be as honest as you've been. I love
you, but I don't want to. God, I don't want to." Her voice
held such hurt he almost reached for her, even as the words
struck at him. "Because loving you means I want all those
things with you that scare you so much—a home, a family, a future. So someday I think—I hope—I'll stop loving
you. And then I'll leave."

Chapter Twelve

She'd gone. She'd said she loved him. She'd said she asked nothing of him. And then she'd left.

Oh, he knew the trip had been planned a long time. But it came down to the same thing. She'd left, and she'd left him behind.

Would she have asked him to come if he'd said yes to the Smithsonian, if he'd proved he was following the "right" path in life? Was that the price of admission to her heart?

The rush of anger receded as quickly as it had come. No. That wasn't fair. That wasn't Bette's way.

More likely she was trying to spare him. If her family was anything like his, bringing someone to a function like this would have been tantamount to an engagement announcement. Five days of expectant looks and probing questions; she'd known how that would rub against him.

Your whole life has been spent opposing your grandfa-ther. Yes, she'd been right there. By the time Walter Mul-holland had died, his junior year in college, the pattern had become second nature. Whatever Walter Wilson Mulhol-land would have approved of, he didn't do.

Including marrying Bette?

He pushed the question away.

Why hadn't he told her the things he'd been tempted to say? He could have told her he'd nearly decided to accept the Smithsonian offer, that after a couple months of talk-ing with them he thought they'd worked out an arrange-ment that overcame the drawbacks. He could have told her he loved her. The words had been there, pushing to es-cape.

Instead, she'd told him she loved him and she'd gone. And he felt as if men with pickaxes were working in syn-copation inside his head, heart and belly.

"Paul." Norma Schaff's voice came through the inter-com. "Grady Roberts is on line two."

With a deep sigh, he dropped his feet from his desk and leaned forward to pick up the receiver.

"Hey, Grady, what's up? But make it short. Some of us work for a living, you know, not just make a few phone calls and rake in a million."

"Paul, I'm in my office and you know how I can see a lot of the financial district from here—"

"If you're calling to brag about your view—"

"Paul, shut up and listen, will you? There's a fire, a big one. It's your dad's building."

Paul was out of the chair without realizing it. "Are you sure?"

"Yes. I just checked with somebody's binoculars to make sure before I called you."

"Thanks, Grady."

He'd already started to hang up, when Grady's voice stopped him. "Paul!"

"Yeah."

"Paul, it looks bad. There are trucks all over. You may have trouble getting close. Be careful."

"Thanks."

He snatched his coat and, after a split second of hesitation, also grabbed the ratty raincoat left over from last spring, plus a hat from an undetermined source. Before he finished his hurried explanation to Norma, she'd dug out two umbrellas, a wool scarf and a pair of gloves, tucking them into pockets as efficiently as an experienced kindergarten teacher.

By the time he gave up on the crawling cab and struck out on foot for the final three-quarters of a mile, he was grateful for every layer. The wind sliced sleet into his raw skin. Running made it worse, but still he ran. Even when the sidewalks became as clogged with pedestrian traffic as the streets had been with vehicles, he ran, dodging and, when necessary, pushing through the crowds. Only when a police barricade blocked the way did he stop, and only then because a slicker-outfitted member of Chicago's finest snagged him by the sleeve.

"Stay back!"

"I've got to—"

"Nobody's got to go in there, buster, but the firemen. Just back up here and let them do their job."

Paul pulled in a couple deep breaths as he considered the pugnacious expression and broad shoulders of the cop. Then his eyes went to the building, belching smoke that seemed to hiss as it met the cold, wet air. Nobody could still be in there, at least not alive—

"The people. Where'd they take the people? They must have evacuated—"

A flicker of understanding lit the cop's eyes. "Around this corner, go to the middle of the block, there's an insurance company, glass all across the front, big open lobby. That's where they've been taking 'em. Leastwise the ones the ambulances didn't take."

Ambulances. The word reverberated in his head even as he started at a run in the direction the cop had indicated.

The lobby was a dizzying mass of people. People with mismatched jackets flung over their shoulders or with blankets wrapped around them. Some sitting quietly against a wall, others talking feverishly to anyone who would listen.

Forcing himself to be methodical, Paul worked his way through three-quarters of the room before spotting a familiar face.

"Miriam!" His father's associate had been out to the house with her husband many times for dinners both business and social.

"Paul. What in the world are you doing here?"

"I heard about the fire. I haven't seen— I can't find—"

"He's fine, Paul. Everybody got out safely."

Some of the tension went out of him. But he'd feel certainty only when he saw his father himself. "A cop said they were taking people to hospitals."

She nodded. "Some smoke inhalation, and some shock, I think. But they've told us everyone's in good condition. Everybody was evacuated in time."

"Do you know where he is?"

"He and some others were trying to find a way to get taxis through the streets to start taking people home. He was going to the next street over to talk to someone in charge of the police to see if they could help."

Leaving the building, he noticed the cold more this time. He wasn't sure whether it was because the temperature was dropping or because fear no longer held such a stranglehold on him. By the time he found his father twenty minutes later, the raw chill was in his bones.

The sight of his father talking to a man with a walkie-talkie a few dozen yards away brought welcomed warmth into him. James Paul Monroe nodded at something the other man said, then turned away and stood coatless and hatless, staring up to where smoke rose against an equally gray twilight sky. His suit jacket shimmered in the huge spotlights the fire department had directed on the area, as if the moisture caught in its fabric had turned to frost.

"Dad." Paul waited until he was close enough that he could say the word without shouting.

His father turned toward him, but slowly, as if he didn't have full control over his muscles. Paul's heart wrenched at the slightly dazed sheen in his father's eyes.

"Son."

Paul pulled his father into his arms, in a fierce and grateful hug, remembering a hug he'd received some twenty years before by the side of a dark and rainy street.

"You'll freeze out here, Dad. Take this."

Quickly, he shrugged out of his topcoat and put it around his father's shoulders. As he pulled on the raincoat, he pulled out the scarf to put around his father's neck. Through it all his father stood, just looking at him. Paul knew he was acting a bit like a mother hen, but he couldn't help it, and he had the oddest certainty his father knew exactly how much he needed to do these things.

A memory flashed through his mind of the time when he'd been fifteen and had broken his arm, of his father each morning neatly rolling the shirtsleeve over the cast while Paul fretted to be off.

"You better put the coat on, Dad. It'll be warmer that way." He helped his father put his left arm through one sleeve, but when he reached for the other arm, a slice of light showed him the red, blistered skin of a burn across the knuckles as his father gripped something hidden in the shadows by his side.

James Monroe glanced down at his hand as if in surprise. "The fire came up the back stairwell. We started that way, but when I tested the door, we knew we'd have to find another way."

Paul swallowed as he realized how his father had tested that door. He reached down, intending to take the object out of his father's hand so he could put on the coat, but before he could, James Monroe tightened his grip, despite the wince the movement produced, and Paul pulled his hand back.

"It's odd how your mind works at times like that," his father said. "When the alarm sounded, it hit me that the smell I'd just barely been catching for a while was smoke. I realized we had to get out. We had to get everyone out of the building right away. I told them all not to stop for anything. But I did. I couldn't leave without it. It's odd how you see your mistakes, how you know what's important at times like that."

Paul looked down to where his father's fingers slowly loosened from the object he'd rescued as he escaped the fire. Paul's brows contracted in a puzzled frown as he saw the dull hard glint of gold. Then his father's hand opened, and the beam of light fell on what it held: the gold-framed photograph of the family taken the summer before Paul's senior year in college.

"But all the things in your office. Your baseball glove, your awards, your pictures..." All the things that had chronicled his father's successes. Paul glanced up at the smoke still billowing into the sky and wondered if a bit of leather and some aging paper could have survived.

"Probably gone."

Paul's gaze came back to his father's face, and he could see no more hint of despair there than he'd heard in his voice.

"I might miss those things, but I took what's most important to me."

His father looked at the photograph held in his burned hand, and standing there in the cold, with the sting of smoke all around them, he smiled.

Paul wouldn't forget that smile, not as long as he lived. That and the way his parents held on to each other when he and his father finally made it to the house in Lake Forest some time near midnight.

His father had insisted on seeing that all the people from his office were safely on their way home and that the fire department had declared the fire out before he agreed to let Paul take him home.

Even on the drive to Lake Forest, Paul knew his father hadn't fully relaxed. That came only when he walked into his wife's arms at the front door.

After his father showered and had his hand bandaged, they sat in the kitchen while his mother fed them, and the three of them talked.

Before his mother went up to bed, she laid her palm along his cheek as she used to to console some childish hurt.

"Mom..." He wanted to tell her...exactly what, he wasn't sure.

She shook her head slowly, wiping out the need for special words. "Everything will be all right, dear." She might have been talking about his father's condition or his business. But Paul didn't think so. Her next words confirmed it. "Look into your heart, and then don't be afraid to go after her. She loves you. And love can survive a lot of hurt."

The words were so soft, so unlike his mother's usual breeziness, that Paul didn't fully comprehend them until she had left the room. How did she know Bette had left? How had she fathomed his turmoil?

The questions had barely formed when he realized his father had lingered. When their eyes met, his father spoke.

"I know you always hated my joining the family firm, Paul. And you blamed your grandfather. But you shouldn't. Your grandfather didn't force me into anything—the firm, the position, the house. I'd never had those things, and I wanted them. So I made a choice—a choice, Paul. Nobody forced me. I still enjoy all those things.

"That doesn't mean I haven't had regrets. There are a few things I wish I'd done differently."

Paul felt the full force of his father's look, a communication as intangible yet as real as the silent connection of twilight games of catch two decades ago.

"Maybe I let being the best lawyer I could be consume me, Paul. Maybe I wasn't around enough, especially in those first years as head of the firm. Maybe I let the image and the externals get to me. Your mother and I...well, she forgave me a long time ago. Now, I hope you will."

"Forgive you? Dad, I—"

"I wasn't there for you like I should have been. It was better when Judi came along, but for you—"

"Dad, you were always there when I needed you."

Paul knew the truth of the words as he said them. He might have wanted more of his father, but what kid didn't? And what kid could be reasonable about it, could comprehend the incessant juggling of career, marriage, family and occasional privacy? He could understand his father's need to be the best lawyer he could be. Hell, he'd inherited the same compulsion to give his clients the best.

His father waved off his objection. "I did you a disservice, Paul, by not overtly stepping in between your grandfather and you."

"I did all right on my own with that fight."

A flash of understanding lit the past: he hadn't fought alone. Why hadn't he seen that before? Why hadn't he recognized that, with no fanfare, his parents had withstood Walter Mulholland? It was so obvious now. If they hadn't, he would have been sent to military school six times over during his adolescent rebellions. And he might have made speeches about not attending an Ivy League college, but who'd paid tuition at the school of his choice?

His father shook his head even as he smiled dryly. "I didn't mean stepping in to protect you from Walter running roughshod over you— I agree, you did a better job of that than anyone else ever could have done—but to prevent you from dismissing everything he believed in. Walter Mulholland wasn't all right. But he wasn't all wrong, either, son."

That night, lying in the bed he'd known as a twelve-year old, Paul thought of those words and his own insights.

The boy he'd been had so desperately fought his grandfather's dictatorial ways that he'd boxed himself in. Even if he'd *wanted* to go to that Ivy League college, he never would have done so. Even if he'd wanted to be a lawyer, he never would have become one. His father's words echoed in his ears. *Walter Mulholland wasn't all right. But he wasn't all wrong, either.*

What an ass he'd been.

But no more.

What was it he'd accused Bette of doing? Trying to live up to every expectation of her dead grandfather? Wasn't he equally as bad—spurning every expectation of his dead grandfather? Time to start weighing decisions against what *he* wanted.

And what he wanted was Bette Wharton.

"And of course, the party is tonight. Then, Saturday we'll go to the Thompsons for cocktails and dinner, but other than that, I really haven't planned very much."

Aware of an expectant pause, Bette filled it, though the words hadn't sunk in. "That's fine, Mom."

"Is it? Well, with Ronald and Clara here, too, I just didn't know how many plans to make. Especially with the children... It's a long trip for the little ones for such a short time, and if there are too many things going on, it gets too much for them."

Her mother had already gone over the weekend plans twice before, once after picking up Bette at the airport on Wednesday and again yesterday. With her mother covering the same information as they sat on chaise longues in the waning sun while the rest of the family enjoyed a boat ride on the lake, Bette didn't have to bother pulling her thoughts from what had occupied them since Tuesday night. Paul.

She'd acted on impulse in his office. Without considering where it might lead or what its repercussions might be, she had said exactly how she felt—about him and what was happening between them. At least half of how she felt. Because she'd told him only about the pain. She hadn't told him about the joy he'd brought her, too. And no matter how much he might hurt her, she could never deny the laughter and the loving he'd given her.

" ... Would you like that, Bette?"

"Sorry. What?"

"A tennis lesson. I said I could set you up with a tennis lesson Saturday afternoon so you'd have something to do. I know we haven't planned much for you this trip."

"No. Thanks, Mom, no tennis lesson. It's all right."

"Is it? I know you like to have things structured. That's another way you've taken after your grandfather. But down here, we've gotten into the habit of taking life easier. And, of course I knew you'd have some work that you'd brought with you to keep you busy."

Her mother's words penetrated this time. "Really, Mom. It's fine."

... Like to have things structured... knew you'd have some work that you'd brought with ...

She *had* brought work, though she hadn't taken it out of the suitcase. And she *did* like structure, though that didn't mean twenty-four hours a day.

Another way you've taken after your grandfather. Took after him or blindly emulated him? That was what Paul had accused her of. *No time for fun, only time for work and advancement.*

"Oh, here they come!" Her mother headed down the path to meet the boat pulling up to the Whartons' small boat house.

She watched her mother and father, Ronald and Clara, and remembered her belief that she couldn't possibly fall in love with Paul Monroe because she saw his faults too clearly. She'd been wrong. Her mother and sister-in-law weren't blind to their men's faults; love just focused beyond the faults. Reason gave way to something wiser.

She hadn't given that to Paul. She'd fought hope so hard that she hadn't admitted there might be cause for it; Paul had changed in the past weeks. Had she?

Her fears for the future had looked over her shoulder at every stage, never allowing her to open herself to him fully. Even telling him she loved him had carried the reminder of the future, and her fears for it. *I love you, but I don't want to. God, I don't want to... someday I think—I hope—I'll stop loving you. And then I'll leave.*

Another thought had her sitting upright and swinging her feet to the patio.

Fears for the future.

Her grandfather had taught her to look to the future. Maybe she'd taken the lesson too much to heart, turning her back on the present, but with Paul she'd done something else. She'd forgotten that hope was also part of the future.

She'd already started out of the chaise, when she heard her father's shout.

"Bette! C'mon down and we'll take you out, too."

"No, thanks, Dad. You go ahead without me this trip. I've got to make a phone call."

No answer at his office. She checked her watch. Nearly five-thirty in Chicago. They were gone.

His answering machine picked up at his apartment. She hesitated, then hurried on before it cut her off. "Paul, it's Bette. Please call me at my parents'."

Hanging up, she wondered if she should call back, tell him more, tell him.... No, the things she had to tell him couldn't be compressed between the beeps of a message tape.

He'd brought so much into her life, the laughter, the passion, the companionship. From him she was learning the value of *now*. With his impromptu reactions and the way he drew spontaneity from her, he'd taught her that today was as important as tomorrow. She could enjoy window decorations now and then without forfeiting the future.

Or take an evening boat ride with her family while she prayed for the phone to ring. And hoped that enough to-days would build a tomorrow.

Forty hours after finding his father, Paul stared at his reflection thrown back by the multiple layers of glass in the airplane's window. He'd spent Friday walking the beaches he'd known all his life, watching Lake Michigan's brooding December power and doing some brooding of his own.

The first answer came with a gust of cold wind that sliced through his clothes. Like a tactile memory, the cold stirred thoughts of Thanksgiving night and he heard Bette asking him, "What are your dreams, Paul?"

He knew now. She was his dream. A life with her. It was what he'd wanted from the start and what he'd fought so hard against. Fought her, fought himself, because he was still fighting Walter Wilson Mulholland.

He remembered his thoughts of earthquakes while he and Bette sat in Jan and Ed Robson's living room and looked at each other across the tiny body of a baby. More like a heartquake, he thought now. Well, the rumbling and shuddering were over—at least as far as he was concerned. His world had shifted and rearranged itself into a new conformation. Into a landscape that had Bette at its center. He wanted to make plans now. Plans for children, for finding a house with a yard, enough room for some twilight games of catch. Plans for college educations, for old age. Plans for a life with Bette.

In a few minutes they'd land at the Phoenix airport and he'd be at the Whartons' house not long after. Then he would tell Bette the things he hadn't told her Tuesday night. Then he could try to make her see what had happened since she left two days before.

Paul Monroe had grown up.

Uncertainty solidified into a sharp-edged rock in Bette's stomach when she answered her parents' door late Saturday afternoon and found Paul Monroe staring back at her.

He hadn't answered her twenty-four-hour-old message, but he'd come after her. What did that mean?

"Paul." She knew her lips formed the word, but she wasn't sure if it had any sound.

"Hi, Bette." One corner of his mouth lifted, but it wasn't much of a smile. "I had to see you."

"Who is it, Bette?" Her mother's voice grew nearer as she came down the hall.

Automatically, Bette opened the outer door to Paul, and stepped back to let him in.

"Mother, this is Paul Monroe." What else to say about him? *My friend?* Too small to be the truth. *My lover?* Only one part of the truth. *The man I love?* Too much the truth. "From Chicago."

"Oh. How nice to meet you." Her mother glanced from one to the other of them. "It's wonderful that you could pay Bette a surprise visit while she is with us. It's a shame Bette's father isn't here right now to meet you also."

"I know it's a surprise visit. I hope it's not inconvenient, but I was...I, uh, I was hoping to take Bette out for dinner."

She didn't think she could remember Paul ever stumbling over his words that way. It terrified her.

"Bette, remember the Thompsons are expecting us at five-thirty for cocktails." Mrs. Wharton looked from her daughter to this intense-looking young man, and put together a clue or two dropped over the past few weeks to arrive at a very satisfactory conclusion. A conclusion that involved one less guest at the Thompsons' dinner party. "So the rest of us will be leaving as soon as the baby-sitter arrives, about half an hour," she finished smoothly.

Bette read the message in her mother's look, and thanked her silently.

"So if we don't see you before we leave," continued her mother, turning to Paul and putting the seal on this revised plan, "I hope you enjoy your stay in Phoenix."

"Thank you, Mrs. Wharton. I'm going to try." Bette knew exactly when Paul turned to her mother and stretched out a hand, because the weight of his eyes left her for the first time. "I hope we'll see each other again."

Bette heard the words, but refused to admit their possible meaning. They were too dangerous. They could elicit too many hopeful, soaring ideas of "what next" if she let them free.

"I hope so, too. If you're not in any hurry for dinner, you should get Bette to show you around the area first. There's a lovely view from the boathouse."

Her mother and Paul exchanged goodbyes, and some how Bette found herself leading Paul down the twisting path to the boathouse tucked away privately by the water's edge.

Bette went directly to the railing and stared out at the water, darkening with night and undisturbed by any human traffic. The shadows under the roofed portion were deep, but she was fully aware of Paul standing behind her.

"I had to see you—" He broke off, then started again. "There are more things that need to be said between us."

She felt him nearer.

"I know, that's why I called you yesterday."

"You called?" His voice was low.

She twisted to see his face, but he was too close, and she saw only her own desire reflected there. She looked back to the water. "I left a message at your apartment."

"I haven't been home." His fingertips brushed her hair behind her ear, perhaps so that he could see her profile more clearly from where he stood behind her right shoulder. "I needed to talk to you, Bette. There's something.... Something happened Thursday. There was a fire."

The strain in his voice chilled her. Turning, she tried to read in his face what this fire had meant to him. He wasn't injured, at least on the outside. But inside?

"A fire?"

"Dad's building."

"Oh my God—"

"No." He gripped the arms she'd instinctively extended to him. "It's all right, Bette. He's fine. Nobody was seriously hurt. There's a lot of damage, and it'll be a mess for a while. For the firm. For Dad. But it's not much compared to what could have happened."

His hands traveled up her arms and across her shoulders, finally coming to her throat. He spread his fingers under her hair to caress her nape with warmth while with his thumbs he stroked the line of her jaw. In the shadows, wavering with the water's reflection, she saw his eyes just as surely caressing her lips.

"I learned something from that fire, Bette. Afterward Dad talked about his life, and my grandfather, and I started to see— I've been wrong. Wrong and blind and stubborn. That's why—" he dropped a kiss on her mouth as light and powerful as a laser's beam "—why I came here." Another kiss. "I had—" Another kiss "—to see you, to tell you...." Desire flared between them without lightening the shadows around them. "Oh, God, Bette. I need you."

He held her face between his palms and sank into her mouth. She felt the need, the tension in him. She felt confused, uncertain— Why had he come? What had this fire meant to him? What was this change in him? But those were questions for the future, because beneath the confusion and uncertainty, she also felt the sure steady beat of her love for him. He needed her now. He wanted her now. Now was the moment she had. She'd take it, and she'd give it.

Instinct led them to the wide cushioned seats that edged the back of the boathouse, because in the inky darkness they couldn't see anything. Not even each other. But touch led them where their eyes could not, the way to ease the ache, the way to fill the needs, the way to love each other.

And even in the dark, she could see the face of the man she made love with, the man she loved. She would always see his face. It was her fantasy, more powerful than any schoolgirl could imagine. Yet it also haunted her, because

it lacked one element—the love, the deep, committed love
of the man making love to her.

"Bette?"

She didn't answer. She didn't want him to know she was
crying. He had come after her, but why? He might have
followed one of his impulses, the desire of the moment to
see her, be with her, make love with her. Or he might have
felt her speech in his office had been an ultimatum, de-
signed to close him in, trap him, bind him. Tears would
only add to that impression.

"Bette, there's something I have to ask you."

She held her silence like a shield, protecting him from
her tears, protecting herself from his questions.

No, not a shield, a restriction. She was doing what she'd
sworn not to do, holding back from him out of fear.

"Bette. Do you really love me?"

The tears slipped loose.

He'd just made it all very simple. Did she really love
him? Oh, yes. She hadn't planned it. It had just happened. But she did love him.

"Yes. I really love you."

Her voice flowed with love, but also with the tears. He
shifted, putting a palm under her chin to lift it and lever-
ing himself above her to try to look into her eyes.

"Bette, don't cry." Paul's hoarse plea made her cry
more, and his fingers, gently rough, couldn't stop the flow.
"God, Bette—"

"It's all right, Paul." She'd known what he could give
her, and she'd risked it anyhow. She'd lost her heart, but
by losing it she'd also found it. This time she had to tell
him that side of it, too. "I knew . . . I knew . . ."

"You knew what?"

"How it would be, but it doesn't matter now—"

"How what would be? You're driving me crazy with these elliptical comments, Bette. I don't know what you're talking about, but experience tells me I'd hate it like hell. We've got to talk. Really talk. That's why I came down here. To talk to you, to tell you—" He broke off as if suddenly struck by the difficulty of expressing what he was about to say.

"To tell you... things," he finished lamely. The emphasis he put on the last word indicated it had great meaning, but she couldn't begin to fathom it.

"Things?"

"Aw, hell. I can't tell you here. Not with this, and with you crying and thinking what you're thinking. I know you, Bette, and you can't tell me you're not looking seven steps ahead and coming out on the totally wrong path."

She felt slightly stunned by the spate of words, and more than a little confused. "Now who's talking in elliptical comments?"

"I am. And it's going to stop. Starting now, we're going to take this one step at a time. And the first step is to tell you— No. Better yet to show you."

"Show me?"

"Yeah. C'mon, I'm going to show you exactly what I have in mind for the first step."

"Paul, this is the airport."

"Boy, I sure am glad I didn't get bus tickets then. We'd have been in a lot of trouble."

He sounded odd, almost giddy and a little nervous. Not at all like himself.

"Paul. Just this once. Answer me straight. What are we doing here? What's all this about a first step, and showing me?"

"I'll tell you. But not until we're inside."

She couldn't sway him from that as they turned in h
rental car and made their way to the main entrance to th
airport.

"Okay, we're inside," she reminded him. "Now tell m
what this is all about."

"See Gate B23?"

She scanned the monitors for B23. "Departing for La
Vegas," she read.

"Right."

"We're going to Las Vegas?"

"That's right. I bought a pair of tickets for this fligl
right after I landed here."

"I don't understand. You want to gamble?"

"I hope what I have in mind is more along the lines c
playing a sure thing."

The husky timbre of his voice sent a thrill down he
backbone. "What is it you have in mind, Paul?"

"I have in mind getting married."

"Married?" Her mouth formed the word, but she didn'
think she spoke it. No matter what tricks her respirator
system might be doing, her mind hesitated to accept wha
she'd heard. "Are you serious?"

"Absolutely. I'm also sure, positive and certain. A li
tle anxious maybe, but also eager."

Behind all the glib words, she saw that there was a doub
in his eyes, though, and when he expressed it out loud sh
feared she'd cry in the middle of Sky Harbor Airport.

"If you'll have me. Will you marry me, Bette?"

Twice she tried to swallow the tears. But she couldn'
stop them, certainly not enough to get out any words. In
stead, she placed her palm against the faintly bristled curv
of Paul's jaw and stretched to touch her lips against his
even as she continued to cry.

He took her face between his hands and kissed the earstains on her cheeks, then returned to her mouth. Deep and hot and dark, he still somehow managed to make the kiss tender. And full of promises for the future. Oh, Lord, so full of promises.

They broke apart to gulp in air and smile giddily at each other.

"I don't have any luggage."

"That's okay, I don't have much myself, only a few things I'd left at my parents' house. We'll buy what we need." The green flecks in his eyes heated, sharing the memory and the anticipation. "After all, we're veteran shoppers for this sort of trip. But first, I have to know: is that a yes?"

"Yes, that's a yes."

They stood, grinning at each other for a full minute before Paul grabbed her hand and headed for the departure gates. "That's us," he said as the boarding of the Las Vegas flight from Gate B23 was announced.

Bette's head was in too much of a spin to notice much except the compact energy of the man next to her as they passed through security and continued toward the gate. Then, as abruptly as he had showed up at her parents' front door, Paul stopped.

Two strides short of Gate B23, he pulled back suddenly on Bette's hand. She felt the smile on her lips freeze as she looked at him. His gaze went from the gate back to her, and she knew what he was going to say before he said it.

"I can't do this, Bette."

She pulled in a breath of pure pain. For an instant she thought she might collapse. But she didn't. Numbness and pride held her up. She felt only gratitude that her legs held steady as she pivoted and started back down the corridor. Later, she knew, the numbness would recede and the hurt

would be nearly unbearable. But she would bear it. An
she would love Paul Monroe despite the pain.

"No! Bette, wait." He caught her after two steps, no
too gently pulling her around to face him. "You misu
derstood!"

"What did I misunderstand, Paul? Your proposal? Di
I take it too seriously? Was it a joke? Were you teasin;
was that it?"

"God, no, I wasn't teasing. And I wasn't joking. Loo
at me, Bette. It's a basic matter of believing. No time t
make a list or keep to a schedule or create a seven-ste
master plan. You either believe me or you don't. Righ
now."

His demand allowed only instinct, no thought. "I be
lieve you."

Some of the tension went out of his hold on her, bi
none of the intensity. "Good. Because I meant every wor
I said. You're in my life for good, whether you like it c
not, and I want to be married to you, Bette Wharton. Bi
not Las Vegas style. We can't get married that way. It's nc
the right way for us."

"I...I don't understand."

"I've sworn to stop doing what my grandfathe
wouldn't have wanted and start doing what I *do* wan
Eloping to Vegas was reflex action. But it's not what I wa
and— Hey!" His eyes lit up with something a shade ho
ter than laughter before his voice changed. "You were re
ally willing to elope with me, weren't you? No plans, n
schedule, just hop on a plane and go get married."

"Yes."

The single word said more than all her explanation
could have.

"What do you know about that?" His grin tilted. 'That's the nicest thing you could ever have done for me, Bette."

He caught her closer.

"But I want the whole damn thing with you, Bette. I want to go back to your parents' house and be introduced as their prospective son-in-law. I want to take you home to Lake Forest and watch my parents' faces when we tell them the good news. I want to hear Judi squeal. I want to get congratulated by Grady and Michael. I want to go looking for the perfect house for us to buy—together. And I want to marry you in a church, with a minister and flowers and a veil and pictures and a cake and one hell of a reception. I want as many of our friends and relatives as we can cram in to be there when we make those promises about forever and ever."

"You do?"

"I do." She watched his eyes acquire a familiar glint, and she realized that her love for this man might never stop growing. "See, I even know my line already. 'I do.'"

She laughed. She couldn't help it. It was one of the things she loved about Paul Monroe, this ability to make her laugh. Because, his joy in making her laugh, in drawing that out of her, was one aspect of his love for her. She wrapped her arms around his neck. "Thank you for making my fantasy come true, Paul," she whispered against his lips. "My whole fantasy."

He couldn't have known what she meant by that, yet she felt he'd understood that she did trust, wholeheartedly and unreservedly, in his love. His arms tightened across her back, almost fiercely. But his voice was soft.

"Any time, Bette. Any time."

Their mouths met with a tenderness that belied the desire trembling in their bodies. The desire that would be as much a part of their lives together as the tenderness. An the laughter.

Paul rested his forehead on hers, though he couldn't resist dipping to take her top lip between his in a caress that evoked memories and promises between them. Then I loosened his arms enough to meet her eyes. "You ever ki me like that again, Bette Wharton, and you better be prepared to tell me you've had fantasies about airports."

Her chuckle was still a little frazzled, and his brows ro above suddenly hopeful eyes. "Have you?"

"No!" This time she laughed outright.

His disappointment sighed deep and long, and I pressed a quick, hungry kiss to her lips before settling h arms more comfortably around her waist.

"So, how long do you think it'll take you to plan wedding like that?"

"Oh, so I'm going to do the planning?"

He grinned. "I'm learning to enjoy thinking about th future, but would you really want me to plan a wedding With schedules and deadlines and stuff?" He seemed take her wrinkled-nose grimace as a no. "I bet you coul get my mother to help. And I'll consult. So, how long wi it take you to plan a big wedding like that?"

"I don't know. Nine months, a year maybe?"

"A year!"

"I really don't know, Paul. I haven't done it before, yc know."

"I tell you what, since you're a rookie at this, I'll giv you eight months and a little time to spare—say the la weekend in August."

"I feel a 'but' coming."

His grin sent a deliciously hot shiver through he "But—" he drew out the word as he ran his hands up h rms and along her shoulders "—the honeymoon comes first."

The pads of his thumbs reached lower, skimming the points of her collarbone, stirring her body to recognition of the sensations those thumbs could create if they strayed lower, and lower still. She felt a small shudder ripple through her, and saw from his eyes that he felt it, too, had wanted to feel it, had been trying to create it.

"We'll turn in these tickets to Vegas and see how far that'll get us toward the most exotic, most romantic, most sun-drenched, most secluded place we can get to with the least possible delay."

She went into his arms without hesitation. "Just like a kid, wanting dessert first."

* * * * *

Bette Wharton and Paul Monroe
request the pleasure of your company
as they celebrate their marriage
(and play matchmaker for Michael Dickinson!)
at their
WEDDING PARTY
Silhouette Special Edition #718
January 1992

This is the season of giving, and Silhouette proudly offers you its sixth annual Christmas collection.

SILHOUETTE

Christmas Stories

1991

Experience the joys of a holiday romance and treasure these heartwarming stories by four award-winning Silhouette authors

Phyllis Halldorson—"A Memorable Noel"
Peggy Webb—"I Heard the Rabbits Singing"
Naomi Horton—"Dreaming of Angels"
Heather Graham Pozzessere—"The Christmas Bride"

Discover this yuletide celebration—sit back and enjoy Silhouette's Christmas gift of love.

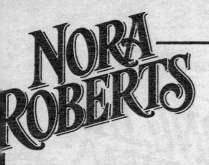

NORA ROBERTS

Love has a language all its own, and for centuries, flowers have symbolized love's finest expression. Discover the language of flowers—and love—in this romantic collection of 48 favorite books by bestselling author Nora Roberts.

Starting in February 1992, two titles will be available each month at your favorite retail outlet.

In February, look for:

Irish Thoroughbred, Volume #1
The Law Is A Lady, Volume #2

Collect all 48 titles and become fluent in the Language of Love.

LOL192

THE LANGUAGE of LOVE

Silhouette Romance®

LONG, TALL TEXANS

DONAVAN
Diana Palmer

Diana Palmer's bestselling LONG, TALL TEXANS series continues with DONAVAN....

From the moment elegant Fay York walked into the bar on the wrong side of town, rugged Texan Donavan Langley knew she was trouble. But the lovely young innocent awoke a tenderness in him that he'd never known...and a desire to make her a proposal she couldn't refuse....

Don't miss DONAVAN by Diana Palmer, the ninth book in her LONG, TALL TEXANS series. Coming in January...only from Silhouette Romance.

LTT192

Silhouette Special Edition®

is pleased to announce

WEDDING DUET
by Patricia McLinn

Wedding fever! There are times when marriage must be catching. One couple decides to tie the knot, and suddenly everyone they know seems headed down the aisle. Patricia McLinn's WEDDING DUET lets you share the excitement of such a time.

December: PRELUDE TO A WEDDING (SE #712) Bette Wharton knew what she wanted—marriage, a home . . . and Paul Monroe. But was there any chance that a fun-loving free spirit like Paul would share her dreams of meeting at the altar?

January: WEDDING PARTY (SE #718) Paul and Bette's wedding was a terrific chance to renew old friendships. But walking down the aisle had bridesmaid Tris Donlin and best man Michael Dickinson rethinking what friendship really meant. . . .